ALWAYS MY OWN

THE ALWAYS LOVE TRILOGY - BOOK 2

TAWDRA KANDLE

Other Books by the Author

The King Series
Fearless
Breathless
Restless
Endless

Crystal Cove Books
The Posse
The Plan
The Path

The Perfect Dish Series
Best Served Cold
Just Desserts
I Choose You

The One Trilogy
The Last One
The First One
The Only One

The Always Love Trilogy
Always for You
Always My Own
Alaways Our Love

The Seredipity Duet
Undeniable
Unquenchable

Recipe for Death Series
Death Fricassee
Death A La Mode

Always My Own

When Elizabeth Hudson and Trent Wagoner met on a Christmas tree lot in Florida, sparks flew, igniting a fire they both thought would burn for a long time.

The problem with fires is that sometimes people get hurt. In this case, both Elizabeth and Trent end up burnt when an impulsive decision results in long-term repercussions.

Trent, still dealing with the aftermath of a painful situation in his hometown of Burton, struggles with the feelings he has for Elizabeth. He's not sure that committing to her is a good idea when everything he touches seems to end badly.

Elizabeth took a risk when she moved to Burton for Trent. Now she's stuck in a job she's not sure she likes, living with people she doesn't know and in love with a man who may not be capable of the forever she craves.

When it seems as if hope has died . . . there's always love.

Trent and Elizabeth's story begins with the Christmas short
Underneath My Christmas Tree

The Burton Books began with
The One Trilogy

The Last One
The First One
The Only One
The One Trilogy Box Set

And continued in
The Always Love Trilogy

Always For You
Always My Own
Always Our Love

Will and Sydney's story is coming!

My One and Always
A short in the anthology
Love Paws
April 18, 2016

DEDICATION

In 2008, in the parking lot of Monkey Joe's, I met a blonde with two cute kids. She was new to homeschooling, and she'd just joined our social group. Little did I know how important she'd be in my life.

Five years later, when I was in the middle of this crazy author life and struggling to keep up, Stacey came to my aid, helping me with proofing, promo and other bookish fun. When I suggested (begged) that she learn formatting, she took a deep breath and dived in.

Since then, Stacey has formatted every one of my books . . . but more important, she's become one of the top formatters in the indie world. She never fails to amaze me with her knowledge and ability!

Stacey has come to just about every local signing and speaking engagement I've had. She threw my first launch party. She helped move my family, twice. And the woman makes a dang good pan of brownies. And pumpkin roll.

So this book is dedicated with love to Stacey, my Florida sister, my shoulder to cry on, my wine buddy, my partner in crime, my friend.

Chapter One

Elizabeth

I

T PROBABLY WASN'T A GOOD omen that the first sign of civilization I came across in my brand-new hometown was a bar.

But even if seeing it was a bad sign, the Road Block looked like a decent joint. It was huge, a building of raw planks that rose out of the empty fields, the sides decorated liberally with neon. The parking lot was pretty packed, even though it wasn't full-on dark yet on a Tuesday night. The sign near the road announced that it was Ladies Night, with half-priced drinks and a DJ spinning tunes.

Sounded like my type of place.

I slowed my packed-to-the-gills car, and for a moment, I debated whether stopping at a bar on my way into a town I'd never seen, where I hoped to run a successful law practice, was a good idea. And then the part of me that'd been talking louder and louder of late told me to give myself a break. One drink wasn't going to hurt anyone. That sounded about right at this point, so I swung into the parking lot and eased into a spot near the back.

Climbing out, I stretched, feeling the muscles in my back ease when my feet hit the graveled ground. The air was chilly now that the sun was down, and shivering, I reached back into the car for my jacket before I headed for the front of the building.

Inside, the Road Block was a wide open space, with dim lights, plenty of round tables, rows of booths and a large dance floor, which was empty at the moment. Apparently the DJ hadn't started playing yet. Still, as the parking lot had indicated, the place was fairly crowded, and mostly with women. I guessed Ladies Night was popular in Burton, Georgia.

I found a spot at the bar and hopped onto a stool, glancing around the area. Two people were working behind the bar: one was a woman who was probably about twenty years my senior, and the other was an incredibly well-built man, with dark cropped hair. Both of them were moving fast, taking orders, filling them and chatting with the patrons. I waited, biding my time until the man spotted me and moseyed down to my end.

"Hey, thanks for waiting. Sorry, we're a little busy tonight." He grinned at me, and I swore my bones melted. *Oh, mama.*

"Um, no problem." I flashed what I hoped was a winsome smile. "Can I just have a glass of white wine? Whatever you're offering tonight for the special is fine."

Mr. Incredibly Handsome folded his arms over that

huge chest and leaned onto the bar, bringing his face to my level. "We have a nice Pinot, but I really recommend the Riesling. It's new, it's from Australia, and my wife absolutely loves it. And she's got a very discerning palate."

My heart, which had been skipping along merrily as he spoke, dropped. *Yeah, it figured.* All the good ones were taken. A thread of uneasiness wrapped around my stomach, but I pushed it away.

"That sounds perfect. The Riesling, I mean."

He winked at me. "You got it." Pulling a wine glass from the rack overhead, he tipped a bottle over the rim, giving me a generous serving. "Here you go." He studied me for a few seconds. "You're not from Burton. Just passing through or coming for a visit?"

I grimaced. "Neither. Moving here."

He raised one eyebrow. "And not very happy about it, apparently. Relax, sugar. We're a very welcoming community."

"Yeah." I took a long drink. "Mmmm, you were right. This is excellent." I leaned back a little and took in the room, surveying the booths with women of all ages filling them and the high-tops with an equal number of females. "So Ladies Night is a big hit, huh?"

He chuckled. "It is. We have live music on the weekends, but the women hereabouts told me they wanted one night where they could just kick back and cut loose. And they wanted to be able to request their favorite songs. So we started Ladies Night. We get a full house just about every week."

"Nice." I drained my glass and nudged it toward the

bartender. "I'll have another, please."

He glanced at me but didn't comment as he refilled my wine glass. "So where're you from?"

I took a much more ladylike sip this time. "You name it, I've lived there. Well, pretty much." I hooked a thumb toward myself. "Army brat."

"Ah." He nodded. "Then I guess I should ask where you came from just now?"

"Florida." I turned my glass in a neat little circle on the paper napkin.

"Oh, really? Whereabouts?"

"East coast." I didn't want to go down that road, not tonight. Deciding to turn the tables, I flashed him a smile. "How about you? I take it you're Georgia born and raised?"

"Better than that. I'm *Burton*, Georgia born and raised." He lifted one massive shoulder. "Went away for a little while after graduation, but I found my way back and opened up this place. Now I'm here to stay."

"Seriously? This is your bar?" I looked at him with new appreciation. "Congratulations. It's great." I tore off a corner of the napkin and rolled it into a little ball. "But still. Owning a business in a town doesn't mean you're stuck here forever. Your bar doesn't have to keep you in town."

The bartender—excuse me, the bar *owner*—spotted someone over my shoulder, and everything in his demeanor changed. His face softened, his eyes went hot, and though I doubted he realized he was doing it, his tongue came out to lick his lips.

"The bar isn't what keeps me in town. My reason for staying in Burton—hell, my reason for doing anything—just walked in the door."

I turned my head to follow the direction of his stare. The only woman walking toward us was a tiny thing with long blonde hair that was nearly white. Her flirty black skirt was a tad longer than I would've worn it, but paired with tights and shorty boots, it looked cute. She'd topped it with a thin-knit sweater in a shade of blue that matched her wide eyes. While the shirt wasn't tight by any means, there wasn't any mistaking the generous boobs under it. I stifled a sigh. I wasn't exactly built like a boy, but neither was I as blessed as the chick who was fast approaching us, her smile wide and her eyes focused only on the man behind the bar as she climbed onto the stool next to me.

"Hey, baby." He reached down, across the oak bar, and slid his hands over her ribs. "I was wondering when you were going to get here. You look . . ." His gaze swept down her, hungry. "Delicious."

"Funny, I was thinking the same thing about you." She raised her mouth to his, and he lifted one hand to her face, holding her chin between two fingers and kissing her with a thoroughness that made me both a little uncomfortable and a little turned-on.

"Mason." Her voice was breathless as she turned her head and caught my eye. "Um, honey, we've got an audience."

To his credit, he didn't immediately pull away from her. His lips teased for one last kiss before he eased her down to the stool.

Flashing me a saucy glance that held no remorse whatsoever, Mason ran his tongue over his mouth again. "Sorry about that. This is my wife, Rilla Wallace. Darlin', this is . . . uh, I'm sorry, I didn't ask your name. Or introduce myself." He pointed at his chest. "I'm Mason Wallace."

I swallowed another healthy gulp of wine. "Elizabeth Hudson." Once again, I congratulated myself that I'd never changed my name. Not officially, and not in my head. I stuck out my hand to the young woman next to me. "Nice pick on the wine, by the way. Your husband recommended the Riesling because he said you liked it."

Rilla glanced down at my glass, frowning as though she'd never seen wine. "Really?"

"Yeah, babe." Mason touched her hand where it lay on the bar. "You had it at New Year's, not this year but last. Remember? With Meghan and Ali and everyone?"

Her face cleared. "Oh, that's right. The white wine." She shot her husband a mischievous grin. "I remember that night."

His smile only grew, and I had the feeling I knew what they'd done that night. I cleared my throat. "I think I'd like another refill."

Mason reached for the bottle. "Darlin', can I pour you a glass, too?"

She cocked her head. "Are you driving me home? Boomer dropped me off."

"Of course I am. That was the plan, right?"

"Then fill me up." Rilla glanced at me, almost apologetically. "I don't usually drink, but this is my first night out in a long time. We have two little ones, and they keep me busy."

"Yeah, and you deserve a little fun." Mason set her glass of wine down. "How was everything at home when you left?"

"Insane." She shook her head, rolling her eyes, but I caught the way her mouth quirked up on one side. "I got the baby fed and down, and then I put Piper in the tub. I was getting ready at the same time, keeping my eye on her, and next thing I saw, she was trying to get Smoky in the bath with her, and that cat was having none of it. There was water everywhere. I almost cried when Millie and Boomer got there to take over."

"Okay, babe, you just earned yourself a second glass of wine." Mason squeezed her hand. "I've got to go give Darcy a hand. You ladies okay for the moment?"

I lifted my glass in a salute. "All good here. Thanks."

Rilla smiled at her husband. "Go forth and charm the masses." Her eyes tracked him as he moved to the other end of the bar, his steps surprisingly graceful for such a big guy. "I realize I'm not exactly an impartial judge, but he's fairly wonderful, isn't he?"

Part of me wanted to sigh, and the other part wanted to gag. I ignored both and sipped my wine. "He seems to be."

"So . . . Elizabeth?" She took me in, checking me out so thoroughly I felt a little uncomfortable. "You're visiting? New in town?"

I shrugged. "New, not yet in town. I'm on my way in. My car's out in the parking lot, packed so full I'm surprised it's not scraping pavement. I just stopped here for a little, um, snack on my way to the apartment."

"Ah." She nodded as if what I'd said made sense to her. "What brings you to Burton? It's not exactly a destination for most people, unless they have family here already or they've moved here for a job."

This was the sticky part. I opted to go with a version of the truth I'd been telling most people over the last few weeks. "I bought out a law practice from an attorney who was retiring. I was looking to move, and I love Savannah, so it worked out for me to be so close."

Rilla regarded me without speaking for a moment. "Uh huh. Is that Clark Morgan's practice? I heard he was moving to New Mexico with his wife, to be closer to their kids."

"That's the one." I finished my third glass of wine, and as usually happened, the alcohol hit me all at once. Everything got a little hazy around the edges, and I wasn't quite seeing clearly, but the dull and constant ache that'd been part of me for the past five weeks? Yeah, it was definitely easing. "I mean, who wouldn't want to be a lawyer in a small town like this? It's practically like Mayberry, right? Just . . . grab your fishing pole and whistle down the street."

"Well . . . not quite. Maybe in some ways."

Rilla, I noticed, still had an almost full glass of wine. Clearly she wasn't in a hurry to forget the particulars of her life, and why should she be? Here she was, this girl who had to be at least five years younger than me, married to that guy who was so hot he practically smoldered, and with two kids to boot? Plus, you could just tell by looking at them that he was head over heels in love with her. I'd bet he'd never leave her. I'd bet he'd walk over fire before he walked out on her.

"If I had your life, I wouldn't be in a hurry to drink all my wine, either." I spoke out loud without meaning to do it.

"I'm sorry?" She paused in the act of raising her glass to her lips.

"I said, if I had your perfect life, I wouldn't want to drink away my memories, either." I rested my elbows on the bar, mostly to keep myself stable.

Rilla smiled, and even as blurry as my eyes were, I saw a little sadness there. "We all have things we'd like to forget, don't we? Even the people you might think have a perfect life." She lifted her glass, almost toasting me. "But you're right. I'm very blessed. I have an incredible husband, two healthy kids and people who love me—and who I love right back. Two years ago, I never would've dreamed I'd have this. I thought I was doomed to be alone forever. So you never know, right?"

"I guess." I turned my glass in circles, the damp paper napkin shredding beneath. "But maybe sometimes things don't work out. Maybe even when you think you've found your happily-ever-after, it turns out to be another dead end."

Rilla started to say something else, but just then, the other bartender approached us. "Hey, Rilla. How're you doing? How are those sweet babies?"

"Hi, Darcy. They're keeping me hopping, but I'm not complaining. How's your family?"

The older woman grimaced. "Driving me nuts. Turns out all the crazy things you did in your youth come back and haunt you through your kids, when they say, 'But Mom, you did it when you were my age!'" She refilled a bowl of nuts and set it down between us. "They're good kids, though. Not going to complain." She glanced my way. "Can I get you ladies anything? What're you drinking?"

I smiled. "I was drinking Riesling, but I'm ready to upgrade. Pour me a shot of Jameson's, please."

Darcy's eyebrows rose. "You sure about that? You got someone to drive you home?" Her eyes darted around me. "Or wherever you're going?"

I dug into the pocket of my purse and fished out my car keys. "Here you go, Darcy. Nice name, by the way. My best friend in law school was Darcy, too. She abandoned me with a law practice so she could marry her one true love. Nice, huh? Anyway, take my keys. Not going to drive. Believe me, I'm a lawyer, I know better." I waved my hand in front of my face. "I'll call a cab or something."

The bartender laughed. "Honey, you must be new in town. No cabs in Burton, unless they got lost on their way to Savannah."

"Mason and I'll make sure she gets where she needs to go, Darce." Rilla spoke up. "At this point, I don't know that the whiskey'll hurt her."

Darcy sighed. "Your funeral, toots. Here you go." She poured me the shot. "Bottoms up."

"Bottoms up." I giggled at the phrase. "If I have too many of these, my bottom'll be up, for sure." I tossed back the whiskey, wincing at the burn. "God, that's good."

Across the room, music began to blare from a set of huge speakers, and at the same time, the lights dimmed. The women in the bar and in the restaurant area all began to cheer as a good many of them made their way to the dance floor.

I recognized the opening strains of a song I'd loved in high school. "Oh, my God, I've got to dance to this." I slid from the stool and grabbed the edge of the bar until the room stopped tilting. Holding out my hand to Rilla, I grinned. "Hey, lucky lady, want to dance? I hate being out there without anyone I know."

Indecision warred on her pretty face. Finally, she shrugged. "Okay. Why not?" She raised her voice. "Darcy, tell Mason I'm on the dance floor if he's looking for me, will you?"

Darcy nodded. "Let me know if you need help, Rilla."

"She doesn't need help. She's gonna boogey." I exhibited a few of my more sophisticated dance moves. "We're gonna get down. Like Kenny says, we're young."

A few steps onto the dance floor and we were both swallowed up by the crowd of gyrating females. For the first time in months, I felt relaxed, wild and pain-free. This was good. I let go, shaking my ass, wriggling my shoulders and letting my hair fall back as every memory melted away into oblivion.

"Elizabeth." The voice that roused me from blissful rest wasn't familiar, but it was kind. I blinked, looking up into the warm brown eyes. Did I know him? Something jarred in my mind. *Oh, yeah, the bartender. Who owned the bar and gave me the nice wine.*

"Yep." I licked my dry lips. "Yep, I'm Elizabeth."

"Honey, can you tell us where you're going? Where's your apartment?"

I struggled to put the pieces together. "Um, Crystal Cove. My house is . . . fuck, no, I don't live there anymore. Moved out." The pain came thundering back as I remembered. "Burton. I'm . . . some apartment. Next to the flower shop, but only until he can build me my own house out in the country. *Our* own house. We're going to plant a garden, and raise food and babies."

The long sigh came from the woman sitting next to me. I felt a soft hand on my hair, stroking it down my back. "Elizabeth, we don't know where to take you."

"Address is in my phone." I tried to sit up, but the room spun, and not in a good, fun way. Gingerly, I lowered my head back to the table.

"Your phone is locked." I heard frustration in Mason's tone. "Is there anyone we can call? Anyone who expects you?"

My lips began to move separate from my brain, speaking before I could stop them. "Yep. Call Trent Wagoner. Call my husband, Trent."

CHAPTER TWO

Trent

WHEN I WAS A LITTLE kid, I was afraid of the dark. It wasn't something I ever told anyone; the foster homes I'd lived in off and on throughout my childhood were actually good ones, run by caring, decent parents, but I'd learned fast that kids in crisis can sometimes be like cornered animals. Even the ones who might not have normally been mean or aggressive kept their eyes open for weaknesses in others, and telling them I was having silent freak-outs after the lights were switched off? Yeah, that was a definite weakness.

Later, when I was a teenager, I realized the dark had certain benefits. In the corner of the school gym during a dance, for instance, the lack of light gave me the chance to feel up any girl I could convince to join me there. If I managed to bum a ride for my date and me to the movie theater in the next town over, the dim and flickering light from the screen was perfect for a hot and heavy make-out session. Plus, I was cool. By that time, I'd learned to hide, to cover up any real emotion I might have had. It was safer that way.

Nowadays, the dark of my bedroom was a relief at the end of the day. It was the one place I could take off the mask of indifference and caution that I wore all day. One place I didn't have to worry about anyone sneering at me behind my back, making snide comments just loud enough for me to hear. One place I didn't have to fear running into—well, anyone.

And hell, let's be honest, it was also a damn relief to be off my feet after a solid eight of lifting bags of feed, hauling crap around the warehouse and working my ass off. I was grateful for my job, no doubt about it. When I'd come back to Burton, I'd assumed I could get back my old position at the hardware store. I'd left on good terms the last time I'd moved out to Benningers' farm to work for the summer, and although I hadn't come back after harvest, since I'd moved up to Michigan, I couldn't think of any reason why Larry wouldn't hire me again.

Until I'd pushed open the door that day and had seen the look on his face when he spotted me. At that moment, I'd remembered the fatal flaw in my logic. Larry Wexler was Jenna Sutton's uncle, her mother's brother. That was how we'd met in the first place; he'd given his niece a part-time job. I'd been so intent on forgetting everything about her, about that time, that I'd blocked out the memory of their relationship.

Still, the man hadn't taken a swing at me the minute he saw me. That was a good sign. He didn't greet me with a hug either, but the expression on his face—somewhere between regret and resignation—was better than what I saw on the dude standing next to him. That guy looked vaguely familiar, but I couldn't place him.

"Trent." Larry sighed, shaking his head. "I heard you were back in Burton." He glanced at the other man. "Heard why, too."

My back went stiff. The last thing I wanted to talk about was what had brought me back home. "Yeah, well . . . it wasn't exactly what I planned, but when does anything ever work out? It's all good. But I need a job. I was hoping maybe . . ." My voice trailed off as Larry's mouth pressed into a hard line.

But the other man didn't have any problem with filling up the sudden uncomfortable silence. "Oh, hell, no. Are you out of your fucking mind? You have balls, Wagoner, to show up here and expect anyone to help you. Either that, or maybe you're strung out like your mama. Heard she was trying to hook some big fish on the corner in front of the Catholic Church."

"Nick, that's enough." Larry's tone was hard. "Keep your mouth shut." His eyes flickered back to me. "Trent, I wish I could say it was different, but I can't give you any work here."

I was nodding before he finished the sentence. "I understand, Mr. Wexler. Sorry for bothering you." I couldn't stand to be in there a minute longer. Without another word, I turned and left the store, only stopping after the door had closed behind me. I stood on the street, staring at the cracked sidewalk, wondering what the hell I was supposed to do next.

"Trent." The door had opened again without me hearing it, but I couldn't miss the rattle of glass as Larry closed it behind him. "Hold up a minute, son."

"It's okay. Really. I just . . . forgot, I guess." I ran a hand through my hair. "But it's okay. I won't come back."

"I'm sorry, Trent. If it were up to me . . . boy, I'm not stupid. And I'm not blind. I saw you last year, when you and Jenna both worked here. You didn't do anything wrong. You didn't mess with her. She's my niece, my sister's girl, and God knows I love that child. But I saw what I saw." He put his weight onto one foot, hands on his hips, mouth pursed. "If it was up to me, I'd give you a job. But if my sister didn't kill me, my wife would."

"I get it." I did. I understood. I didn't hold anything against Larry, but I wanted to get away from there. I needed to be gone.

"Listen. You came back here for your mother, and that means something. Knowing what I know, you could've walked away from her, and no one would think worse of you. But you stood up and you came back. Maybe some won't think that makes a difference, but it does to me."

"Thanks." I stared over his shoulder, my jaw tense. I could feel a tic jumping in my cheek.

Larry blew out a long breath. "What I wanted to tell you is this. Grainger's hiring over at the feed store. You head over there now, and I'll call him, tell him you're coming. I'll give you a good recommendation. He'll hire you, I know it. Might be hard work, but you're young. You can handle it."

A small wave of relief covered me. "You don't have to do that."

"'Course I don't, but I'm going to. Get going." He paused. "I hope things work out with your mom. I knew her, when she first came to town." Larry cleared his throat, and his eyes dropped from my face.

"You did?" I wanted to gag a little. I couldn't picture my mother, the thin brittle shell of a woman she was, involved with Larry Wexler, a tall, strong Baptist who didn't drink or smoke.

"Not that way." Larry's brows drew together. "I just knew her a little. She went to church with us for a time. She was a sweet thing, always wanting to help out." He shook his head. "I see her nowadays, and I just try to remember what she was like back then."

I couldn't imagine my mother in church any more than I could see her with Larry. She'd never darkened the door of any religious building as long as I could remember. Still, I knew the man was trying to give me a piece of her I didn't have. For that, I stuck out my hand. "Thank you, Mr. Wexler. Appreciate the referral, and, uh, the . . . what you said about my mom. I'll be seeing you around."

"Yeah, probably. Good luck, son." He pumped my hand briefly before he turned to go back into the store.

And that was how I ended up working at Grainger's Feed Store. Paul Grainger was a good man, fair to his workers, and he didn't seem to hold anything against me. As a matter of fact, he was all business and wasn't interested in anything that happened beyond the walls of the warehouse and shop. That was perfectly okay with me. I would've been happy to forget everything else, too.

But it was damned hard work. I never stopped moving,

lifting and hustling all shift. So lying flat on my bed in the dark was pretty much the best part of my day. Okay, not pretty much. It was. No one was bitching at me, no one was whining, and no one was staring daggers at me.

I'd just relaxed enough that my eyes were drooping when my cell phone went off. For a few minutes, I considered turning it off. Who was going to be calling me, anyway, unless it was someone at work—and they never did—or my uncle Nolan, who was always asleep before ten o'clock? My number hadn't changed since I'd lived in Burton before, but there wasn't a soul in this town who'd have been phoning me.

But in the end, I rolled over and lifted the phone. My eyes took a second to focus on the screen, but there was just a number there—no name. It was a local call, and that kind of freaked me out. I pushed to sit up, reaching for my pants so I could run across the hallway and make sure *she* hadn't snuck out after I'd watched her go to bed.

I swiped my finger over the phone and held it to my ear. "Yeah?"

"Trent?" I didn't know the voice, though it sounded slightly familiar. "That you?"

"Yeah." I repeated the word. "Who's this?"

"It's Mason Wallace, down at the Road Block."

Of course. That's where I knew it from. "Okay. What can I do for you?"

"Uh . . ." Mason hesitated, and I got the feeling he wasn't sure how to answer that question. "The thing is . . . there's a woman here. She says she's your wife."

Shock took away my ability to speak. And apparently

made it impossible to breathe, too, because for a minute, I was gasping like a bluegill on the bank of the river. My mind, however, continued to spin out of control.

Elizabeth? Elizabeth was here, at the Road Block? In Burton?

". . . and I don't know, Trent. She's kind of, uh, well, wasted." Mason had continued speaking during my temporary paralysis. "She didn't drink that much, but she's sort of passed out. So maybe we misunderstood her. Or maybe she's just batshit crazy, man."

"No." I recovered enough to answer him. "I mean—is she blonde? And is her name Elizabeth?"

He was silent for a beat. "Yeah."

I rubbed my forehead. "Okay. Can you keep her there just until I can drive out? It'll be ten, maybe fifteen minutes."

"Oh, yeah. Don't worry, I don't think she's going anywhere for a while." I couldn't miss the thread of subtle amusement. "But we'll keep our eye on her."

"Thanks." I ended the call and for the space of a few minutes, sat unmoving, staring down at my hands.

Elizabeth was here, in Burton. To say I was surprised was a massive understatement. Part of me had believed I'd never see her again. I'd expected divorce papers would find me at some point, mostly because I couldn't imagine that she wouldn't want to get married again. Married this time to someone worthy of her, of course, which was something I was never going to be. I'd proven that and fast.

But now she was not only here, in my hometown, but she'd told someone that she was my wife. Yeah, Mason had said she was drunk, but still . . . obviously I'd been on her mind. When she was vulnerable and in trouble, it was me she'd told them to call.

I got dressed as fast as I could and slipped out of my room. The rest of the apartment was dark and still, and I counted that as a blessing. I was careful to close the front door quietly behind me before I jogged to my truck, parked in the street.

Burton was just as still as my apartment had been. The night was mild for February, but regardless of the temperature, it was winter, which meant everyone was cocooned in his own house. When spring came, there'd be people out sitting on front porches, watching the world pass by. But that was months away, and that worked in my favor. The last thing I needed was the neighborhood noticing the guy Burton loved to hate skulking around at midnight.

I didn't pass a single car until I was nearly to the club, and even then, I only saw one, turning out of the nearly-empty parking lot. I pulled up in front of the large wooden building and swung out of the truck.

Once upon a time, I'd spent every Friday and Saturday night at the Road Block. Before Mason had come home and opened up the club, I'd had to drive a town over to find a decent place for drinking, dancing and dicking around. This place had been a huge timesaver—not to mention helping me to conserve gas and wear and tear on my truck. And of course the music was a damn sight better, since Mason used the contacts he'd made while living in Nashville to make sure his club hosted the hottest up-and-coming bands.

But I hadn't set foot in the place since I'd been back in town this time. It held too many memories. Plus, I figured there was a better than average chance I'd be lynched or at least beaten up if I showed my face there. Not that I'd wanted to, anyway. Between work and—the other responsibilities I had now, there just wasn't time or energy for anything frivolous like dancing. Sure as hell wasn't interested in looking at any woman, let alone touching one.

Well, maybe just *one* woman . . .

I gave myself a full body shake, the way I used to when I was a kid and I needed to snap out of my head. I had to get real. I wasn't going to sail into the bar and find Elizabeth standing there waiting for me to rescue her. I'd get her out of there, she'd sleep off her drunk and then tomorrow morning, she'd be gone.

Although, another voice in my head reminded me, *I still had no idea why she was in Burton to begin with.* Was she here to find me? If that was the case, why hadn't she called? My number hadn't changed.

The only way to get the answers I wasn't sure I wanted was to go inside and face her. I took a deep breath and opened the door.

Most of the lights were already out. Only the bar was lit, and I could see Mason standing behind it, leaning over with his elbows resting on the solid oak. The blonde perched on the stool in front of him, whose lips were really close to his, was his wife, not mine.

That thought jarred me a little. Elizabeth and I'd had so little time together as a married couple that I'd only just begun thinking of her as my wife right before I'd left. I remembered the first time I'd referred to her that way out loud. I'd run into a coffee shop while she waited in the car, and the barista—a flirty brunette—had made a comment about the extra whipped cream I'd requested.

"It's not for me. It's for my wife." I'd felt an odd and unfamiliar twinge of pride and possessiveness when I'd used the word. *My* wife. Precious little in this life had been mine. I didn't have any siblings, I'd never known a dad, and my mother wasn't necessarily someone I wanted to claim. But Elizabeth . . . she was the most beautiful woman I'd ever seen. She was scary-smart, funny, sexy as hell, and somehow she loved me. She'd chosen me.

Now, watching Mason murmur something in his wife's ear that made her both giggle and blush, I was brutally aware of what I'd lost. What I'd never have again.

I didn't know if I made a noise or moved, but Mason spied me and straightened to stand up. He jerked his chin in my direction, and Rilla swiveled in her seat. I remembered her only vaguely; she hadn't been part of our crowd growing up, since she was both younger than us and had been homeschooled. She'd never been one to hang out here, even after she married the owner of the place.

But when I saw the expression in her eyes—the same wariness I'd seen in so many faces on the streets of Burton before I'd left last spring and since my return—I remembered that Rilla Wallace was also Boomer Sutton's niece. Jenna's cousin. And apparently, she hadn't forgotten what had happened a year ago.

"Trent." Mason came around the bar. "I heard you were back in town, but I haven't seen you around."

"Been busy." I jammed my hands in my pockets, but to my surprise, after the barest hesitation, Mason extended his hand. I shook it, absurdly grateful for the gesture.

Next to us, Rilla sighed.

"Yeah, I bet." Mason stood with his hands on his hips. "So . . . Elizabeth is over here. In this booth. She kind of passed out, and we thought that would be the safest place for her.

"Thanks." I swallowed hard. I wanted to run over and scoop her up, hold her against me again. And then again, I was afraid if I did, I might not ever let her go.

"So . . . wife, huh?" Mason quirked an eyebrow at me. "There's a story there, I guess."

There was, but it wasn't one I was going to share here tonight, with Rilla watching me, her eyes narrowed. I just nodded. "Sorry if she caused you any problems tonight. She's not like this. I've never seen her drink more than a glass or two of wine." They both regarded me silently, clearly expecting more of an explanation. "We, um, had a misunderstanding, and I didn't know she was coming to Burton."

"Yeah. She didn't actually mention you until right before she went under, or I probably would've called you sooner. She said she was just moving to town."

I didn't respond, but surprise made my stomach clench. *Moving to Burton?* That was news to me. But then again, just about anything having to do with Elizabeth would be news to me at this point.

Rilla slid to her feet. "She seems like a nice girl. I hope . . ." She glanced over in the direction of the darkened dance floor. "I hope things work out for you two."

Tension twisted my gut. I didn't want this chick's pity, not when she hardly knew me and probably had an opinion of me colored by her family. I gritted my back teeth together. "Thanks. I'll just get Elizabeth. We'll be out of your way."

I could see her feet hanging off the seat nearest the bar area, but the rest of her body was shrouded in the dark. I made my way to her, my heartbeat stuttering a little when I saw her face.

She lay on her side, with one hand tucked under her cheek, just as she always had done when she slept with me. Messy blonde curls tumbled over her shoulder and onto the smooth vinyl of the booth. Her eyes were shut tight, but her lips were slightly parted, as though she were waiting for me to kiss them.

I remembered the first time I'd done just that, standing on a chilly beach in Florida. I'd never forget the surprise in her eyes as they went soft, and the way her mouth had felt beneath mine.

"Her car is outside." Mason spoke quietly behind me, and I shot him a glance. "I went to check before I called you. She gave us the keys earlier." He dangled them in front of me. "It should be fine in our lot for tonight. If you want to bring her over tomorrow morning . . ."

I shoved the keys into my pocket and raked one hand through my hair. "I got work first thing. Okay if we leave it 'til about five or so?"

Mason lifted one large shoulder. "Sure. If she wants it before that—it looks like she's got all her crap in it, it's completely stuffed—tell her to give me a call, and I'll be happy to drive her out here."

"Got it." I bent to lift her beneath the arms, and Mason moved the table away to give me some room. Elizabeth was dead weight, her head lolling back over the crook of my elbow as I held her. I couldn't resist breathing in her scent, one quick fix after weeks of denial: she smelled like sunshine, honeydew and . . . whiskey. Yup, that was definitely whiskey.

I moved toward the door, but before I could leave, Rilla darted over to me, holding a jacket and a brown leather handbag I recognized. She laid it carefully on Elizabeth's middle, whispering to me, "The purse is zipped up, so you shouldn't have to worry about it spilling out."

"Thank you." I kept my voice low, too, although I had a hunch we could've screamed at the top of our lungs and not disturbed the woman in my arms. I started for the exit again, and Mason held open the door, giving me a thoughtful nod as I passed him into the chill of the night. Rilla came out with us, and I was grateful when she opened the passenger door of the truck.

"Good luck, Trent. I'll see you around." Rubbing her hands over her upper arms, she ran back up the steps to her husband.

I eased Elizabeth into the seat, leaning over her to fasten the seatbelt. I tugged it tight; the door on this side wasn't exactly the most dependable, and I didn't want her flying out.

"Trent? Is that you?" Her voice was soft and only a tiny bit slurred. My heart stuttered a little.

"It's me, baby. I got you." I tested the seatbelt one last time before I straightened.

"I dreamed you went away. I didn't know where you were." Her eyes fluttered, the lids heavy with the effort to stay open.

"I'm right here." I gave in to temptation and touched her soft cheek, still warm from sleep. "Just sit tight, okay? I'm taking you home."

"Mmmmm." She laid her head against the seat back again. I stepped away to close the door, and then had another thought.

"Elizabeth, if you feel like you're going to puke, tell me, okay, baby? So I can pull over?" The last thing I needed was that smell in my truck.

"Not gonna puke. Just so damn tired." She sighed, her head rolling again, and I knew she'd faded away again. Probably better that way, I decided. Neither of us was up to a long talk tonight about why we'd found each other in Burton.

She slept all the way back to the apartment. I focused on the road, only letting myself glance over at her at stop signs. I was afraid if I looked at her too much, I'd never be able to tear my eyes away.

We pulled up in front of the apartment, and I shut off the truck. Turning in my seat, I waited to see if Elizabeth would wake up. But she didn't stir. Her face was peaceful, and her breathing was even. I sat in the chilly silence for a few minutes, thinking that if I could just keep things like this, I wouldn't mind too much. If we could hold the world at bay, we'd probably be all right. As long as we'd stayed in our own little bubble of existence, we'd been happy and in love. It was the intrusion of real life and other people that'd screwed us up.

Elizabeth shivered, her lips pressing together and a small line forming between her eyebrows as she frowned in her sleep. It was getting colder, I realized, and she wasn't wearing her coat, which I had tossed onto the seat between us. Staying outside wasn't a realistic option. It was time to face the music.

I got out of the truck and closed the door behind me as carefully as I could. On the passenger side, I unlatched Elizabeth's seatbelt and slid my arms beneath her knees and behind her back, drawing her against my body again. She clung, her arms snaking around my neck and her face burrowing in my shoulder. I stepped back and kicked the door shut before making my way up the cement steps to the door of the apartment.

I hadn't locked the front door, since this was Burton, and no one in town ever turned a lock. I slipped inside, letting my eyes get used to the dark of the small living room while I figured out what to do next.

"Where are we?" Elizabeth's lips moved against the skin of my neck, and a shot of red-hot want rocketed straight to my dick. *Great.* All I needed was for her to feel my hard-on and freak out.

"Home." I kept my voice low, dropping my head closer to hers so she could hear me better. "Shhh. I'm just going to get you settled in bed—"

"Home where?" She was still a little fuzzy, I could tell, but her blinking eyes were starting to look clearer, which likely meant any moment she'd remember who I was and what I'd done. And then the shit would hit the fan.

"My—the apartment." I was careful about the semantics, because she'd have a pretty solid case against the idea that I had any rights to this place. "Just sleep for now, and we'll talk in the morning. It's really late."

Her eyelids fell again, as though they were too heavy to hold open. "I . . ."

"Trent? What're you doing out here?" The hall light clicked on, flooding the living room with brightness. My mother stood in the doorway of her bedroom, wearing the perpetual frown I'd gotten used to seeing. Her long hair hung limp over her bony shoulders, and her eyes were narrow as she stared at me.

"Go back to bed. Everything's fine." I hoped my tone told her I wasn't going to take any nonsense, not right now. "I'll talk to you in the morning."

"Why're you carrying that girl? What's wrong with her? What did you do?"

Of course it always came down to me doing something wrong, which was ironic as fuck seeing as I wasn't the one who'd been picked up for solicitation a month ago. And I wasn't the one who'd been in and out of jail and rehab for over twenty years.

"I didn't do anything. She's fine, just . . . tired. I'll explain tomorrow. Go to bed."

But because listening to me and respecting my needs was something utterly foreign to my mom, she stalked into the living room, craning her neck to get a good look at Elizabeth.

"You all right there, lady? He didn't hurt you, did he? Can you hear me?"

Elizabeth opened her eyes again, confusion warring with apprehension. "Hurt me? No . . ." She wriggled against me, and I loosened my arms, letting her slide to her feet, though she kept her weight against me, and I knew if I

28

moved, she'd probably collapse. "I'm okay. Who're you?"

My mother straightened up, her mouth twisting into an ugly scowl. "I'm this guy's mother, if it's any of your damned business. The better question is, who the hell are you?"

"Elizabeth." She answered as though it were a question in school. "I'm this guy's wife."

If we were living in a cartoon world, my mom's eyes would've bugged out of her head along with an ah—OOO—gah sound effect. Her mouth was a perfect round O, but for once, nothing came out of it.

I swallowed a long sigh. "Like I said, we're not dealing with this tonight. I'm getting her to bed, and then I'll tell you everything in the morning." *Yeah, not likely.* I'd give her just the bare minimum to get her off my back.

"Ooooh, boy. I can't believe this." She started to laugh, and the sound was as ugly as the rest of her. "You went and got yourself married, and you picked a drunk just like your dear old ma, didn't you?" She wrapped her arms around her stomach and gasped. "That's just perfect."

"She's nothing like you." The fierceness in my voice sobered her up fast. "Now get the hell into your bedroom, or I swear to God, I'll throw you out. I'll do it tonight, and I'm telling you, it's fucking cold out there. Get back into bed and thank Jesus you've got one."

Her gaze flicked between my face and Elizabeth's, but in the end, she didn't say anything. Turning on her heel, she stomped down the hall and slammed the door shut behind her.

"That's your mother?" Elizabeth swayed a little. "Wow. She's . . . ummm . . . pretty much exactly how I imagined her.

Why the hell's she here?"

My chest tightened. "That's something we can talk about tomorrow. For now, you need to go to bed." I gripped her shoulders and steered her toward the hallway. "My bedroom's down here. You can have the bed, and I'll sleep out on the couch."

She twisted around to look up at me. "You don't have to do that. We're married, remember?"

As if I could forget that. "I know, but . . . just trust me. I have to get up early for work, and you're not going to feel so great in the morning. You'll thank me after you've gotten some sleep."

She frowned but allowed me to nudge her along until we reached my door. I leaned around her to open it and guided her toward the bed.

"I don't have my bag with my pajamas." She stood next to the bed, hugging her arms around her ribs, looking like a forlorn little girl. I wanted to scoop her back into my arms and just cuddle her close, keep her safe and give her comfort. But I knew danger lay down that road. Instead I folded my arms over my chest—mostly to keep from touching her.

"Yeah, I know." I jerked my chin toward the cheap composite wood dresser along the wall. "I've got some T-shirts in there if you want to wear one of them, or you can just . . . undress. Whatever." I had a sudden and vivid mental image of Elizabeth peeling off her clothes and climbing naked into my bed. *Yeah, I had to get out of there and fast.* "If you need anything, I'll be on the couch. Bathroom's at the end of the hall. There's a clean towel under the sink." I was ridiculously glad I'd done laundry right after work, the only reason that the towel—which was mine—was clean.

"Okay." She dropped down to sit on the bed, kicked off her shoes and then, with a deep sigh, fell onto the pillow, curling her legs up.

For a moment, I just watched her, waiting to see if she would say anything else or need me for anything. When I heard the first soft snore, I took one step forward, lifting up the sheet and thin blanket and draping them over her slight body. Smoothing the covers over her shoulder, I gave myself permission to breathe in her scent, that intoxicating mix of lilac and roses I'd been missing since the night I'd left. And since I was down there anyway, leaning over her, I took the extra five inches and brushed my lips over her cheek.

"'Night, Elizabeth. Sleep well."

CHAPTER THREE

Elizabeth

PAIN. PAIN. PAIN.

My head pounded. I was pretty sure something inside was trying to claw its way out, and I probably couldn't feel any worse. And then I shifted a little on the bed, and a wave of nausea rolled over me.

Yeah, turned out I was wrong. I could feel worse. I groped for my comforter, to pull it up over my eyes, but instead of downy fluffiness, I found only an unfamiliar blanket. I managed to pry one eye open and focus on the room.

It wasn't my bedroom in the Cove. Instead, it was smaller, and the walls were painted a bland off-white. The floors were hardwood, but they didn't gleam like my mother's did. A scuffed old dresser was pushed against the wall between two small windows. Other than that and the bed, the room was empty. It felt temporary and impersonal.

Memories of the night before began to come back to

me. The Road Block . . . several glasses of wine . . . music, dancing and then a very unsettling image of Trent, coming to take me home.

"God." I turned my face into the flat pillow and breathed in. Immediately I was immersed in pure Trent, a mix of the soap he used and something else that reminded me of pine trees and cool breezes. I had a quick flash of him carrying me, holding me tightly against his body . . . and had I imagined that he'd brushed a kiss over my cheek? No, that must've been a dream. I didn't have the foggiest idea why Trent was here in Burton, when he'd told me he'd live in hell before he came back to this town. But no matter what, I had to be steely strong and remember that he wasn't the man I'd thought he was. He'd left me without so much as a backward glance, and that was something I couldn't afford to forget.

But I did have to figure out what the hell was going on and locate my car, which at the moment held all my worldly possessions, including a change of clothes which I needed pretty badly. I pushed to sit up, pausing long enough to let the room stop spinning. Taking several deep, cleansing breaths—just like they'd taught us in yoga class—I stood, bracing one hand on the wall.

"Okay then." I gritted my teeth and looked around the floor for my shoes. I found one at the foot of the bed and risked kneeling down to look underneath for the other one. After giving my head a minute to get over the dizzy, I rose to my feet again and slid them into my shoes. Time to face the music.

The first thing I realized when I stepped out into the narrow hallway was that it was much earlier than I'd thought.

The light seeping in from the small living room windows was weak and cast a gray glow. I slid along the wall, tentative, unsure of who I might see.

"Good morning."

I hadn't spotted Trent standing in the corner of the living room near the front door, one foot propped on the seat of a wooden chair as he tied the laces on a formidable work boot. His long legs were encased in worn jeans that I recognized, and a fitted blue T-shirt rode up a little on his back, revealing a strip of skin that was still tanned from the summer. I remembered what the skin felt like beneath my fingertips, and suddenly they were itching to touch it. My mouth went dry.

"Bet you're feeling kind of rough." He finished the laces and dropped his foot to the floor. His blue eyes assessed me, though his face stayed carefully neutral.

"My head hurts." I meant it to sound as though it wasn't a big deal, but my throat was still rough, and instead the words came out scratchy and almost bleating.

"Yeah, I guess it does." Trent hooked his thumbs in the front belt loops of his jeans. He glanced over my shoulder, and when I turned my head, I saw an old wall clock. "Listen, I have to get to work. But—"

"Work?" I sounded inane, but in my defense, when we'd been together in Crystal Cove, he hadn't yet decided what he was going to do next career-wise. I was mystified about what kind of job he might have here in Burton.

"Yeah. At Grainger's Feed." He gave his head a little shake, as though reminding himself of something. "Not that it means much to you, since you've never been in this town before. But anyway, that's where I work. And I got to go. I can't be late. But when I get home, we'll . . . talk." He sounded grim.

"Okay." The single word was all I could manage.

"Your car is still out at the Road Block."

I blanched, the memory of that place suddenly quite clear. "Shit." I pressed both hands to either side of my throbbing head. "I can't believe I got drunk on my first night in a new town. A town where I just bought into a law firm and plan to be a respectable member of the community." Saying it aloud made my eyes burn.

Trent's eye twitched, but he went on speaking as though I hadn't. "I'll run you out there after I get home from work, so you can pick it up."

Panic bubbled in my chest. "But all my stuff is in the car. My clothes and everything. I don't have anything else to wear." I pulled my shirt away from my stomach.

"Mason said he'd drive you out today if you wanted. He lives just a little bit across town, so if you want to call him, I can leave you his number."

The idea of asking for a ride from the guy who'd had to put up with my drunken ass the night before was considerably less appealing than waiting for Trent to be able to take me out there. "I'll wait for you. I'm not scheduled to go into the office until tomorrow anyway."

"Okay. Well . . . I'll be home a little after four. There're a couple places you can walk to around here—Kenny's Diner is about three blocks away if you turn left. Ah, and some kind of craft store in the other direction. I don't know what-all else there is."

"Okay." That was apparently the official word this morning. *Okay.* Trent put his hand on the doorknob, but before he could leave, I remembered something else. "Oh, hey—did I dream it, or was your mother here last night?"

His shoulders slumped. "You didn't dream it. More of a nightmare, anyway."

"So she's here, in your apartment?" I looked behind me, as if she might be creeping up.

"Yeah, but you don't need to worry about her. She'll sleep most of the day, probably. And Mrs. Price across the street watches the house for me." At my blank look, he pointed through the front window, nudging aside a tired looking bit of lace curtain. "She's homebound. Elderly. She sits in her chair all day, staring out into the street, so I made an arrangement with her. She watches the house, and if my mother leaves, Mrs. P. calls me. I do all her grocery shopping and take care of anything else around the house for her. It works for now."

"Got it." I nodded slowly. "But why do you have someone spying on your mom? Is she under house arrest or something?" I meant to be flippant, but Trent nodded.

"Or something. She's a drunk, Elizabeth. And she's mean, manipulative—" He stopped and shook his head. "Never mind. Just ignore her, if she wakes up. I'll try to get home as soon as I can, so you don't have to deal with her any longer than necessary."

I lifted one shoulder. "I'm a big girl. I'm sure I can handle it."

"Maybe, but you don't have to. She's not your problem." His jaw tensed before he blew out a long breath. "Yeah, so

36

. . . I need to leave." He repeated the words, but he didn't actually move yet. "I have my phone with me all day, and I try to check it, in case you need anything. Your purse is in the bedroom, by the way." He pointed down the hall. "So I'll see you later. This afternoon."

"And we'll talk." I wrapped my arms around my ribs. "Okay. See you later."

"Yeah." This time he swung open the door and went through it, jogging down the steps to the sidewalk. I stayed frozen in place until I heard his truck start up and pull away.

And then . . . I turned in a slow circle, checking out Trent's place in the dim sunlight just starting to fill the living room. It was very basic. An old sofa was pushed against the wall; it was covered in a faded quilt, but I could still make out the lumps beneath it. Other than that and the chair near the door, the room was empty. It felt temporary and somehow sad.

I sighed, thinking about my cozy little place back in the Cove. It hadn't been spectacular by any means, but it had felt like home, even more so after Trent had moved in with me. Of course, that meant it had turned into my own personal den of tears after he'd left me. Not that I'd ever let him know that.

I went back into the bedroom and found my purse on the dresser. My phone was still on, but barely; the little battery icon at the top of the screen was blinking like mad, screaming for me to charge it up. Since my charger was in another bag in my car, the phone was going to have to die for now. I tucked it away and dropped back onto the bed.

The apartment was quiet. I had long, empty hours

stretching out in front of me, and God knew I should've been exhausted. I burrowed my face back into the pillow, breathed deep of Trent and willed myself to go back to sleep.

But it wouldn't happen. I tried deep breathing, counting sheep and reciting Bible verses from my childhood. Nothing worked. Heaving a sigh, I rolled over and settled down again. The problem was, my mind wouldn't quiet. Even with the blaring headache, my thoughts were coming fast and furious, darting from one worry to another.

I'd stayed last night with Trent, the man I thought I'd never see again. The man who I'd fallen madly in love with at Christmas, married on New Year's Eve and lived with for two amazing months, before he'd suddenly left me, with no warning or explanation. The man who'd broken my heart so utterly that I'd thought I'd never stop crying.

What made it worse was that my grief had been tinged with anger at myself. I'd spent countless hours beating myself up for the choices I'd made. After all, Trent had been honest with me from the minute we met. He'd told me that he was a man-whore who was trying to reform. He'd deflected my flirting and my not-so-subtle invitations, and I'd accepted that we were destined to be only friends. His change of heart had been a huge surprise, but it wasn't one I overthought. After all, I'd been slowly falling for this man for four weeks; the fact that we were finally on the same page felt . . . right. It was as though everything was working out at last.

And for a while, that was true. Just as I hadn't expected him to fall in love with me, his leaving came as a shock, too. Yes, we'd had a little spat. I knew he'd been upset that I'd jumped the gun on moving to Burton, but when we went to bed that night, both of us stiff and silent, nothing had prepared me for the fact that I'd wake up alone.

I clamped my jaw together and pressed one palm over my eyes, willing all the pain to pass. It didn't. After a few more moments, I snarled under my breath, tossed back the blanket and pushed myself out of the bed again. I was too restless to lay still any longer, and even though I wasn't really sure what I was going to do to occupy myself for the next . . . I calculated the time in my head. *Nine hours.* Well, I'd figure out something. I couldn't hide in the bedroom all day.

Down the hall from Trent's bedroom, I saw the open door of a bathroom. That cheered me slightly; I might not be able to change my clothes, but I could get clean at least. I tip-toed past the other closed door—where Trent's mom was sleeping, apparently—and slipped into the bathroom as quietly as I could.

This was clearly the domain of a male. One thin towel hung from a hook on the back of the door, and the hand towel ring was empty. A cake of soap sat on the counter by the sink next to a toothbrush and a nearly-flattened tube of toothpaste. Nothing was dirty, exactly, but neither did it have the extra touches most women might add.

But beggars can't be choosers, so I decided to suck it up and make the best of the situation. Squeezing a tiny bit of toothpaste from the tube, I used my fingers to scrub at my teeth and then rinsed my mouth with a handful of water. It wasn't the same as a toothbrush, but it would do for now.

I rummaged under the sink and found a folded towel that seemed to be clean. There wasn't much else there other than a bottle of toilet cleaner and an old black nylon shaving kit that once upon a time had sat next to my own makeup case in the bathroom I'd shared with my husband. I gave into temptation and unzipped the bag, touching the handle of Trent's razor, still damp from when he'd used it this morning. His shaving cream and deodorant were tossed in there, too, along with a small folded piece of red paper tucked in the side. Frowning, I dug my fingers further in and retrieved it.

As soon as I touched the paper, I knew what it was. And when I unfolded it, I saw I was right; my own loopy handwriting covered the tag.

Merry Christmas, Trent! Love and kisses, Elizabeth

I traced the T in his name with the tip of my fingernail, remembering. I'd been at a loss as to what to buy my new boyfriend for Christmas. He didn't need anything, really; he didn't have a house, just his truck. He wore jeans and T-shirts most of the time, along with the occasional flannel shirt. There were plenty of things I might've bought for him, but one thing I knew about Trent Wagoner already, and that was that he was a proud man who wouldn't take kindly to his woman splurging on a big gift for him. The thought that I was 'his' woman had given me a shiver of delight; at that point, we hadn't made any commitments, but I could tell how he felt by the way he looked at me.

Finally, I'd settled on something simple. I'd run by Matt Spencer's surf shop and picked up an inexpensive pair of board shorts, since Trent had confessed to not owning any swimming trunks at all, and on impulse, I'd also grabbed a kitschy Crystal Cove souvenir key ring. His truck keys were on a plain ring, so I thought something fun might make him laugh. At the last minute, I had an extra key to my apartment made and added that to the ring.

When we'd opened presents on Christmas morning—well, it was more accurately Christmas afternoon, since we'd kept each other awake most of the night, making love first under the tree, and then on the bed, and then to Trent's amusement, on the narrow fainting couch in my living room—Trent had laughed at the board shorts. But his face had gone still when he'd seen the key ring and key.

For a moment, I'd forgotten to breathe. I'd bitten my lip, wishing like hell I could rip the thing from his hands and make him forget I'd done this crazy thing. But the eyes he'd raised to mine were filled with wonder. I'd barely had time to stammer out the beginnings of an explanation when he'd pulled me into his arms, kissing me speechless.

"No one's ever given me something like this." His lips brushed over my temple, his warm breath fanning my hair. "Trusting me with . . . with you. Thank you."

I swallowed over a lump in my throat, thinking about it. That day, he'd taken the tag I'd made and tucked it into his pocket. Apparently, he'd saved it even beyond Christmas. Not for the first time, I wished I could read his mind and get some insight into what made this man tick. If nothing else, I wanted to know why he'd gone from apparently loving me to leaving me without a word.

Tucking the paper back into his shaving kit, I pulled the zipper shut again and replaced it under the sink. Trent would never know I'd been snooping, but the thought of him holding onto that small scrap of paper stayed with me as I stepped into the shower and turned on the water.

Putting back on my rumpled clothes—the same ones I'd been wearing since I'd left Crystal Cove the morning before—was not much fun. I grimaced as I performed the nasty task of turning my underwear inside out before I pulled it on again. I hadn't done that trick since my college days, during finals. I shook out my jeans and stepped into them and then tugged the shirt over my head. Luckily, I had a brush in my purse, so I was able to finagle my hair into a ponytail. I'd washed my face clean of makeup, and between that lack and my hair up, I looked like I was about sixteen years old.

I hung up my towel on an empty bar and ventured out of the bathroom. I'd just stepped into the living room, which was now flooded with bright sunlight, when I heard a raspy voice behind me.

"So the princess finally makes an appearance."

I startled and turned slowly. "Good morning. I'm sorry we didn't really get to meet last night. I'm—"

"Yeah, the wife." She cackled then, and I winced. "Which is a huge joke, because my boy, he don't do long-term. He's not exactly the staying kind, if you know what I mean."

Oh, did I know what she meant . . . But I wasn't going to discuss Trent with this woman. During our short time together, one thing I'd come to know was that his mother had been neglectful and cruel during his childhood. Trent had spent the better part of his growing up years in foster homes. I wasn't really clear on why his mother was living with him now. And I certainly wasn't going to ask her.

"I don't think that's any of your business. Matter of fact, I don't want to talk with you about anything to do with Trent. You don't know anything about—us."

Her faded eyes narrowed in the sullen and sunken face. "I know enough. I know my boy's not the kind to settle down. Probably takes after his father, whoever that was. He's the love 'em and leave 'em type. So what'd you do to tie him down? Get him drunk first? Or did you tell him you were knocked up? That might do it."

My fingers curled into fists, the nails digging into my palms. "No and no. I didn't get him drunk. I've never seen Trent drunk, ever. And I'd never lie about something like that. About having a baby. I'm not pregnant, and I didn't trick him into anything. If you want the truth, getting married was Trent's idea." I stopped abruptly, wishing I could pull back those last words. They were true, yes, but the last thing I wanted to do was give his mother any ammunition.

"Oh, it was?" She grinned then, and I saw gaps between chipped and crooked teeth. "Ah, okay. I get it now. You're loaded, aren't you, princess? My boy saw his chance at a payday." She laughed that horrid, hurtful laugh again. "So he left you, huh, when you wouldn't fork over the cash, and you came sniffing after him? Isn't that always the way?"

"No, actually, it's not. But like I said before, it's none of your business. If you were any kind of decent mother, you'd be worried for your son, and maybe wondering why he got married so fast. But I know about you. I know what you did to Trent when he was growing up, how often you left him. I know about the drinking and the drugs—"

"You shut your fucking mouth, you little bitch princess." In just three steps, she was in front of me, in my face, one bony finger poking into my chest. "You don't know nothing about nothing. Trent whines about a lot of shit, but he's just lucky I didn't get rid of his sorry ass before he was even born. Know how many times I wished I had? Plenty. But he don't ever say thank you for that, does he? No, it's all 'my mother did this' and 'my mother did that.' Fucking whiner is what he is."

I didn't have anything to say to that. This woman made me want to gag, and I took an involuntary step backwards.

"That brother of mine fills his head with how bad my boy had it. How'd he know? He never bothered to come down from Michigan when I needed him. When I was knocked up and alone, he wouldn't come. But then it's real easy to blame the mother, isn't it?"

I thought of Trent's Uncle Nolan, who I'd met in Crystal Cove. He owned the Christmas tree farm where Trent had been working since last spring, and they'd come down to Florida together to sell the trees. From what I'd seen, Nolan was a decent man who loved his nephew. He'd always been kind to me, too.

"Nolan's been good to Trent. I met him in Florida, and he seems like a nice guy."

She snorted. "Sure, to you he would." She popped both hands to her hips and smirked. "You just listen, princess. Don't get comfy here. It's not going to be long before Trent gets tired of babysitting me and takes off again. I can tell you I'm not counting on him hanging around, and neither should you. You're not his type." She let her gaze wander down my body in derision. "Yeah, not his type at all."

Nausea and misery rose in my chest. I couldn't stay in that room for one more minute. Reaching blindly for my purse, I yanked open the door and stumbled out into the cold air. I fumbled in my purse for my sunglasses and shoved them onto my face, both to protect my eyes from the brilliant sunshine and to hide the threatening tears.

At the edge of the sidewalk, I hesitated. I didn't really have any place to go. I glanced back up at the door to the apartment, hugging my arms around my waist and shivering. For the first time, I noticed that there was a flower shop next door to Trent's apartment. Suddenly, something clicked in my memory.

It's a small apartment, right next to the florist on the main street in town. Just two bedrooms and one bath, but it was the only thing coming up for rent in town right now. I figured later we could find something else. That little house out in the country you were talking about, maybe. Once I get settled in at the law office, anyway, and you figure out what you want to do next.

My voice that night had been filled with hope and happiness. I'd done something on impulse, but I just knew Trent would be okay with it. Surprised, sure, but in a good way. And that was where I'd been terribly wrong.

But the dawning realization—*that son of a bitch is living in the apartment I rented for us*—took away some of the guilt and amped up the mad. I'd been the one to choose this place and to put down the deposit. It was where I intended to live in Burton, and it had been my destination the night before. My lips curled. Here I'd thought it was mortifying that in my drunken state I'd blurted out Trent's name as my emergency contact, but it seemed I was doomed to run into him even if I'd bypassed the Road Block and driven into town stone cold sober. Because he was living in my damn home.

Following close on the heels of the annoyance was the knowledge that I couldn't do anything about that right now. Trent was at work, his mother was firmly ensconced in the apartment—*my* apartment—and I was standing out here on the street looking like an idiot. What was I going to do, march back in and toss the horrid woman out on her ear? Yeah, that wasn't going to win me any points with Trent. Not that I was looking to appease him, of course, but still—he had come to my rescue last night. I supposed I owed him at least the courtesy of explaining how he happened to be living in the apartment I'd intended for the two of us.

Meanwhile, a stiff breeze blew, and I shivered. I kicked myself for not having grabbed my jacket before I'd fled the apartment, but no way was I going back in there now. And there wasn't anything to be gained by standing here freezing to death until Trent came home.

I headed in the direction of the diner he'd mentioned, since that seemed like the most promising destination, and I did have my purse and wallet with me. I could get some breakfast, drink some coffee and at least warm up a little. But once I reached the small restaurant, something held me back from actually going inside. I still felt a little queasy thanks to last night's fun, and just seeing the place full of people gave me pause. Through the shaded windows, I could see the filled booths and tables and waitresses moving between them. They looked cozy and comfortable with each other, and I felt like an outsider. Yeah, I didn't need that.

Instead I kept walking. A few people passed me, and I felt their curious glances; whether that was because I was a stranger or because I looked as though I'd slept in my clothes—which of course I had—I wasn't sure. I kept my head down and my eyes on the pavement in front of me.

I was wandering without any sense of where I was headed, turning corners and hoping I'd figure out how to get back to the apartment by the time Trent was home from work. Of course, Burton wasn't exactly New York City, so I had a hunch getting lost would be difficult.

At the third corner, I hesitated. I was back at the main drag in town, having executed three sides of a square. Across the street was an older house that had been converted to a doctor's office, and to my right sat a dry cleaner. But it was when I turned to see what was behind me that I caught my breath.

The building was brick, two stories, with double doors painted white. The sign on the lawn was made of weathered wood, and words carved into it made me grin.

McAllister Memorial Library of Burton

From my earliest memories, libraries had been my sanctuary. As soon as we moved into a new town or onto a new Army post, the first thing I'd do once the moving trucks had pulled away—and sometimes even before, if I could sneak off without my mom knowing it—was find the public library. I'd get my new library card, if I could scrounge up proof-of-address, or at the very least, I'd make friends with the librarians. And then I'd be back at least once a week, finding new books and getting lost in a world that felt warm, accepting and safe. It was my haven in a life that often seemed chaotic and out of control.

Before I could stop to think about it, my feet were moving up the stone steps to the doors. I turned the doorknob, testing it, half expecting the door to be locked, as I wasn't sure it was even nine o'clock yet.

But it opened, and I stepped into the warmth with gratitude, breathing deep the familiarity of books, wood polish and silence. For a moment, I was in utter bliss.

"Good morning. Can I help you?"

The voice belonged to the woman standing against the check-out desk, her arms folded over her chest. She was about my height, I judged, probably in her late forties, with light brown hair and wide blue eyes. She regarded me with mild surprise and the hint of a smile.

"Um." I twisted the strap of my purse between my fingers, all too conscious of how I probably looked. I wondered if she thought I was homeless or down on my luck, on the prowl for a place to hang out.

Then again, maybe she wasn't that far off.

"I'm new in town." I blurted out the words. "I don't start working until tomorrow, and my, uh, stuff, my bags with my clothes, haven't caught up with me yet." I tried for a confident smile. "I don't know anyone here, and I don't have my car yet, either, so I was just . . . taking a walk. And I saw the library. I love libraries."

The woman laughed softly. "Well, that's good to hear. I always think a love of libraries is the sign of a kindred spirit." She extended her hand to me. "I'm Cory Evans. Welcome to Burton."

"Thanks. I'm Elizabeth Hudson."

"Nice to meet you, Elizabeth." She tilted her head, studying me. "I just put on the kettle for my morning tea. Would you like to join me? My daughter-in-law made me some delicious cinnamon buns, and they go very well with a hot cup of tea."

My stomach chose that minute to emit a loud growl, and I met Cory's gaze sheepishly. "I guess I can't very well claim I'm not hungry, huh? Thank you. Tea and cinnamon buns sound heavenly."

The staff room beyond the desk was small, but with a small round table in the center and several overstuffed chairs set up around it, I could feel the coziness. Cory waved for me to sit in one of the chairs as she prepared to pour the tea.

"My daughter Maureen gave me this tea for Christmas, and I've been enjoying it every day since. It's a holiday spice, and it just warms me up." She lifted the lid from a small white china pot and pulled out a silver ball infuser. "Do you like honey in your tea? The Nelsons send me jars of the honey from their bees."

When I had the cup and saucer in my hand and a cinnamon bun on the plate in front of me, Cory sat down, too. She took a dainty sip and closed her eyes, humming.

"So, Elizabeth. What brings you to Burton?"

I stalled by taking a drink and using my fork to cut into the bun. "Ah . . . it's kind of a long story. But the short answer is that I bought a law firm."

Cory raised one eyebrow. "Clark Morgan's firm? I knew he was retiring, but I had no idea he'd actually sold the practice. His wife's been pestering him for the last three years.

She wants to move to New Mexico, to be near their grand-children."

"Yeah, he seemed pretty happy when I called him." I closed my eyes as I bit into the bun. "My God, these buns are incredible."

Cory's mouth tightened on the corners. "Yes, Ali's got a gift." She shook her head and laughed a little. "I'm sorry. I'm a real stickler about swearing, and I'm always on top of my girls about it." She rolled her eyes, apology sketched on her face. "You remind me of my daughters. I was about to give you a hard time for taking the Lord's name in vain."

I swallowed the bite I'd just taken. "I'm sorry. My mom's the same way, but I was the only girl in my family. She pretty much gave up by the time I was a teenager."

"Ah, so you have brothers?" She leaned back in her chair. "I have two daughters and one son. Well, clearly, since I have a daughter-in-law. And I have one granddaughter, two grandsons and another of one kind or the other on the way."

A wistful sense of longing rose in me. "Sounds like you have a wonderful family. You're lucky."

"I am. Very blessed." Cory fiddled with her napkin. "My husband and I were married for over thirty years before he passed last year. I would've given anything for more years, but the time we had together was . . ." She paused. "More than any woman could ask for."

"I'm sorry." On impulse, I reached across and gripped her hand. "I can't imagine being with someone that long, and then losing him." I thought of Trent, and my heart stuttered a little.

"You're not married?" Cory glanced at my left hand, and my thumb rubbed against my ring finger.

"I'm . . ." I didn't know why, but I couldn't lie to this woman. Yeah, we'd just met, but she'd invited me in, made me tea and . . . well, she was a librarian. If I couldn't open up to her, who could I trust? "Actually, I am married. But it's kind of complicated."

"Oh, sweetheart, the best ones always are." She grinned, kicked off her black heels and tucked her feet beneath her in the chair. "Do tell. I love a good story."

I worried the corner of my lip between my teeth. "Okay, well . . . I was living in Crystal Cove, in Florida—"

"Oh, I know where that is. My daughter-in-law's sister-in-law Meghan is from there. I was down for the wedding last year."

My eyes narrowed. "Is everyone in Burton related to everyone else? I know of Meghan. Her mom Jude is a friend of mine. And I rented office space from her stepfather Logan."

"It's a small world, for sure. And no, we're not all related . . . quite. But sometimes it feels like we are. Anyway, go on. You were living in Crystal Cove. Were you working there?"

I nodded. "I moved down there right after law school graduation. My best friend talked me into opening a practice with her." I thought about Darcy and her giddiness that had convinced me moving to Florida was a grand idea. "Unfortunately, right after we opened, she met a guy, married him and moved to Ohio. I had to buy her out and stay in a town where I didn't know a soul."

"Oh, honey. That's terrible. What about your family? They weren't in Florida?"

"No. My dad's in the Army, and they're always moving. It was my decision to move to Florida, so I had to deal with the consequences." The truth was, I'd never asked for help or even complained to my parents about what had happened with Darcy. I'd been taught well the importance of keeping a stiff upper lip—and that didn't include whining about something I couldn't change. My dad would've told me to put my head down and get through it, and my mother would've pretended everything was fine. It was our family's MO.

"Anyway . . ." I brought my focus back to the present, or at least to the near-past. "Logan rented out the parking lot of his office building to a guy selling Christmas trees last November. The owner's nephew was working for him there, and that's how I met Trent."

"Trent?" Cory looked startled. "Trent Wagoner?"

Of course, she would know him. Hadn't we just established that everyone knew everyone else in this town? "Yeah, Trent Wagoner." I waited for her reaction, not sure what to expect. When Trent talked about his hometown, it was with a mix of wistful nostalgia along with an odd bitterness. I couldn't remember much about how Mason Wallace and his wife had reacted the night before when I'd named Trent as my husband. I wondered if Cory would give me more insight.

"That's who you're married to? Oh . . . hmmm. I'd heard that he was working for his uncle up in Michigan. Well, that's nice." Cory didn't give away anything in her tone or expression.

"It all happened so fast. We were just friends at first, because he—Trent was kind of on a fast from, uh, from girls."

Talking about his self-imposed sex fast with the woman who'd admitted swearing made her uncomfortable didn't seem like a good idea. "But then one thing led to the other, and we spent Christmas together." And what a Christmas it had been. Every minute together, we'd made new memories I'd expected to be just the beginning of our life together. "We were so happy, and it felt right . . . and I know it sounds insane now, but he asked me to marry him, so on New Year's Eve we drove up to Georgia and got married in Kingsland, just before midnight."

"Wow." Cory set down her tea. "That was very fast, wasn't it? How long had you known each other?"

I felt my defenses rising. "We'd known each other since before Thanksgiving. And we'd been—uh, together since Christmas." My shoulders slumped. "Yeah, it was fast. Probably too fast."

"That's a call only you two can make. Some of the best marriages begin impulsively." Cory smiled and patted my hand. "So that's how you came to be in Burton?"

"Kind of." I squirmed in my comfortable chair. "Trent talked about this town a lot. And we were trying to figure out what our future was going to look like. I'd just finished paying off what I owed from buying out my friend Darcy, and the world seemed wide open. One night, Trent started telling me about Burton, and he said if I came here and opened a practice, we could live in town at first, and then maybe buy some land just outside and have our own little farm. He talked about building us a house, and about what he wanted our lives to be like."

That night had been one of my favorites from our brief

time together. Trent had held me in his arms as we drowsed in bed, both us sated and warm and optimistic. It had felt like anything was possible.

"And stupidly, I thought he was serious about coming back here. I never had a hometown. I had moving trucks and Army posts and a suitcase. So I guess I idealized what it would be like. I thought he'd be pleased, but I guess I jumped the gun." I turned my teacup in a circle on its saucer. "The next day, after we'd talked, I went onto my law school alumni website and started looking for openings near Savannah. There was a posting about Clark Morgan's firm, and I should've talked to Trent first, but I thought it'd be a good surprise." I twisted the hem of my shirt between my fingers.

"And it wasn't?" Cory gave me a sympathetic grimace.

"Not exactly. I called Clark and we worked out the deal—he was so excited—and he gave me the name of a woman who could rent me an apartment in town, until we could find something more permanent. I called her, found out she had a place available, and I put down a deposit on it. When I got home that night, I couldn't wait to tell Trent what I'd done. But he was less than . . . appreciative."

That was putting it mildly. He'd gone eerily quiet, his face shuttering into stark emptiness the longer I talked. When he finally spoke, it'd been in short, terse sentences, questioning me about why the hell I'd thought he'd ever want to go back to his hometown. When I'd tried to explain, he'd stalked into the bedroom, closed the door and gone to bed without another word.

Cory sighed. "Oh, honey. Here you thought you were doing something good . . . I'm sorry. Trent's history here isn't easy."

I nodded. "But I still thought we'd work it out. I figured once he'd gotten over his mad, we'd talk and I could explain why I'd done it." My throat tightened. "But I woke up the next morning, and Trent was gone. He texted me later that day and said he'd realized we'd rushed into everything. That it had been a mistake, and we'd be better to walk away now, before things got too tangled up." I spread my hands in front of me. "And that was it."

"And yet here you are." Cory tipped the teapot over my cup and then her own. "What made you decide to come to Burton anyway?"

"Mostly because I'd already made the commitment to Clark. And I know it sounds stupid, but I never thought Trent would be here. The way he'd talked about this town, I assumed it was the last place he'd be." I picked up my cup. "I have no idea why I told Mason . . ." My voice trailed off. Sharing the story of my quickie wedding and crazy impulsive ideas about buying into law practices was one thing, but telling the kind librarian that my first action upon entering this fine town was getting shit-faced drunk was altogether different. And I really didn't know why I'd mentioned Trent's name to Mason, let alone confess that he was my husband. It must've been the wine.

"Mason? You already met Mason Wallace? I thought you just got to town."

I winced. "I did. But I stopped at his bar on the way in. That's how I found out Trent was here."

"Uh huh." Cory looked like she was biting back a smile. "So you've seen Trent?"

"You could say that. I'm kind of staying at his apartment. Which I figured out is actually my apartment. He had to leave early this morning to go to work, so I don't know why he's in Burton, why he's living in the apartment I'd arranged to rent or . . . well, I don't know anything. He says we're going to talk this afternoon."

Something I couldn't read passed through the librarian's eyes. "How much did Trent tell you about his childhood?"

My mouth tightened. "I know about his mother. He didn't say much about her, but what he did mention didn't paint a very pretty picture. And then I met her this morning." I paused, remembering the spiteful bitterness on her face. "Let's just say it didn't go well. She didn't exactly welcome me into the family."

"I'm sure." Cory sighed. "Donna Wagoner is—well, my mother taught me that if I didn't have anything nice to say about someone, I shouldn't say anything at all. So I'll keep my mouth closed, I guess." Her spoon clicked against the saucer as she lay it down. "I've known Trent since he was in kindergarten. He was in my son Flynn's class, and it was pretty clear from the beginning that he had, uh, challenges at home. I didn't know Donna before that, but I met her then."

"What was he like as a little boy? Trent, I mean?" Imagining the strong, stoic man I knew as a child was almost impossible.

Cory grinned. "He was a cutie. Those big blue eyes, and he was blond in those days. A little towhead. But he was very serious. He almost never smiled, it seemed to me." She focused over my shoulder, her gaze going soft. "I always remembered one thing, from when the kids were in third or fourth grade. Flynn and Trent were both playing soccer then, and they'd usually come over here after practice, then I'd drive Trent home. I used to invite him to stay for dinner, because I had a feeling he didn't get much in the way of home-cooked meals. But he'd always say, 'Oh, no, Mrs. Evans. Thanks, but my mom is waiting for me. She bakes me cookies every day for when I come home from school. I don't want to miss them.'

"Of course, I knew that wasn't true. I doubt his mother was even home most days after school. By that time, he'd been in and out of foster care at least twice. It just broke my heart when he said that."

Pain twisted in my chest as I pictured Trent, an earnest eight- or nine-year old, telling the story of how he wanted his life to be. Somewhere along the way, he'd come to grips with his reality. It hadn't exactly made him bitter, but he was guarded and more than a little cynical, I thought.

"I can't understand why he'd want to come back here and live with his mother after the way she treated him. I got the impression he tried to stay as far away from her as possible." I finished my second cup of tea.

"You don't know that he *wanted* to come back." Cory arched one eyebrow. "I'm not going to say anything else, Elizabeth, because it's up to Trent to share with you what he will. But I'll just give you a little insight into the male psyche, if you don't mind. No matter how much little boys grow up into men, inside there's still that child who wants to be wanted. Who wants to be loved and wants to trust the people who are supposed to provide that love. It's the same reason women return to their abusers time and again, and why kids are sometimes reluctant to talk about mistreatment. We're programmed to want to believe the best in people. And no matter how horrible a mother Donna was—and is—somewhere deep inside, Trent wants to believe she can change. He probably wouldn't admit it, but it's something for you to keep in mind." She reached over to pat my knee. "And that's all I'm going to say on the topic. Now, I've got books to reshelve and other work to do, but you're more than welcome to stay here until Trent gets home. I can't imagine you want to go back and hang out with Donna."

I shuddered. "No, thanks. I think I'd end up saying something I might regret if I had to spend any more time with her."

"Hmmm." Cory looked as though she might say something else, but in the end, she only shook her head a little. "Well, make yourself at home. And I hope you won't be a stranger, even once you're settled here in town. We need more appreciators of libraries in this world."

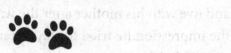

I stayed at the library until it was nearly four o'clock, and then, with no little reluctance, I thanked Cory for her kindness and began to wend my way back to the apartment. Trent's pickup was nowhere in sight, and there was no way in hell I was going back inside before he came home. I dropped onto the cement step, shifted against the chill of it, and waited.

Not five minutes later, the old truck rambled down

the road and came to a halt at the curb in front of me. My eyes followed Trent's movement from the driver's seat and around the front bumper. He slowed as he caught sight of me, and I heard his sigh. Without missing a beat, he sank down next to me, mirroring my position with his elbows on his knees.

"The fact that you're sitting out here says my mom was driving you crazy, huh?"

I slid him a sideways glance. "I'm sitting out here because I didn't want to go back inside before you got here. I spent the day at the library."

"The library?" Faint surprise tinged his voice. "You've been there all day?"

"Yup." I stared out into the street. "I met Cory Evans. She's really nice."

Trent stiffened just a little. "Mrs. Evans . . . yeah, she is. I know a couple of her kids."

"She said you used to play soccer with her son." I played with a string from the hem of my jeans.

"She did? Oh, um, yeah. Long time ago." His tone was cautious, tentative. "Did she say anything else?"

I lifted my shoulder. "No, not really. She mostly talked about her kids and her grandchildren, and how she knows Meghan and Jude. Oh, and she filled me in on some other stuff in the town, like who's related to who. Not that I'm ever going to remember it, since she wouldn't let me take notes."

He laughed then, a genuine chuckle that made my heart skip. "That sounds about right. And lately, Crystal Cove is all wrapped up in that, too. Now that Meghan's up here, and Alex—that's Alex Nelson, he was in my class, too—he and his boyfriend moved down to the Cove last fall to run the bed and breakfast."

"I know Alex and Cal. I'd forgotten that they were from Burton."

"Well, Alex is, originally. He grew up on a farm outside town, next to Sam and Ali Reynolds. I don't know where his boyfriend is from, though. Not here."

"Hmm." I twisted a little to face Trent. "And now here I am. One more Cove connection?"

"I guess." Trent moved a little, as though he were trying to maintain distance from me.

Silence stretched between us. I was waiting for him to say something, anything that might give me some insight into why he was here, in the hometown he'd sworn he never wanted to see again. Why he'd left me without warning or explanation.

But he didn't speak. His gaze was fastened on some spot just beyond the sidewalk, his mouth tight and his eyes shuttered again.

"I know this is my apartment." I blurted out the first thing that crossed my mind, even though it wasn't at all what I wanted to say. Trent frowned, the corners of his mouth curling slightly. I should have stopped there, but instead the words came tumbling past my lips. "This is the place I arranged to rent when I bought the practice. I paid a deposit on it. And you just waltzed in and took it? How did that happen?"

Trent closed his eyes, and steepling his fingers, he pressed them against his forehead. "I know. I didn't think you'd end up coming to Burton once I—well, after. I figured you'd change your mind and stay in the Cove, or go some-where else. And I was going to pay you back for the deposit. I've been saving it up, a little each week. I can give you what I have so far."

"I don't want your money." I knew I sounded like a pet-ulant child, but I didn't give a damn. "What I want is an ex-planation. And a place to live that doesn't come with a mean old lady who hates me."

He huffed out a laugh, shaking his head. "Yeah, I'd like that, too. To live without my mom, I mean."

"How did this happen, Trent?" I worked hard to keep my tone softer, less accusatory. "I know we argued, and I know I was stupid in making the plans without checking with you—but I didn't think it was so bad you'd leave."

"It wasn't. I mean—" He blew out a long breath and raked one hand through his hair. "Elizabeth, I was stupid. I was an idiot to think I could be good enough for you. Over Christmas, all during that time, it was okay, because it was almost like we were living in a bubble. We were together, we didn't have to deal with the real world, and it was okay. But then you went back to work, and I was sitting at your apartment all day, nothing to do, no job, no plans. And even then, we maybe would've been okay. If it wasn't . . ." His jaw clenched.

"It was me, wasn't it? I just thought you missed being in Burton. You talked about this place like it was a perfect hometown. I thought I was doing a good thing. When I saw that partnership for sale pop up on my alumni page, it seemed like it was kismet, you know?"

"It wasn't you. At least, not the way you think. Yeah, I

was kind of pissed about the whole Burton thing, because this town? Last place I wanted to live again." His Adam's apple bobbed as he swallowed. "But that night, after we fought . . . I was out on the sofa, just brooding. Being stupid. I was just about to head into the bedroom, tell you I was sorry for exploding that way, when Nolan called."

"Your uncle?" I frowned. "What did he want?"

"He called because there wasn't anyone else but me. He's still my mother's emergency contact, and when she was arrested, they called him. He was back up in Michigan, and I was closer, so it made sense for me to be the one to bail her out."

The pieces were falling into place. "That's why you left? Because your mother was in trouble, and you went to take care of her? Why the hell didn't you just tell me that?"

Trent's shoulders stiffened. "Because you don't need to deal with my shit. When Nolan told me what she'd done, I knew I was right—I'm no good for you. I'm only going to drag you down, Elizabeth. We were fools to think it could work between us. We're too different."

My stomach clenched, and I struggled to hold back the sob that wanted to rise. "So you just made that decision for me. No checking to see if I felt the same way. No explanation. You just left. You took off, and the only thing you gave me was a text that said this wasn't going to work out. And I was supposed to be okay with that."

"It was for the best." His tone was measured and neutral. "I figured you'd get mad, but then you'd get over it. And you'd do what was best for you. Maybe get a job in a city where you could meet people like you. I expected I'd get a letter from you one day, asking me to sign divorce papers or whatever, so you could get married again, for real."

"Oh, really? And just where did you think I'd send those divorce papers, Trent? I had no fucking idea where you'd gone, remember? I texted you, I called, and you never answered me. I guess when I met this imaginary man and decided I wanted to get married, I'd have to hire a private detective to track you down. Thanks so much."

"I didn't have much choice." He gripped the edge of the steps. "And I didn't mean to take the apartment, either. I got here, got my mother out of jail, and I planned to get the hell out of town right after that. But then I found out the situation was a little more complicated than I'd thought."

I waved my hand. "Oh, do go on."

Trent rolled his eyes, but he kept talking. "When I got to the courthouse, the judge and prosecutor took me aside. They said with a habitual offender like my mother, they tended to look the other way as long as she had someone looking after her, someone in town who took responsibility for her. But since I'd left, and given the nature of these new charges—"

"What were the new charges?" I interrupted him, curious and yet dreading his answer at the same time. I was thinking she'd hit someone while driving drunk, or maybe robbed a liquor store.

Trent looked pained, but he went on nonetheless. "She was arrested for solicitation. Someone saw her on the street corner between Kenny's Diner and the Catholic Church, stopping men and offering her . . . services."

"Oh, my God." I understood now why he hadn't wanted

to say it. "God, Trent. I'm sorry."

"Yeah, she sank to a new low, even for her. But anyway, since she wasn't just walking around sloshed or whatever, and since I'd left Burton, the prosecutor told me they were going to press charges against her. She'd end up going to the county prison, and with her record, even though nothing had ever been done before, it probably would've been for at least a year." He turned his head to meet my eyes, and I saw in them both deep pain and defeat. "I couldn't just turn my back on her and let that happen. I know I'm a sap. I know it sounds crazy. But I had to do whatever I could, even if she'd never given a shit about me."

"So that meant you had to move back to Burton?" I could see it more clearly, why he'd come back.

"Well, yeah. But there was more. The judge told me about this program. It's a private rehabilitation place north of Atlanta, and it costs a shit-load of money. But there's a sort of scholarship deal the state offers for hardship cases, like my mom. The biggest requirement is that there has to be a . . ." He cast his eyes upward, as though the words were printed on the clouds above us. "'A demonstrable and dependable support system in place before and after the client participates in the program.' Judge Roony and the prosecutor told me they'd recommend my mother if I could keep her out of trouble for four months."

"Four months." One hundred and twenty days. After meeting Trent's mother, I could imagine what a daunting task that was. "Of course, you said you'd do it."

"Yeah, I did." He had the grace to look a little ashamed. "I had to have a place to bring her back to, a steady place to live. After I graduated high school, I didn't have my own place. I lived out at the farms in their bunkhouses, or I rented a room in town when I was working at the hardware store. My mother'd been taking rooms wherever she could get them. So I started looking around, asking around, and someone told me the only place empty was this one." He slid me a guilty grimace. "I called the landlady—she doesn't live in town—and I told her I was your husband and I'd come to town a little earlier than we expected. She had the management company give me the key. I've been paying the rent and the utilities."

"Oh, thanks, so good of you to do that." I couldn't help the sarcasm. "I mean, nice to know I don't owe back-rent on the apartment I haven't even been living in." I crossed my arms over my chest. "Did you look for some other place to live? Or did you plan on just squatting here indefinitely? I guess me showing up really is putting a kink in your plans."

Trent ignored my last jab. "I looked at the beginning, but there isn't any other apartment available. Burton isn't exactly a real estate mecca. And if we moved now, it would put my mom back to square one—she has to maintain the same address for four months, or she's disqualified."

I felt the walls of inevitability closing in on me. "There's got to be some place else." I took a deep breath, willing away the sense of claustrophobia. "I'll look for somewhere I can live. You and your mother can keep this place, since you're here already and she needs it. I can find a house to rent or something. Even if there's no other apartments in town, I can always drive in from the country."

Trent was shaking his head before I even finished. "I

called the management company today and the real estate office, too. They said there's nothing available for rent for at least six months, and what's more, there's not really anything for sale in town, either. Most of the houses hereabouts are sold as soon as they're available. So unless you're willing to pay a couple hundred grand for a six-bedroom farm house twenty minutes from town, you're out of luck."

"So what the hell am I supposed to do now?" Panic seeped into my voice.

Trent cleared his throat and gripped his denim-covered knees. "You could just stay here."

Before I could open my mouth to respond, he went on, in a rush. "I know it's not the best plan. But I can't think of anything else. I'll sleep on the sofa, and you can have the bedroom. I'll do everything I can to keep my mother out of your way." He looked at me again, this time his gaze pleading. "I know I don't have any right to ask you for anything, Elizabeth. But I am anyway. For my mother's sake. Please."

I stared at him for the space of several heartbeats. This man, this beautiful, broken man, had just about destroyed me when he'd left. And now he was begging for me to do him this favor—not for himself, no; I suspected he'd never ask me for anything for himself—but for his mother, the woman who'd abandoned him, probably abused him emotionally if not verbally or physically, and who'd never shown herself capable of caring.

"I know it doesn't make any sense." As though I'd spoken aloud, Trent answered my thoughts. "What has she ever done for me? Not a damn thing but make me miserable. But see, Elizabeth, I don't want to be like her. If I turn my back on her when she needs me, I'm no better than she is. I'm just the same. And I won't be that."

There was steely determination in his tone, and I knew he wouldn't be moved. He'd do everything possible for his mother, even if it meant giving up his own chance at happiness. And God help me, I was still so in love with him that I couldn't sabotage his efforts, even when I knew we'd lost our own shot at happily-ever-after.

I nodded my head. "Okay, Trent. We'll try it your way. For now."

Relief flooded his face, and he reached across to grip my hand. "Thank you, Elizabeth. I promise, I'll make it work."

Staring out into the dimming light, I swallowed. "Trent, I don't want to tell anyone—about us." I saw his wince of hurt and hurried to explain. "Not for me, but for you. Your mother said some stuff this morning, and I don't want other people jumping to the same conclusions about why we— well, why we got married. If we're not going to be together, there's no reason to make a big deal out of it, right?"

He was silent for a moment. "Sure. You're probably right. We'll get through these next three months, and then the minute she's in the rehab program, I'll figure something out. Don't worry, Elizabeth. You won't regret this. I'll make sure of it."

But he was wrong, because I already knew I was making a huge mistake.

CHAPTER FOUR

Trent

WHEN I'D GOTTEN BACK TO Burton and realized I was going to be staying awhile in the apartment that wasn't even rightfully mine, I'd driven over to Farleyville to get some cheap furniture. Nothing too fancy; I bought beds and simple dressers for my mom and for me, a coffee table and a sofa. The latter had been a really good deal, since the stuffing had seen better decades and the fabric was faded nearly into nothingness. At the time, I'd congratulated myself on how little I'd paid.

Tonight, I was wishing I'd shelled over a few extra of my precious bucks to get something with a little more support, a little more cushioning and maybe even a pull-out real boy bed. Every time I moved, the wood of the sofa's frame jabbed into another part of my body. My feet stuck up over the arm opposite my head, and the pins and needles I felt warned me they were falling asleep faster than I was.

And close up, with my nose near the material, there was a distinctive odor that spoke of every body that had ever sat here, every meal prepared near this couch and maybe even a few assorted animals who'd snoozed on the cushion. I rolled onto my back and took a cleansing breath.

I knew I didn't have any right to complain. Elizabeth hadn't kicked my worthless ass out of the apartment I'd stolen from her. She'd been quiet while we drove out to the Road Block to retrieve her car, and once we'd gotten back to the apartment, she'd ignored my mother's jabs while we ate take-out from Franco's Pizza. As soon as she finished her salad and slice, Elizabeth had stood up, wished me a terse good-night and then disappeared into the bedroom that used to be mine.

I'd hauled a couple of suitcases into that bedroom earlier, so I figured she was probably unpacking. But she didn't come out, even after my mom stomped down the hall to her own room. Finally, I'd shucked off my jeans, yanked an old threadbare afghan from the back of the couch and settled onto what passed for cushions.

It felt a little surreal to be under the same roof as Elizabeth again. I remembered the last time we'd been together. She'd come home from work with Chinese food, and we'd eaten it in bed, while she giggled and told me about her friend Abby who had a strict policy about always eating Chinese leftovers under the covers. I'd accidentally on purpose spilled a little duck sauce between her boobs, which had led to me licking it off, which had led to me licking even more of her smooth and warm skin . . . which had led to lots more action with tongues, hands and—and *shit*, I was hard just thinking about that night.

We'd been good together, while it worked. When we'd first met, I'd thought she was a crazy, flighty lawyer, one of those career women who had more degrees than common sense. And then she'd come onto me, making it very clear that she'd be interested in hooking up. I was pretty sure she saw me as the perfect one-night stand: I was the guy selling Christmas trees in the parking lot of her office building, the guy who'd be gone in a few weeks.

If she'd made me that not-so-subtle offer a year before, I'd have jumped on it—and her. But after what had happened with Jenna Sutton, I'd changed. I'd made a vow to swear off casual encounters with women. As long as I'd worked for my uncle Nolan up in Michigan, I'd been celibate, keeping to myself and avoiding any situation that might lead to what I'd begun to think of as trouble. Women meant trouble in my mind. I'd spent years having fun without any consequences, and now I'd learned my lesson the hard way.

It could've been worse, of course. Jenna had flirted and charmed me into one night of hot and heavy fun, nothing much different than what I was used to getting with other girls. But Jenna *was* different: she wanted more. She'd shown up at the Road Block the next time I was there, sidling up to me, slipping her arm around my waist, insinuating we were more than what we were. For the first few hours, I humored her. After all, I liked the girl. She was younger than me, sure, but she was legal—I was damned careful about that. We'd been friends when I'd worked with her at her uncle's hardware store, but I'd never seen her *that* way until she'd come to the Road Block to celebrate her birthday and made it clear as hell that she wanted more. But even if she was a good lay, I didn't want her again, and I sure didn't want her as a girlfriend.

So I'd had to make that clear, and I hadn't exactly been nice about it. Jenna wasn't taking no for an answer, and I'd had to be harsh. I'd seen the look on her face when I'd spoken. She was hurt, devastated, her big eyes filling with tears. Seeing her that way, something broke in me, but before I could say anything to soften the blow, she'd turned and run out of the bar.

A few drinks made short work of her memory, and the redhead with the big boobs who had no compunction about going down on me had taken care of any lingering regrets. Honestly, I hadn't thought about Jenna again until I'd heard her name at the bar about a month later.

"You hear about Boomer's girl?" I couldn't remember the name of the guy talking to me. He was another regular at the Road Block, someone I saw at the bar or on the dance floor, chasing skirts.

"No, what happened?" I expected a report of a new boyfriend or maybe she was getting married. Chicks were crazy. Who knew what they might do?

"Tried to off herself."

I choked on my beer. "What? What the hell did you say?"

"Took a buncha pills. Boomer found her, got her to the hospital. Heard it's touch and go."

My heart was pounding, and bile rose into my throat. *Fuck.* Could this really be true? I craned my neck to look up the bar. Mason stood with his hands braced on the shiny wood, talking on the phone. When he hung up, he turned around, and his eyes met mine. I watched him make his way toward me.

"Is it true?" My voice sounded strangled, even to my own ears.

Mason nodded. "Boomer stopped home at lunch and found her. She was unconscious. He called 9-1-1 . . . I just talked to Rilla, and they think she's going to be okay. She was just coming around."

My hands were shaking as I gripped the edge of the bar. "Do they know—was there any warning? I mean . . . she never seemed depressed to me. She was always smiling and happy."

"I don't know." He leveled his gaze at me. "You were with her a little while back, weren't you? I heard talk she left here with you, one night last month."

"Her birthday." I managed to get out the words. "She was here celebrating . . . and she wanted . . . she asked me if she could come home with me."

Mason exhaled a long breath and ran his fingers over his short hair. "Trent, I see what happens around here. I don't think you're that way, but by God, if you did anything to her—"

"*No.*" I ground out the word. "No. I didn't. I mean, yeah, we—she—you know. She spent the night. But I didn't force her, and I swear to God, Mason, I tried to talk her out of it. She said she just wanted to have one night of fun, and she wouldn't let up. So yeah, I took her home with me. But I never make any woman do anything with me. I don't drug them. I don't even sweet-talk them. Sex with someone who isn't a hundred percent into it isn't exactly my idea of fun."

Mason shook his head. "I get it. Like I said, I don't miss much, and I've seen you turning down more women than dragging them off. Still . . ." He raised one eyebrow. "You better hope this shit with Jenna doesn't have anything to do with you. And you better hit your knees tonight and pray Boomer never finds out you hooked up with his baby girl."

Of course, my prayers about both of those topics went unanswered, because apparently Jenna confessed that her suicide attempt was mostly a result of her regret over losing her virginity to me—and my inability to return her feelings. And Boomer, hearing that explanation, came gunning for me. Not literally gunning, thank God, but close enough. The sight of the man heading for me, fire in his eyes and both fists clenched wasn't something I was going to forget any time soon. If it hadn't been for Mason and a bunch of other guys pulling him away, I was pretty sure he would've beat me unconscious.

Even before that night, though, I'd made my decision. No more women. No more casual hook-ups. The thought of Jenna lying across her bed, wanting to end her life because I couldn't be who she wanted—it killed me. I couldn't take a chance on breaking another heart.

But it had been Boomer's threats and rants that had solidified my choice to leave Burton. I'd called my uncle and asked if I could come up to work for him, and Nolan, being the exact opposite of my mother, had said yes without hesitation. I'd come clean with him about why I wanted to leave Georgia for Michigan, and he was supportive. So I'd sold my few possessions—my guitar, my tools, everything other than my truck—and hightailed it north.

That was a story I'd never shared with Elizabeth. When we'd become friends at Logan and Jude's Thanksgiving gathering, I'd given her a vague answer about why I was on a sex fast. And once I'd broken that fast—when I knew I had strong feelings for this woman that went beyond both friendship and lust—that topic hadn't come up again. We were too busy making up for lost time.

I'd almost told her on New Year's Eve. We'd been together non-stop since Christmas Eve, when I'd moved out of the motel and gone to stay at her house. Each day, I fell a little more in love with her. I'd known she was funny, smart and wicked sexy, but seeing her softer, more vulnerable side made me want to hold her in my arms forever. She'd talked about her family now and then, about the trials of being an Army brat and her parents' expectations. They'd texted her on Christmas Day, but there hadn't been any phone calls or video chats.

"Well, they're in Germany visiting one of my brothers." Elizabeth had shrugged. "The time difference makes it hard, and they called me before they left. And they sent my Christmas box."

I'd seen the package of gifts her family had sent, and by its contents, I could tell that I knew more about her after about six weeks than they did after twenty-some years.

On the last morning of the year, I'd lain in her bed, watching the pink glow of the sun creep into the room. Elizabeth had sighed in her sleep and turned toward me, snuggling against my side as she wrapped her arm around me.

"Don't leave me, Trent." She'd whispered the words, her

voice still slurred with sleep and her breathing unchanged. I knew she was dreaming, talking in her sleep. But still, what she said pierced me, and I knew in that moment that I'd never want to be apart from her. By some amazing stroke of luck, I'd found the woman who felt like my other half. The fact that she loved me, too, was even more of a miracle. I wanted to make it permanent. More than that, I needed to do it.

So when she'd finally opened her eyes, smiling sleepily at me, I hadn't hesitated.

"Marry me, Elizabeth."

At first, she was confused. I could tell by the way her forehead wrinkled. I'd taken advantage of that, threading my fingers through hers as I kept talking.

"We could leave this morning, drive up to Georgia. There's a place where you can get married with no waiting. Before the new year, you'd be my wife."

I'd watched her eyes go soft and thoughtful. For several moments, she didn't answer, and I was terrified that she was going to laugh at me and say no. But then excitement and joy suffused her face, and she smiled.

"Yes. Okay. Let's do it."

All the way up the coast, we'd sung along to the radio, laughing together when I botched the lyrics, which I did on purpose most of the time. I'd sung to her for real, too, telling her a little more about my high school band, back when I'd played the guitar. We'd just crossed the state line when she turned to me.

"Hey, how did you know about this place, that we can get married without a waiting period? You're not one of those crazy serial grooms, are you?"

I'd laughed. "No, ma'am. Never been married before." I snagged her hand and lifted it to kiss her knuckles. "Never wanted to before now." I winked and then added, "I looked it up on my phone this morning while you were still asleep. I thought we could do it on the beach, at sunset, right there in Crystal Cove, but the waiting period's required in Florida."

"Ah." Elizabeth had nodded. "That's okay. I'd rather it be just the two of us, anyway. Unless you wanted to call someone from your hometown? We're not that far from Burton, are we?"

My jaw tightened a little. "Yeah, we're close, but no. There's no one in Burton who I want attending my wedding."

"Good. Then it's just us and the crazy Elvis impersonator who'll be presiding, right?"

I'd squeezed her hand. "That's Vegas, baby. Here in Georgia, you'd be more likely to get a guy who's dressed up as Rhett Butler or maybe Ted Turner."

In the end, the man who had performed our wedding ceremony looked more like Jimmy Stewart. Elizabeth kept staring at him and smiling as he spoke the necessary words.

She said I do and I will, and so did I. Within a few short minutes, Jimmy Stewart was pronouncing us husband and wife.

We ran from the tiny chapel, laughing. My new wife turned to me and grinned.

"So what now?"

I looked around the small town square. "How about dinner at the Starlight Diner?"

Elizabeth feigned a dubious look. "Sure we can get into

that place? It's New Year's Eve, after all."

"Baby, stick with me. I got connections."

So our wedding dinner was waffles and chili cheese fries at the diner. Afterwards, we checked into a small family-run motel right off the highway. The owner, Earl, was working the front desk, and he eyed us both with some distrust, looking at the bare ring-fingers on our left hands. We hadn't taken the time to buy rings, though we did once we returned to Florida.

"We just got married this afternoon." I dug into my pocket and produced the marriage license. "We didn't get a chance to buy rings yet. Tonight's our wedding night."

Standing next to me, Elizabeth nodded, trying her best to look virginal and inexperienced. I coughed away a laugh.

"Well, that's just fine. Just fine! Nancy, c'mere. We got newlyweds here. What do we have we can give them, to make their wedding night extra-special?"

In the end, Nancy produced a bottle of non-alcoholic wine and a basket of crackers with a tub of cheese. We thanked her and Earl and retired to the small motel room, both of us giggling like naughty teenagers.

"Wasn't that sweet? I was afraid he was about to give you the sex talk. And Nancy kept patting my arm and whispering, 'Just try to relax, dear. It gets better as time goes on.'"

"Oh, really? And what do you think? Should we put that advice to the test?"

Elizabeth stepped out of her shoes and pulled her thin white sweater over her head. Standing before me, her full breasts spilling over the cups of her bra, with her short skirt still on, I thought I'd never seen anything so beautiful and sexy in all my life. I tugged her close to me, and kissed her, breaking away only to murmur in her ear.

"I love you, Elizabeth Hudson Wagoner. My wife."

She gripped my ass, molding it in her hands. "I love you, too. My husband."

I'd made love to her that night with brand new tenderness. It really did feel like our first time, our hands gripping together as I moved within her, holding myself over her slim body. I'd never felt such a sense of peace and of belonging.

"I'm home," Elizabeth had whispered to me, her lips skimming my throat. "Wherever you are, that's my home. Now and forever and ever."

"Amen." I'd added it with fake solemnity, but neither of us laughed, because we knew it was true and right.

When she'd fallen asleep in my arms, after we'd rung in the new year in the best, most romantic way possible, I'd remembered that I had planned to tell Elizabeth about Jenna today. I'd wanted her to know everything before we made those vows. But I hadn't told her, and after that, the time never seemed right. I reasoned that there wasn't really anything to tell. I felt guilty about what Jenna had done out of despair for what she thought was her love for me, but I didn't regret telling her I could never love her. Now that I knew what real love was, I was all the more convinced that pretending to be Jenna's boyfriend would've been less kind than being straight with her from the get-go. But really, what was there to gain from spilling all those details to the woman who was now my wife? Not a damn thing. After all, it wasn't like we were ever going to go back to Burton, if I had anything to do with it. No damned way I'd be back in that town.

I shifted on my creaky sofa, smothering a moan as a particularly aggressive spring jabbed into my back. In the dark of night, I could admit that I'd hoped when Elizabeth had agreed to share the apartment with us for now, she'd suggest I sleep in the bed with her. I mean, we were married, for God's sake. We wouldn't be doing anything wrong. But she hadn't offered, and I'd been too chicken-shit to ask. Maybe once she got over her initial mad, she'd change her mind. I didn't expect her to have sex with me, but just letting me sleep in half of the bed I'd paid for would be a kind gesture.

"My God, you scared the living shit out of me. What're you doing here on the couch?" My mother stood in the arched doorway between the living room and the hallway. Her thin cotton nightshirt accentuated her boney frame, and her bleached blonde hair, which was now more than half gray, hung in ugly strands down her back and over her shoulder.

"Go back to bed, Ma." I kept my voice down, which was more than I could say for my mother.

She cackled then, sounding so much like a witch that I wanted to shake her. "Kicked you out, did she? Yeah, I know her type. Princess Prissy, she is. Too good for me, and too good for you, or so she thinks. Fucking rich bitch."

I pushed myself to sit up and leveled one finger in my mother's direction. "I told you to go back to your damn bed. Now get in there and shut up about Elizabeth. You don't know shit about her, and she's being kind enough to let us stay here."

"Oh, ho, the truth comes out. *She's* letting *us* stay here? Shouldn't it be the other way around?" Before I could explain, she was speaking again, opening her mouth and almost yelling the words.

"She's been sending you money all this time, hasn't she? That's how you could get us this place and all the furniture at once. All your whining about needing a job and all that shit—it wasn't for real, was it?"

I closed my eyes and gritted my teeth, pain shooting through my jaw. It wasn't any wonder I'd had almost constant headaches since I'd moved in with my mother; the stress of living with her made me grind my teeth all night. "No, Ma, it's nothing like that. She hasn't given me a cent. And you know what? I'm not getting into this with you tonight. I'm just telling you, be nice to Elizabeth. Or if you can't handle that, at least shut up around her. If it weren't for her, we'd be looking for some place else to live, and you'd probably lose the chance of going to this rehab program."

"I told you over and over, I'm not going to any fucking rehab. That's bullshit. I don't need to be rehabbed. I need you to get out of my business and let me live my life." She shifted her weight from one foot to the other, a mean smile curling her lips. "Never knew you to be such a mama's boy. What's wrong, *son*, you making up for lost time? Did some therapist tell you to try to climb back into the womb or some shit like that? My fucking brother make you see a head shrink?"

"Would you shut up?" I ground out the words. "Would you just fucking stop talking? You don't know anything. I have no fucking idea how you and Nolan came from the same family, because he's the only decent, normal family I

80

have. And I'm only here, keeping your ass out of jail, because I'm *not* like you, Ma. I'm different. I don't run away from my responsibilities. So if that makes me a sap, then sure. Whatever. Say what you want. But I'm not walking away from you, no matter how much shit you give me. I'm keeping you here until you go to rehab. And you *are* going to rehab, Ma, because the alternative is going to prison. How do you think you'd make out there? You think you look good in orange?"

She opened her mouth, as though she was going to make some comeback, but nothing came out. Something flickered in her pale, washed-out eyes, and I thought it might be fear. She stood staring down at me for another few seconds before she wheeled around and stamped back to her bedroom, slamming the door behind her.

I fell back onto the sofa, letting out a long breath. She exhausted me. Being with my mom these last four weeks had been like living with a toddler—or at least how I imagined a toddler might be. She was demanding, self-centered and had a tendency to throw tantrums. She wore me out; going to work at the feed store was actually a relief each day, because it meant I got a break from her constant haranguing and whining.

The house was quiet again now, though, and I let myself relax a little. My mind wandered to the bedroom again, where Elizabeth—*my wife*—was sleeping in my bed. I wondered what would've happened if I'd admitted I knew I'd made a mistake when I'd left her back in the Cove. What if I had asked her to forgive me, to give us a second chance? Would she have welcomed me back into our bed tonight, or would she have thrown my apology back in my face? I couldn't be sure.

It didn't matter, anyway. Everything that had happened since I'd driven away from her house in Crystal Cove had only confirmed what I'd decided in the early hours of that morning: being with me could only hurt Elizabeth. My life, my past, my mother—all of them would bring her down, tinge her perfect world with my own particular brand of fucked-up. I wasn't going to do that. I loved her too much to see that happen. We'd get through this period of time, and then I'd be out of her life for good. Once my mom was in that rehab program, I planned to get the hell out of Burton, this time for good. I figured I'd find a job and rent a house somewhere up near the rehabilitation facility, so that we'd meet the requirements of the program and give both of us a fresh start.

And Elizabeth could start over. She could stay here in Burton, where I had no doubt she'd be welcomed by the town, since they loved a good success story. She'd meet a man who was worthy of her, and they'd live here, raise a family and make the home I knew she'd always wanted. Even though I'd never see her again, I'd have the satisfaction of knowing I had played some small part in giving her that home, since I was the one who'd brought her to Burton. That would have to be enough. I'd never love anyone the way I loved Elizabeth. That I knew for sure. I loved her enough to put her needs above my own, and that was something I'd never done before.

And it was with this depressing thought that I finally drifted off into an uneasy sleep.

CHAPTER FIVE

Elizabeth

THE LAW OFFICE OF CLARK Morgan was located three blocks off the main street of Burton, in an old house tucked beneath a canopy of huge trees. It rose out of the ground as though it had been born there, not constructed. A sign post by the front walk informed passers-by in the most discreet and genteel way that this building housed not only the law office, but also the Downy Firm of Accountants and the Burton Gazette and Printing Company.

I sat in the front seat of my car, staring up at the front door, wondering what the hell I was doing here. Law had never been my passion. It was what I'd studied so that I could justify staying in college three more years, since I didn't know what else I wanted to do. True, I'd been excited about starting my own office with Darcy after graduation, but that enthusiasm had dimmed once she'd fallen in love and left me on my own in the Cove. The fact that I'd also had to buy out her half of the partnership, thus crippling my business from the get-go and requiring that I stayed in Crystal Cove until I'd paid off my debt, hadn't helped at all.

Making the offer on Clark Morgan's practice hadn't been something I'd thought about too deeply. Trent had been waxing nostalgic about Burton at dinner one night, talking about growing up in a small town where everyone knew him.

"You're so lucky." I'd picked up my wine glass and tipped it back, drinking the last drops. "No one ever knew me. Just when I'd get around to making friends, it would be time to leave again. I want a hometown, too."

"You can share mine." Trent had leaned over and dropped a quick kiss on my lips, his tongue darting out to catch a taste of wine. "I'll take you back and we'll . . . hmmm . . . we'll buy a farm. Live outside of town. I'll build you a house."

I slid out of my own chair and onto my husband's lap. "You will? Where will we live while you're building it?"

"Well, we'll have to rent something in town until I have our house done. You can get a job at one of the law firms, and I'll work at the hardware store until we've saved up enough."

"Mmmmmmmm." I'd nuzzled his warm neck. "I like that idea."

Trent had chuckled, and his arms tightened around me. "I have a lot of ideas you might like . . ." His hands crept around to cup my breast, and I'd been lost . . .

Our discussion that night had ended in bed, which was where I'd decided all good talks should wrap up. But the idea of Burton had lingered in the back of my mind, and it was with that thought that I'd opened up the alumni page of my law school's website, where I'd seen Clark Morgan's classified ad.

It had seemed perfect, the first step in that dream Trent had woven for the two of us. At least it had felt that way until I'd filled him in on what I'd done, and he'd flipped the hell out.

And now here I sat, about to go in and officially take over my new practice. I was about as excited as if I were going to the dentist for a root canal. I dreaded the prospect of getting back into the groove in a new town, learning the quirks of the local judicial system—which judges were hard-asses, which ones were more easy going—and winning the trust of Clark Morgan's clients so they didn't take their business elsewhere. All I wanted to do was curl up in the backseat of my BMW and take a nap.

But that wasn't the Hudson way. I could almost hear my father's voice, informing me that he expected more of his daughter. So with a deep and heavy sigh, I opened the car door and climbed out. Hoisting my fancy leather briefcase over my arm, I squared my shoulders and climbed the steps to the front porch.

It swung open silently, and I stepped into a bright and welcoming foyer. The hardwood floor, buffed to perfection, gleamed in the sunlight that streamed in through large windows. A staircase curved up to the second floor, its polished banister ending in an ornate newel post. I stood for a minute, breathing in the welcome and familiar scent of lemon polish and aged wood.

"Miss Hudson?" A deep voice interrupted my reverie. "That you?"

I put on a wide and professional smile. "Yes, I'm Elizabeth Hudson. You must be Mr. Morgan." I lifted my hand, and the older gentleman took it in both of his.

"Welcome to Burton, Miss Hudson. We're glad to have you here." After giving my hand a thorough if refined shake, he released it and gently guided me toward the back of the hallway.

"Happy to be here. Are you excited about your move?" Clark Morgan had confided in me that his wife was anxious to move to New Mexico, where their daughter lived with her family. While he pretended to be reluctant to leave Georgia, I'd heard the hint of anticipation in his voice, even over the telephone.

"Well, you know, my wife's got us all packed up already. Turning everything over to you is the last thing on our list. I feel a little funny, leaving you so soon, but you'll have my number if you have any questions. And Gladys probably knows more than me about anything that goes on in this office."

Mr. Morgan reached around me and turned the brass doorknob, stepping back to let me enter. I was immediately taken by the floral print on the pretty love seat and coordinating solid rose on the overstuffed chair in the small anteroom. An antique pine coffee table held a few magazines and a newspaper. The whole effect was charming and warm, nothing like a typical law office waiting room.

In the alcove adjoining that space, a woman sat at a large desk. She was older, though I couldn't figure out exactly how old she might be. Her blonde hair was clearly from a bottle, since its color was at odds with the lines on her face. Eyebrows were drawn on over icy blue eyes that examined me critically.

"Gladys, lookit here. This is Miss Elizabeth Hudson, your new boss."

I cringed on the inside. I was easily thirty years younger than this lady, possibly more. The last thing she would want to be reminded of was my position at the head of the office. I amped up my smile and extended my hand again. "So pleased to meet you, Miss . . ." I sensed we weren't quite on a first-name basis yet, so I let the question of her name linger.

"Gladys West. *Mrs.* West." She stood, and I noticed that her posture was impeccable. "Pleased to meet you, Miss Hudson." Mrs. West crossed her arms over her chest, as my hand hung between us, awkward and forlorn.

"Now, Gladys, you be nice. Miss Elizabeth is our lifesaver, you know. If it weren't for her, I'd have just closed up this office and you'd be out of a job. As it is, you have the responsibility of training a new lawyer. Again."

Gladys had stared down Mr. Morgan as he spoke, and when he finished, she addressed me. "Do you plan to come in this late every day? Because that's not how to practice law in this town and certainly not in this office."

My hackles rose, and I opened my mouth to make a stinging retort. I'd been raised with the importance of bowing to authority, wherever that might be and whatever it told you to do. But this woman wasn't my boss. She continued to hold her job at my favor; it had been part of our contract that I would keep Gladys at the office for at least another year. I was really regretting that I'd agreed to that caveat so easily.

But just as I'd heard my dad's voice earlier, I knew what my mother would tell me in this situation. "If you can't say something nice about someone, don't say anything at all. Just remember, if they're unpleasant, likely they had a bad day or even a bad life. Give everyone the benefit of the doubt."

I nodded my head and answered the secretary. "Today is not a typical day, of course. I'll be coming in to the office by nine on most days, I'd think."

"Nine?" One sketched eyebrow raised. "Mr. Morgan is in the office by seven every single day of the week."

Before I could answer her—and I didn't think what I said was going to be very pleasant this time—Mr. Morgan interceded. "I seem to recall that Cornelius never strolled through those doors before eleven AM. And when I was the new attorney, you gave me a hard time for being here so early."

A faint pink flushed the secretary's cheeks. "Better to start out on the right foot and be here all the earlier, I'd say. Now that you've trained the clients to expect appointments and meetings first thing in the day, they'll be unhappy if they can't meet until later."

"I'll keep that in mind." I glanced at Clark, and he seemed to sense that it was time to move on. Wise man.

"I'm taking Miss Elizabeth into my office—well, her office now—to sign some papers and go over some of the details. I doubt anyone's going to need us, but I'd prefer we not be disturbed, Gladys. I need to get home and finish up packing, and Miss Elizabeth will want to bring in her things and get settled, I'm sure."

He opened an oak door to the left of the reception desk and ushered me down the hallway to another large room. It was dominated by a huge desk made of shiny cherry wood, flanked by two tall matching filing cabinets. An ancient desktop computer sat on one sideboard, and a black leather office chair was tucked under the desk.

"I'm leaving all this here, as part of the office package." Clark motioned me to a chair in front of the desk as he sank into the black leather rolling seat. "I don't have any use for it where I'm going, and my wife would kill me if I tried to bring it. Besides, Cornelius left the desk here for me, so it seems only right for me to pass it on to you."

"Did he leave you Gladys, too?" I didn't want my words to sound so bitter, but damn, the woman was mean. I dreaded putting up with her for a solid year.

Clark chuckled. "Matter of fact, he did. She came to work for him when she was young, and by the time I joined the practice, she was running the place. I know she comes off a little brusque, but she'll warm up to you. What you need to remember is that this office, this business, it's her life. She doesn't have any family. She lives by herself, and she eats, breathes and sleeps everything that goes on here. So if she seems a little intense, know that it's because it's all she has."

I snorted. "That sounds unhealthy to me. Maybe she should look into expanding her horizons a little."

"Good luck convincing her of that." He smirked and flipped open a manila folder. "I printed out everything we agreed on digitally, so that we can sign the final paperwork today. The confirmation of your admission to the Georgia bar came through last week, and I've got that right here. All of the client files have been transferred to you, and you've been added as counsel to anything active in the courts right now."

"Thanks." I skimmed the official looking document. "I appreciate your help with the motion to admit me without examination. It was so helpful to have someone on the ground here, so to speak, who knows the ins and outs of the system."

Clark smiled, looking pleased. "Happy to be of help. And listen, if you need the skinny on anyone in the courthouse, just give me a call or shoot me an email. I know it's not easy navigating unfamiliar waters."

"Thanks." I scooted closer to the desk. "Show me where to sign."

We spent the next fifteen minutes taking care of the final details in the document that changed the Law Office of Clark Morgan to the Law Office of Elizabeth Hudson. When the last *i* was dotted and the last *t* crossed, I expected to experience relief or maybe even excitement. Instead, I only felt numb.

"Do you need help bringing in your things? Do you have boxes in the car?" The departing Mr. Morgan handed me the keys to the front door of the building and to our office then stood before me, rocking back on his heels.

I closed my hand around the keys. "Just a few, but no, thanks. I've got them. Nothing's too heavy. Most of it's stuff for my desk." I pointed to it. "Your desk, I mean."

"No, darlin', it's all yours now." Clark winked at me.

"Hey, did I dream it, or did you tell me that you'd married a boy from Burton? I never did ask you who, and my wife was pestering me about it."

I bit the side of my lip. "Uh, well . . . it was Trent Wagoner. But actually, things there are sort of unsettled right now, so I'd appreciate it if you didn't say anything to anyone. I'm not sure what's going to happen."

Frowning, Clark nodded. "Of course. Well, if there's a person who knows how to keep secrets, it's a lawyer in a small town, right?" He fiddled with the key ring in his hand. "You might not want to say anything to Gladys just yet, until things are more certain. She can be a little persnickety about that kind of thing. High moral fiber, you know."

I sniffed. "I don't see myself confiding deep, dark secrets to her. But thanks for the warning."

"Of course. Now don't forget what I said. Call me if you have questions at all. And keep me posted on how things go. I just know you're going to get along fine."

With that comforting thought, Clark Morgan squeezed my hand and turned to leave, without even a backward glance at the office that was formerly his. I guessed he'd said his good-byes earlier.

For a few minutes, I stood in the middle of the room, enjoying the silence and the peace. It reminded me a little of the library, which in turn reminded me that I wanted to stop by and pick up my library card this afternoon, now that Trent had provided me with a copy of our lease as my proof of address. I had a feeling Cory Evans might've overlooked the rule and given me the card regardless, but I didn't feel right asking. When it came to libraries, rules were rules.

Taking a deep breath, I ventured out into the hallway and through the reception area. I paused in the doorway to the outer foyer, calling over my shoulder to Gladys. "I'm running out to my car to bring in my boxes. Be right back."

"Hmph." She managed to convey disapproval and skepticism in that single syllable. I decided to ignore her and keep going.

I hadn't been fibbing to Clark when I'd said I didn't have much to tote inside. One box held the desk set my parents had given me for my law school graduation, complete with a brass name plate. The other had in it a few framed pictures, my diplomas and all the essential documents I needed to keep on hand. I was glad that the advent of e-books and computers meant I didn't need to haul tons of heavy law books from pillar to post; I'd seen those suckers, and having to move them would've given me a hernia. Instead, everything I needed was in one handy-dandy program on my laptop.

I purposely kept my eyes averted from Gladys as I marched through her domain again. Still, I could feel her glacier glare on my back until I closed the door of my office and began pulling things from the cardboard boxes.

In the sunlight streaming in through the windows, I could see a fine layer of dust on the surface of the desk. I hesitated, considering my options. My mother had taught me never to set up anything on a dusty surface, whether it was china on a table or knick-knacks on a shelf. But I didn't have any furniture polish or rags with me, and the idea of asking Gladys for them wasn't appealing.

I ran an experimental finger over the edge of the cherry

wood. Yeah, that was a substantial amount there. No way I could feel good about setting up my blotter, pens and Elizabeth Hudson name plate on a dusty desk. Girding up my loins, I stepped into the small hallway and called her name.

"Gla—Mrs. West, do we have stuff for dusting the furniture? I want to make sure I do it right. Can't have my desk getting dusty, right?"

For a beat, there was no answer. And then the woman herself appeared at the far end of the hallway, hands on her hips. "I just dusted everything in that office yesterday. It's fine."

I waved my hand. "Oh, I'm not complaining, and thank you for dusting, but you know how things get. If you just point me in the right direction, I'll take care of it."

Her lips pursed into a pucker. For a second, I thought she wasn't going to tell me where the cleaning supplies were kept. But in the end, she jerked her head toward me.

"Behind you, in the closet at the very end of the hall. Coffee filters and bathroom tissue are also stored there." She stalked back to her desk, and I heard the chair squeak as she sat back down. I did a little dance to celebrate my small victory and went to fetch the dusting supplies.

Getting the desk and filing cabinets dusted and set up took me all of about fifteen minutes. I flipped through some of the files Clark had noted as being more pressing than others, but frankly, nothing was urgent. This firm handled the full gamut of small-town law, without getting involved in any criminal cases outside of the occasional traffic violation. Mostly, it seemed, they'd dealt with family law—wills, divorces and custody cases—and property sales. The calendar was heavily dotted with real estate closings.

It was nearly noon when I finished organizing my office. I wandered out to the front, where Gladys was pulling a thin clear plastic cover over her computer monitor and keyboard. She glanced up when she heard me coming.

"I take my lunch from twelve noon until one PM every day. On pleasant days, I eat on the back deck of the house. On days with inclement weather, I have my lunch here in this room. During that hour, I switch the telephone over to the voicemail system and turn off my computer." She pointed to the desktop unit.

"That's fine. I'm going to walk down to the library, and I'll be back . . . sometime this afternoon." I picked up the pink message pad from her desk along with a pen and jotted down my cell phone number. "If something comes up, just give me a call and I'll take care of it."

Her face puckered up again, but she only gave me one brief nod. "Fine."

I decided that was as good as it was going to get, so I left before she could come up with anything else to say.

Outside, the air was a little warmer today than it had been the day before. I hitched my pocketbook a little higher on my shoulder and checked my phone, which I had programmed to guide me to the library, since I wasn't familiar enough with the layout of the town to figure it out on my own. My eyes were trained on the dotted blue line as I turned left from the walkway that led up to the front door of my office. Preoccupied, I didn't see the tall figure lurking on the sidewalk until I plowed right into him.

"Oomph!" I staggered backward, rubbing the top of my

head. "I'm sorry, I wasn't watching where I was going."

The man I'd run into didn't seem as fazed as I was. He was at least a foot taller than me, with tousled, dirty-blond hair and deep dark brown eyes under thick lashes. Those eyes regarded me with amused interest.

"Apparently not." A crooked grin lit up his face. "Was there something intriguing on Facebook, or were you texting your BFF?" He was teasing, I could tell, and that was the only thing that kept me from bristling at his suggestions.

I held up my phone. "I was following the blue-dotted road." I said it in a Dorothy-in-Oz-type cadence.

"Ah, I see. And just where do the blue dots lead you to?" He hunched forward, dropping his voice. "And where are the munchkins? And Toto?"

I laughed. "The munchkins are on lunch break, and since I'm allergic to dogs, Toto isn't an option."

"Well then, I won't even ask where the Tin Man, the Lion and Scarecrow might be." He straightened and crossed his arms over his chest. "And please don't say anything about me being the Scarecrow. That used to be my nickname growing up, and I'm not too macho to admit it still stings."

"Scarecrow? You?" I let my eyes travel up and down the guy. He was lanky, sure, but the chest beneath his folded arms was broad, and the arms themselves weren't bad at all. He wore a red and blue plaid button-up shirt, with the cuffs rolled up, showing forearms corded with muscles and covered with a liberal sprinkling of light brown hair. Yeah, *scarecrow* was hardly a word I'd use to describe him.

"Sweetheart, that's the best compliment anyone's paid me in months." He laughed and stuck out a hand. "I'm Will

Garth. Former scarecrow. And you are . . .?"

"Elizabeth Hudson." I slid my hand into his, and it disappeared into his grip. "And my blue dots lead to the library. I'm heading there to get a library card."

Will cocked his head. "Well, that's an unexpected answer. The library, huh?" Panic passed over his face. "You're not a student, are you? Like, in high school?"

It was my turn to laugh. "Now I know you're just trying to repay the compliment. No, I'm post-high school, post-college, post-law school. High school is a distant memory. I just happen to be a big fan of libraries, and since I just moved to town, I wanted to get my card as soon as I could."

"That's admirable." Will nodded. "Do you need an escort? I'd be happy to show you where it is."

I shook my head. "Thanks, but I was there yesterday. But I wasn't coming from my office then, and I'm still trying to figure out my way around town."

"So you're new to Burton, huh? You're working here, in this building?" Realization dawned on his face. "Elizabeth Hudson, you said? Oh, you're the new lawyer, aren't you? Taking over for Clark?"

"Guilty." I winked. "But I didn't know word of my arrival had spread."

"Hey." Will hooked his thumb at his chest. "I'm a newspaper man. Knowing all the goings-on in this town is my bread and butter."

"Really?" I brightened. "Do you work for the Burton Gazette? I saw the sign." I pointed behind me at the hanging shingle.

"Honey, I *am* the Burton Gazette and Printing. President, CEO, owner, general manager, janitor . . . you name it, I do it. Got my finger on the pulse of Burton."

"Aha, so you know all about me, do you? Did you do your research?" My heart beat a little faster. I didn't exactly have skeletons in my closet, but my marriage to Trent was a matter of public record, if someone wanted to look it up.

Will shrugged. "Clark filled me in a little. But I'd love to do an interview and write a piece about Burton's new hot-shot legal mind."

"I'm hardly that." I rolled my eyes. "As for the interview . . sure, I guess. But right now, I need to get down to the library and then back to the office before Gladys reports me to the Georgia Bar for insubordination."

"Oh, Gladys." Will shook his head. "She lives in perpetual disappointment with those around her. Don't even try to win her over—it's a thankless job. According to Clark, she's been riding him since he joined the firm way back when. She only started acting like he was a saint once he announced he was selling the practice and leaving. Now you're the new meat."

"Wonderful." I felt as glum as I sounded. "Thanks for the warning." I took a step around him. "It was great to meet you, Will Garth, newspaper man. I guess I'll see you around the office?"

"You can count on it." Admiration filled his gaze. "I think I might've forgotten to mention that I'm actually Will Garth, *single* and *eligible* newspaper man. So keep that in mind, once you're settled in and thinking you might be ready for an evening of fun."

I laughed again. "I'll definitely keep it in mind. See you

later." I swiveled on my heel and headed down the sidewalk again, intensely aware of Will's eyes on me as I went.

Having a handsome guy find me attractive was an ego boost I badly needed. Since my early teens, I'd been used to males looking at me with interest; I wasn't cocky about my face, my hair and my body, but false modesty was never my thing, either. I'd gotten gorgeous thick blonde hair from my beautiful mother, wide blue eyes from my dad, and a body that had decent curves from my grandma, who'd been a local pin-up girl in her day. None of it was my own doing, so being aware of my looks didn't seem like vanity to me.

Still, I always enjoyed the attention. At least I had until I was finishing up law school, and one of my professors had made a snide comment about me toning down the pretty before I went job-hunting.

"No one takes flighty blondes seriously," the woman had told me, her lip curling in obvious derision. "They'll see you as window dressing, but you'll never get to do more than look pretty in the office. Maybe an occasional appearance in court, if they have a man-heavy jury."

Her words had made me mad—I'd worked my ass off to graduate in the top five percent of my class—but they also hit home. So before Darcy and I had moved down to Florida, I'd dyed my hair brown and worn less makeup, being intentional about keeping my look more serious. It hadn't really mattered, though; the legal world of coastal Florida was an entirely different ballgame, and no one was going to judge me on my looks. Blonde females abounded in that part of the country.

For the first time in my adult life, though, I hadn't been

fighting off men. Looking back, I didn't think it had anything to do with my new hair color. Rather, it was more likely my attitude. When Darcy had left me holding the proverbial bag, I'd buried myself in work just to keep my practice
afloat. Most nights, I'd fallen exhausted into my bed, most
definitely alone. I hadn't had time or energy for even the
most casual of hook ups.

And then Trent had entered my life. At first, I'd seen
him as the perfect candidate for helping me end my unin-
tentional sex fast. Once he'd put the kibosh on that idea—
he'd been on his own break from meaningless sex, for reasons he'd never quite made clear—I'd been happy to have
him as a friend. A friend I could fantasize about, a friend
with whom I had clear and present sexual energy . . .

When we'd given into that mutual attraction, which had
morphed into sincere like and then love, I'd let myself truly
fall for the first time in my life.

"And look how well that worked out." I muttered the
words to myself as I yanked open the library door and
slipped inside.

"I'm sorry?" Cory stood behind the desk, just as she
had the day before, looking at me with a quizzical smile.

"Just talking to myself." I shook my head. "Hello, my
name is Elizabeth Hudson. I just moved to town, and I'm
here to get my library card."

Cory tilted her head. "I must be losing my mind. I
could've sworn I met Elizabeth Hudson yesterday. Unless
you have an identical twin?"

"No, see, yesterday I was sad and scruffy Elizabeth. You
need to forget you ever saw her. Today I am professional

and has-it-all-together Elizabeth. Oh, and I'm also clean-clothes-and-showered Elizabeth. Trust me, today's me makes a much better first impression." I dug into my bag and pulled out an envelope. "I brought in my proof-of-address so I can legally apply for a library card."

"Excellent." Cory reached to take it, but she didn't unfold the paper right away. "So is today's Elizabeth still living with her maybe-husband and her sort-of mother-in-law?"

"She is." I sighed and leaned against the counter. "It turns out that Trent only took the apartment because it was an emergency. His mother had been arrested, and . . . and you already knew all this, didn't you?"

Cory lifted one shoulder. "I'd heard talk. I wasn't going to say anything to you when I didn't know the whole story. And I'm not a gossip."

"I appreciate that. Anyway, Trent needs to keep his mom on the straight and narrow for another few months, so she can qualify for some intense rehab place. I agreed to let them stay there with me until . . . well, as long as they need to."

"Uh huh." The librarian quirked an eyebrow. "Does this mean you and Trent are married for real now? Living as husband and wife?"

"Not exactly." I fiddled with a bookmark on the desk. "We didn't really talk about us. I mean, he told me why he left. Nolan had called him about his mom being arrested. And . . ." I hesitated. "Trent said he realized that getting married was a mistake. That *we* were a mistake. He said he wasn't good enough for me."

Cory winced. "That doesn't surprise me. There's not

much in his background that would give him reason to think otherwise." She reached below the counter and pulled out a form. "Don't get me wrong. I love my town. Burton has been very good to me, and I'm thrilled that two of my three kids have settled here permanently. And even Flynn lives here part time. But I'm not so blind that I think this place is perfect. Any community can have trouble accepting those who don't fit the mold, who aren't exactly the same." She paused, her pen poised over the blank form. "I can't imagine Trent would ever feel comfortable living in Burton permanently. As much as I'd like to believe it's possible for people to have open minds, I'm afraid most of the town will always see him as Donna the drunk's poor kid. Or as the guy who was maybe, ah, less than discriminating about who he spent his nights with when he was younger." Cory flushed. "I'm sorry. I said I wasn't a gossip, and I'm not. I shouldn't have said that."

"No, it's okay. You're not telling me anything Trent hasn't." I remembered him describing his man-whore days. "You know I've never lived in any place long enough for people to have an opinion of me one way or the other. I didn't think about what it would be like for Trent to be back in a place where memories are probably pretty long."

"Exactly." Cory nodded and began writing on the library card application. She turned the paper around and tapped her pen on a blank space. "Just fill out this part and sign it, and I'll start making up your card." She knelt to pull out a small machine and then rose to tap something onto her desktop computer. The machine began to buzz.

"Elizabeth, did Trent ever mention why he left Burton

last spring?" She regarded me with curious eyes.

I frowned. "I don't think so. I just figured he was ready for a change. He went up to Michigan to work with Nolan, right?"

Cory nodded. "Yes. I think you're right. He left a little abruptly, and I wondered if there was a specific reason. But it probably just seemed that way to me." The card maker stopped its subtle roar, and a plastic card slid out with a soft ping. "And here's your library card. You're now a full-fledged member of the McAllister Memorial Library of Burton." She handed me the card. "The borrowing period is two weeks. Overdue notices are sent out after the fifth day delinquent. Charges are twenty-five cents a day." She fixed me with a stern look. "I'm sure you won't have to worry about that, though."

"I never have." Yeah, I sounded a little smug. "I've been going to libraries for over twenty years, and I've never had one overdue fine yet."

"Impressive record." Cory pursed her lips in a silent whistle. "See to it that you keep it up here. The head librarian is very strict."

I was a little confused, since I'd had the impression Cory was the only employee. "Who's the head librarian?"

"You're looking at her." She grinned and patted my hand. "Elizabeth, do me a favor. Keep an open mind about Trent. I can see why he looks at you and thinks you're way out of his league. No one's ever told him he's worth more than a quick—uh, tumble. But he's a good boy. He's got a lot of potential, if the right person comes along."

I closed my eyes. "I feel like I'm in a state of limbo right now. Trent and I agreed we wouldn't tell anyone here that we're together. Were together. I'm married, but not living that way." I thought of Will and his flirting eyes, and guilt stabbed my gut. "Living in an apartment with a mother-in-law who hates me and a husband who can barely look me in the face." I peeked out at Cory with one eye. "And I'm pretty sure the secretary at my new office thinks I'm an idiot."

"Gladys West?" Cory laughed. "Oh, sweetie, don't pay her any mind. Gladys . . . she's just a bitter old woman. I know I said I don't gossip, and I don't, but this is more history than current events. She was born and raised here, and the word is, she fell in love with a man passing through on his way to shipping out to Korea, during the war. He promised he'd come back to marry her, but he was killed over there."

"Oh, my Go-gosh. That's so sad. Now I feel terribly about thinking she's an utter bitch." I side-eyed Cory. "Sorry."

"In this case, I'm pretty certain it's warranted. Anyway, just a few weeks after this man was reported dead, Gladys up and married another man, Harry West. I've heard there were all kinds of rumors that she'd gotten herself in trouble with the soldier and sweet-talked Harry into saving her from being ruined. But they never had any kids, and he left her six months after their wedding. She went to work for Cornelius Sparks, and that became her life. She ran the firm for him, and then when he retired and Clark took over, she ran it for him, too."

"She looked at me like I was something she'd scraped off her orthopedic shoes."

Cory giggled. "That sounds about right. Don't let her get you down. Remember, you're the boss."

"Between Gladys and Donna, the only place I feel welcome in my new town is right here." It sounded pathetic, but it was the truth.

"Honey, it'll get better." She paused, watching me with narrowed eyes. "Elizabeth, let me ask you something. Do you think marrying Trent was a mistake?"

I shrugged. "I didn't at the time. And if he hadn't left me . . . no, I probably wouldn't think so." I swallowed over the lump that had risen in my throat. "But he did leave me. I still love him, Cory, but I don't think I can trust him. What if I let myself fall in love again, and then he breaks my heart all over?"

"Love's always a risk, sugar. It's just a matter of deciding if it's a risk you can afford to take—or one you can't afford *not* to take."

"Thanks. Can't you just tell me what to do? You were married forever. And your kids are all happily matched up, right? You must have all the answers. Enlighten me, oh wise one."

She smiled, shaking her head. "I wish I did have the answers. But all I can tell you is to follow your heart. Oh, and remember that everyone has his own struggle. Trent's doing the best he can with the hand he's been dealt. Give him the benefit of the doubt. I don't know that anyone's ever done that for him before."

I went back to the office for a few hours after I left the library, mostly because the alternative was going back to the apartment where Donna was undoubtedly waiting to pounce. At least at work, I could hide in my office and ignore Gladys.

She thawed just enough to show me how they did billing. Nothing was computerized, I realized with dismay; Gladys used her desktop unit only for typing letters and forms, but everything on the business end of things was still done with old methods most offices had abandoned at least a decade ago.

"I used an hours and billing program at my old office, and I'd like to switch over to that." I flipped through the tissue-thin time sheets Gladys had set in front of me. "It might be a learning curve, getting used to it, but in the long run, it'll be easier for both of us."

She stared down her nose at me. "I don't care for fancy computerized things."

"It's not fancy. It's very basic." I glanced at the wall clock opposite my desk. "Well, it's just about five, and I'm sure you're ready to head home. Thank you, Gladys. I'll see you tomorrow." I pushed my chair back and reached for my purse.

The older woman sputtered something, but I didn't pay any attention. Instead, I shot her a bright smile as I passed by on my way out.

"Thanks for all your help today, Gladys!" I congratulated myself on having taken control of the situation, but just as I reached the outer office door, her voice boomed down the hall to me.

"It's *Mrs. West.*"

"Whatever," I muttered, stamping through the dimming light in the foyer and out to my car. When I'd turned the ignition, I paused for a moment, thinking. I was hungry, having skipped lunch in favor of my library visit, and I knew there was nothing to cook in the apartment's small kitchen. It seemed Trent and his mother had been existing on sandwiches, canned soup and take-out food, but that wasn't going to fly with me. I had a hankering for fried chicken and biscuits tonight.

I got lost a few times getting to the grocery store, but once I found the place, it didn't take long to gather what I'd need. A whole chicken, a bag of flour, some baking powder, assorted spices, a small jug of milk, white vinegar and tub of lard all went into my buggy. In the produce section, I tossed in some collard greens, too. While I was at it, I picked up a bag of coffee. I'd need that come the next morning.

There was a dollar store next to the market, so I loaded all the food into the trunk of my car and ran into the small shop. I found a frying pan and a small sauce pan that weren't up to my normal standards, but they would do for my purposes tonight. The baking sheets were pretty flimsy, too, but I could work with that. I made a mental note to go online and order a few essentials to get me through until I had time for a trip to the closest department store.

Trent was sprawled on the sofa when I staggered through the front door, both arms full of bags. He jumped to his feet.

"Hey, let me help you. What do you have there?" He lifted two paper bags from me.

"Food for dinner. Can you put them in the kitchen,

please?" I followed behind and set the plastic bags on the counter. Once I had everything down, I tugged my shirt back in place—it had ridden up as I'd carried the bags and turned to Trent, my hands on my hips.

"I'm making fried chicken for dinner. I had a long day, I'm hungry, and I just want to eat good food. I don't care if you eat it or not, or if your mother—" I tried unsuccessfully to hold back a twist of my mouth. "If your mother wants to eat it or not. Whatever. Do what you want. I'm making it and I'm eating it. This is my home, too, and damned if I'm not going to cook in my own kitchen."

Trent watched me, waiting until I'd finished my rant. A smile played around his lips. "Fried chicken sounds freaking amazing. I'm starved. Can I please eat some of your fried chicken with you?"

He sounded so much like an obedient little boy, humoring me, that I couldn't completely hold onto my mad. "You may."

"How can I help?" He unbuttoned the cuffs on his long-sleeved shirt and began rolling them up as he turned on the water to wash his hands.

I stood looking at this man, his unbelievably sexy body encased in worn jeans and a thin shirt, ready to lend me a hand. I remembered what Cory had said today about how hard it must have been for him to return to Burton. I couldn't understand why he cared what happened to his mother after she'd made his childhood such a hell, but I had to admire a man who honored his commitments. That he hadn't found it so hard to walk away from me still smarted, but . . . I drew in a deep breath. One step at a time, I reminded myself.

"You can cut up the chicken." I lifted the bird out of a bag and plopped it on the counter. "I had to buy a knife at the dollar store, since I didn't figure you had one, so it's probably crap, but it's all we have. Knock yourself out."

Trent grinned at me. "Working with what I have is my specialty." He tackled the chicken while I started on the buttermilk biscuits and the collards. We cooked in companionable silence, at first only speaking when we had to, but by the time I'd dredged the meat and had it crackling in the pan, I was telling him about my first day at work, describing Gladys and Clark. For the first time in days, I relaxed and felt almost at home.

And my fried chicken dinner? It was damned good.

CHAPTER SIX

Trent

"WAGONER!"

I was just about out the door of Grainger's, heading for my truck after my normal eight-hour shift, when I heard Paul's voice. I paused, turning to look at him.

"Yeah, boss?"

He motioned me over. "Can I have a minute, please?"

Dread twisted in my belly, but I played it off. "Sure." I moved out of the way of two other guys who were leaving, trying to ignore their glances of open curiosity. I kept to myself at work; I didn't interact more than was strictly necessary, and I knew that they probably talked about me. I didn't give a shit about any of them. It was a job to do, and the best thing was to keep my head down and get through.

Paul's office wasn't very large. It was in a corner of the warehouse, with a door to the main store, as well. He had an old scarred desk and an ancient office chair that shrieked every time he sat down in it, which wasn't often. He liked to be on his feet, lifting feed sacks with us or loading trucks when he wasn't working the storefront.

"I'd say sit down, Trent, but I don't have any damn chairs."

"Not a problem, Mr. Grainger. Everything okay?" I cast my mind back over the past few weeks. Nothing had happened that I remembered; no accidents, no trouble. I'd been on time every single day since I started working here, and I'd never taken off a day. I did my job, and I thought I did it well.

"Yes and no, Trent. First of all, you've been a great worker. I've been impressed with you from the minute you started. You keep your mouth shut, your head down and you don't make trouble."

"Thank you." I swallowed hard.

Paul heaved a sigh. "That's the good news part. The bad news part is . . . business is slow just now. It happens every year, but this one's been worse. New place opened up over in Duberville, and a lot of the customers who were coming to us are going to them now, since it's more convenient. Profits are down, and cost of business is going up." He fidgeted in his chair, but to his credit, he looked me right in the eye.

"I want you to know, this has nothing to do with anything else. I don't listen to rumors or judge a man by anything other than his work. If I could do it, I'd make a different call. But this is company policy. If we have to let someone go, all things being equal, it's got to be the last one hired. And that's you."

My heart sank so low that I swore I could feel it pounding in my gut. I opened my mouth to protest, but what the hell difference was it going to make? The man was being straight with me, I could tell that. He wasn't doing this out of spite or meanness. It was just business, and I couldn't argue with numbers.

So I only nodded and tapped the old worn baseball cap I was gripping in my hand against my thigh. "I understand, sir. Thank you for giving me this chance. I—" My throat closed. *Fuck*, I wasn't going to break down like a damn baby. "I just really need this job. It's been great, and you're the best boss I've ever had." My voice sounded pleading, and I wasn't going to have that. I straightened and arranged my mouth into something that looked like a smile. "I get it, though. Thank you for being honest with me."

"Trent, listen. You find another job and you need a reference, you give them my name. I'm more than happy to write a letter, make a call . . . you name it. And if you're still looking come summer, assuming business starts looking up . . . I'll take you back on." He stood up, the chair protesting with a loud squeal, and clapped a hand on my shoulder. "I'm sure you won't have any trouble, though. You're a good man and a hard worker."

"Thank you." I had to get out of there before I lost it, but running from the man's office wouldn't be cool. Instead I sketched him a brief salute and turned, moving as fast as I could through the door, across the warehouse floor and outside into the cool of the late afternoon. I made my way to the truck on auto pilot, climbed in and started her up.

And then I sat there, because I wasn't sure what was

supposed to come next. I'd gotten into a routine in the last few weeks, since Elizabeth had moved in with my mother and me. I got home around quarter after four, grabbed a shower and changed my clothes, retrieving a clean set for the next morning, too, so that I didn't have to disturb Elizabeth while she slept. I'd listen to my mother grouse at me about how awful her life was while I went about my business. By the time I'd drop onto the couch, exhausted from a day at work, it would be about time for Elizabeth to get home.

That was the high point of my day. When she breezed in the front door, usually with a bag of groceries, it was like the sunshine and fresh air came in with her. She'd begun greeting me with a smile, and that was the juicy red cherry on top of the delicious ice cream sundae that was Elizabeth. She'd head right into our tiny kitchen, and while she was opening bags, she'd tell me what she was making for dinner.

I had offered to share the cooking duties with her, but she'd cast me a doubtful glance, complete with raised eyebrows.

"Did you take a cooking course between the time you left the Cove and now?"

I'd smirked, shaking my head. "Nope."

"Then I think I'll take care of the food, thanks." Her lips had twisted into a half-smile. "You can handle something else. How about laundry?" Her smile had begun to fade. "Wait—you don't have a washer and dryer here, do you? Where's the Laundromat?"

"About ten minutes away by car. I usually go on Saturdays and Tuesdays." I'd leaned a hip against the worn Formica counter. "I'll do yours, too. It's only fair, if you're cooking and buying the food."

"That's a deal." Elizabeth had held out a hand to me, just to seal the deal. I knew she'd done it without thinking, but I'd stared at her small white hand as though I'd never seen it before. Before she could think better of the gesture and yank it back, I closed my fingers over hers, relishing the skin-to-skin contact I'd been dying for since she'd come to Burton. I didn't shake her hand; I merely held it within my own, gently, as though it were something very precious and fragile. I'd been tempted to pull her against me and kiss her until I was thoroughly sated. But I knew I'd never, ever get enough of this woman, and I didn't want to scare her off.

So I'd finally let go and stepped back, waiting for my heartbeat to return to normal before I could speak again. Elizabeth had stared up at me, her expression inscrutable.

Now, sitting in the truck in the emptying parking lot, I let my head fall back onto the seat and closed my eyes. The thaw between Elizabeth and me had been slow and gradual, and I still couldn't read what was going on in her head. There were times I'd look up and catch her staring at me, and I'd almost swear I saw longing there. But she never made a move, and I couldn't talk myself into doing it, either. Not when I knew we didn't have a future.

Nothing had changed, after all. I was still the same loser, the same bad bet, that I'd always been. I was still Trent Wagoner.

And dammit, now I was Trent Wagoner who didn't even have a fucking job anymore.

I couldn't sit there any longer. I didn't want to go home

yet and deal with my mother or put on a happy face in front of Elizabeth. I put the truck into gear and backed out, turning onto the highway in the direction opposite town. I didn't know where I was going, but the open road sounded good.

My truck hugged the curves along the winding country roads. The farms I passed were still mostly brown and bare, though I saw a few ploughed fields. I slowed a little as I neared the Reynolds' place; in a few weeks, their farm stand would still be open this time of the afternoon, but right now, before spring had really sprung, it had probably closed an hour before. I'd heard that with Ali and Flynn living in New York part of the year, Sam had hired a few people to run their stand during the off-season. Of course, this year Ali might not be working on the farm at all, even though I knew she was back in town. Elizabeth had struck up a friendship with Flynn's mom, and she'd told me that Mrs. Evans was excited that her son and daughter-in-law were in Burton waiting for Ali to have her baby.

I'd nodded when Elizabeth had shared that information, waiting for the sting that used to hit me whenever I thought about Ali Reynolds. Well, Ali Evans now. But it hadn't come. Maybe I'd finally shaken off the doomed crush I'd had on her since we were in fifth grade. At least that would be one positive result of marrying Elizabeth.

Of course, there'd been lots of wonderful things about being Elizabeth Hudson's husband, even for that short time. All the years I'd spent mooning after Ali were nothing compared to the weeks I'd loved Elizabeth. She'd made me laugh more than I ever had, loved me with abandon, accepted every part of me . . . well, every part of me she knew. And the sex? *God.* It was like nothing I'd ever experienced. Random hook ups were all I'd ever known, but making love to Elizabeth was incredible. The connection between the two of us was real and deep, and when I was buried inside her, staring into her eyes . . .

"*Shit.*" I banged my hand against the steering wheel and dropped the pedal, flooring it around the next bend just to drive the memory away. I didn't need to be skulking past farms out here or remembering the tiny little bit of happiness I'd managed to grab for a few short weeks. I just needed to drive until I could convince myself to go home and break the news to Elizabeth that I was unemployed.

I knew she wouldn't kick my mother and me out. Elizabeth was too decent a person. I knew she could easily cover the rent for us as long as I needed. But I didn't want that. God, how I hated the idea. I wasn't a sexist jerk. I was proud of her career, and I'd never given a second thought to the fact that she earned more than me. But I still didn't want her paying for my apartment. It would be one more nail in our marriage's coffin.

Why that mattered to me when I already knew we were doomed was something I didn't want to examine too closely.

I slowed the truck at the next crossroads, glancing in both directions for traffic. These roads were notorious for speeders—hell, I was one of them—and the last thing I needed was a car slamming into the side of my truck. Although the thought of all the angst, the pain, the stress and the strife melting away as my life seeped into the black asphalt was dangerously tempting right now.

My mind darted to Jenna, to the image that had haunted me for nearly a year. I hadn't actually seen her sprawled across her bed, surrounded by empty pill containers and a bottle of Jack, but I'd tortured myself so often with how I imagined it must've looked that by now it felt like memory. I saw her pretty young face—God, so damned young—slack and blank, her hands reaching and empty. Yeah, that was on me, too.

A car horn sounded behind me. I'd been so preoccupied that I hadn't realized a car had pulled to a stop behind the truck. Without really thinking about it, I hung a left, and within a few minutes, I was approaching the glowing neon lights that outlined the Road Block.

I hadn't been to the bar since the night I'd rescued Elizabeth almost a month before, and up until then, I hadn't been there since my return to town. But right now, I wanted the noise, the crowds and a chance to make all the memories recede. I wasn't planning to get plastered, but one drink wasn't going to break me or kill me.

It was early enough that I nabbed a spot toward the front, and when I swung open the door, only a few people sat at the bar. I made my way across the room and eased onto a stool.

Mason was talking with a guy in the corner who was nursing a beer. He glanced over and spotted me, surprise spreading over his face. I watched as he slid a bowl of nuts toward the beer drinker and moseyed my way.

"Hey there, Trent. Haven't see you in a while. How's everything going?"

I lifted one shoulder in an approximation of a shrug. "You know. Same old shit."

"Get you a beer?"

I nodded. "Yeah. Please."

He grabbed a mug and filled it from the tap before setting it down in front of me. "So. Same old shit, huh?" He
cocked an eyebrow. "Everything going okay with Elizabeth?
You know, your wife?"

I rolled my eyes. "Yeah, I know. She's good."

"Funny thing. I've been hearing about the new lawyer
in town, and I've even heard some people talking about how
the pretty new attorney's shacking up with Trent Wagoner
and his mama, but no one ever says anything about the two
of you being married."

I snorted. "Guess it's not something she wants anyone
to know, huh? And it's not like . . . we're just living in the
same apartment because of—it's complicated. We don't need
to tell anyone about the quickie wedding on New Year's Eve,
mostly because our uh, 'marriage'—" I gave it the required
air quotes. "—has an expiration date. I'm just waiting for
Elizabeth to tell me when that is."

"That's a damn shame." Mason wiped at the bar with
a rag. "She seems like a pretty decent chick, though. Even
when she got sloshed, she was polite. Are you sure you can't
make it work?" He leaned in toward me, lowering his voice.
"I get that complicated deal. Remember Rilla and me? We
got married just so I could save her reputation. I never
thought it was going to be more than that. Never thought I
wanted any more. But now, I can't imagine my life without
her. Rilla, our kids—they're what keeps me sane and happy and steady." A wide smile split his face. "Sometimes you
gotta get through the complicated to get to the good and

steady."

I took a gulp of my beer and wiped some foam off my lip. "Good for you. I mean it, man. I'm happy you and Rilla made it work. But it's not really the same with us. You know me, Mason. I'm no good. Not for long term shit. I'm strictly a one-night-of-fun-and-done guy. Elizabeth deserves more than an asshole like me who can't even manage to hold onto a basic job hauling feed sacks."

"Whoa there, buddy." Mason braced his hands on the bar in front of me, scowling. "First off, I don't want to hear you talking shit like that. Yeah, used to be you had a rep you deserved. I'd see you in here, hitting on anything in a skirt and scoring most of the time. But not lately. You came back into town, and the only time I've seen you in here was when you came to pick up your wife. What I hear—and trust me, I hear just about everything in this place—is that you're working your ass off down at Grainger's and during your off time, making sure your mother stays off the streets."

When I started to interrupt, Mason held up one hand. "I'm not saying anything about your ma, Trent. Man's got a right to be protective of his own, I get that, but we all know your mother didn't make your life easy. Most guys would've let her hang, but you didn't. You came back here, bailed her out and now you're making sure she stays out of trouble. All of this in a town where half the people hate you for what you used to be and the others don't seem to give a rat's ass about you."

I lifted my half-drunk beer. "Thanks for the feel-good talk, Mason. You've really got this sympathetic bartender crap down."

He gave me a half-grin, but he kept talking. "It's straight talk, Trent, because that's what you need. I'm telling you, I get what you're going through, as much as I can. I'm also saying, I admire the hell out of you, because changing who you were isn't easy. I don't want to hear this shit about you not being good enough, because it was obvious to both Rilla and me that Elizabeth—your wife—didn't feel that way. When we asked her who we could call to come help her, she didn't even hesitate. She said your name. She said, 'Call my husband.'"

Yeah, hearing that gave me a spike of happy, but I shook my head. "She was drunk."

"She was. Which means she was honest and real. No bullshit, just reaching out for who she needed. Who she wanted." He paused, his brows knitting together. "Hey, wait a minute. Did you say a while back that you lost your job at Grainger's? Sorry, I just realized what you said."

I sighed. "Yeah. Business is slow, numbers down, last one hired, first one fired. Same old. And where the hell I'm going to find another job in this town . . . I don't know." I drained the rest of my mug.

Mason stood across the bar, studying me. "It's got to be in Burton? You could just go back to Michigan and work for your uncle again, right?"

I shook my head. "Not an option right now. My mother . . ." I hadn't told anyone other than Elizabeth the truth about why I was staying in town. "She needs to stay at the same address for four months to qualify for this rehab deal. This is her last shot, Mason. Her last chance to get sober and maybe figure out how to be a real person. I have to do everything I can to make sure she gets it. So yeah, I need to find something in town or close enough I can make the drive and be home to keep my eye on her at night."

"What about Elizabeth? Can't she help?"

I clenched my jaw. "She could. She would. I don't want that. My mother isn't her problem, and I don't want her fucking supporting us."

"I get it." Mason nodded. He exhaled and looked down the bar, then across the room, where now the door was opening with steady regularity and tables were filling on the restaurant side. Business was booming at the Road Block.

"What would you think about working here?"

The noise in the bar was starting to amp up. People were talking, background music was playing, and so I was pretty sure I'd misheard Mason. I leaned up.

"What'd you say?"

He glanced down the bar to where Darcy, the other bartender, was just tying on an apron to start serving up drinks. "Hey, Darce, you got this for a little bit?"

She winked and nodded. "Got it, boss."

Mason turned back to me. "Do me a favor. Come back to my office for a minute. Let's talk."

An hour later, I left the Road Block with a new job.

"Here's the deal, Trent. For a while, I've been feeling like I'm getting pulled in too many directions. I have a gorgeous wife, two beautiful children, and I don't get to see them nearly enough, because this place is just blowing up. I'm happy as hell about that, don't get me wrong. But I'm not ready to give up my family to keep it going. I have Rocky, and I have Darcy, but neither of them want more hours or more responsibility."

I nodded. "Okay. But Mason, I don't have any experience in working at a bar or a restaurant."

He shrugged. "You'll learn. You're a smart guy, Trent. What I need is someone I can train to do exactly what I need. I want someone to take my daytime hours so I can be home, spending time with Rilla and the kids and my mom. It would mean some weekend days, too, so I hope you'd be all right with that."

"I think I could do that." As long as it was daylight, Mrs. Price could see across the street to keep an eye on my mother. Elizabeth would probably be around, too, but I wasn't going to ask her to have anything to do with my mother.

"Great. So you come in starting tomorrow, and for a week, I'll give you on-the-job training. If we get to the end and we're both happy, it's a steady gig. If for any reason you don't like it or if I feel like it's not a good fit, we'll call it a day, no questions asked, no hard feelings. What do you say?"

I rubbed a brass tack on the arm of the leather chair where I sat. "Mason, I got to ask you one thing. Why're you doing this? Is it because you feel sorry for me? Because I sure as hell don't need pity or charity."

"Chill, dude. This isn't pity. This is me seeing an opportunity and taking it. Sometimes things happen for a reason, and you just have to be smart enough to see it. I've been considering this for a while, and you got to think, it felt like it was—what do they call that? Serendipity? When you walked in here tonight, and you needed a job, I felt like something clicked. Meant to be, buddy. So it's not charity. And I don't feel sorry for you. I admire you for standing up when most people would turn away, for having the balls to come back to this town when I know it was probably the last thing you wanted to do."

I didn't answer, but I met his eyes, and he nodded.

"And I think you got a chance to really turn shit around, Trent. You might think you and Elizabeth aren't going to make it, but I think you could be wrong. Why not give it a shot? You said you're bad news. Well, that's some fucked up shit. You have everything you need, Trent. You're a good guy. I see it. Elizabeth sees it. And the longer you hang in here, others will, too."

I took a deep breath. "You're sure? You think I can do this?"

He leveled a gaze at me. "I know you can." He stood up and offered me his hand. "Now go home and tell that beautiful wife of yours that she's going to have to come back over here now that her husband's helping to run the joint. I'll have Rilla come over one night, and the four of us can get to know each other a little better."

My head was spinning a little. "Okay. I'll mention it." I paused. "Mason—thank you. I know you didn't have to take a chance on me. But I just—thank you."

He grinned. "Seeing potential is my specialty, dude. And I see a shitload in you." He winked. "Prove me right."

"I will. Don't worry."

I felt like I was practically walking on air as I left the bar. I wondered if Elizabeth was worrying about me being late. I couldn't wait to get home and tell her my news.

I opened the door to the apartment after jogging up the steps from the sidewalk. Stepping into the living room, I ducked just in time to avoid being hit in the head by a red shoe that was flying through the air.

"You fucking bitch! Get out of my way. You can't make me stay here."

Across the room, just beyond the short hallway, my mother stood in one high-heeled shoe. Its mate was the one that had just missed beaning me. In front of her, arms crossed over her chest, my wife was blocking her path. The glance she tossed over her shoulder at me was positively murderous.

"Where the hell have you been?" The two women spoke almost in unison, though my mother's words were hissed and Elizabeth practically screamed hers.

"Uh . . ." I paused, deciding that blurting out that I'd both lost a job and gotten a new one was probably not the way to lead here. "What's going on?"

"She's holding me against my will!" My mother screeched, jerking away from Elizabeth. "I want to go out, and she won't get the hell out of my way."

"She came out here and announced she was going out tonight." Elizabeth turned to me, her eyebrows shooting up. "Like, you know, it's something she does every night. I told her she couldn't, and she's been fighting me ever since."

"You can't keep me here against my will. It's illegal. I can call the cops." My mother's bottom lip stuck out petulantly.

"Oh, yeah? And just how do you think you're going to do that? You have a phone?" Elizabeth dug into the back pocket of the jeans that were covering her very excellent ass—*not now, Trent, focus!* She pulled out her cell phone and dangled it over my mother's head. "On second thought, you know what? Go right ahead. Call the police. Tell them I'm keeping you inside. Tell them I'm torturing you. I bet they give me a medal."

I choked back a snort of laughter. I'd forgotten how feisty my wife could get. It was one of the things I'd loved about her early on, but since coming to Burton, she'd been subdued and guarded, with only brief glimpses of the firecracker I'd known and still loved. Like the night with the fried chicken.

But now, she was out in full force, the mad gleaming in her blue eyes. My mother glared at her, and then shifted her attention to me. When she realized whose side I was going to take—and really, could it have been that big a surprise?— she wilted, her shoulders slumping.

"Fine." With one swift kick, she sent the other shoe flying through the air. Elizabeth darted out of its way, and I managed to catch it before it went through the front window.

My mother stomped back down the hall to her room and slammed the door so hard, the entire house vibrated. In her wake, she left a deafening silence.

Elizabeth turned around to face me. "Where were you all this time? I got home, changed my clothes and started dinner, and you still weren't here. And then Madame comes prancing out of her room, cool as you please, and makes it almost all the way to the front door before I stopped her."

"I'm sorry." Guilt battled with my eagerness to tell her about my new job. "I should've called. I never even thought—Elizabeth, I'm really, really sorry."

For a minute, I was afraid she was going to launch into a full-blown rant. And maybe it would've been a good thing. But instead, she shook her head, waved her hand and closed her eyes.

"No, I get it. I mean, you must feel like you don't even have a life. You get up early, go to work, and then come home and babysit your mother until it's time to go to sleep on this crappy couch before you get up and do it all over again. And I'm not making it any easier. I get that you needed to blow off some steam. It's okay. I was just—I was worried, is all."

"Elizabeth." I took two tentative steps toward her, reaching out a hand to touch her arm. "It wasn't that. I don't mind anything. The stuff with my mom is what it is. But I was a little upset when I left Grainger's, because he had to lay me off."

Understanding and sympathy filled her face. "Oh, God, Trent. I'm sorry. What happened?"

I shrugged. "Nothing really. Just one of those things. He said he'd like to hire me back once things pick up again in the summer, but he can't keep me on right now. Not his fault. But still . . . I drove around a little, and I ended up at Mason's. At the Road Block."

"Oh." I saw the pink tinge on her cheeks. She hadn't been anywhere near the bar or Mason and Rilla since her dramatic entry to town a month before. I knew she was mortified that she'd gotten rip-roaring drunk before she'd even really arrived.

"Yeah, I wanted to . . . I don't know what I wanted, but I talked to Mason, and this is the good news part." I raised my other hand so that I was holding her lightly by her upper arms, my thumbs stroking over her thin cotton shirt. "He offered me a job as assistant manager at the bar."

Elizabeth blinked. "Really? And you—I take it you said yes?"

I nodded. "Yeah. It's just days, and I won't have to be there until nine every morning. The pay is really good, and I won't be hauling feed sacks." I slid my hands to her shoulders and squeezed them lightly. "I couldn't believe Mason offered it to me."

Her face lit up as her lips curved into smile. "Trent, I'm so happy for you. That's wonderful." She stood on her toes and lifted her arms around my neck to hug me.

The minute I felt her softness crushed against me, my body went into overdrive. I wrapped my arms around her, holding her closer to me, and without giving any thought to the past or to the future, I lowered my head and covered her mouth with mine.

For a few beats of my heart, Elizabeth didn't respond. She was frozen stock-still, though I could feel the pounding of her pulse against my skin. And then as though she'd been suddenly set free, she made a small sound in the back of her throat and kissed me back with abandon.

Her boobs pressed into my chest, and her hips canted toward mine. I went hard, my response immediate and intense. All the blood in my body was either rushing to join the party between my legs or roaring in my ears. My brain had only one thought, and it was to get my clothes off—and hers, too—lay her on the sofa behind us and slide into the paradise that was her body.

My hands roamed south, molding her ass and lifting her up so that I could grind against the heat of her sex. She dropped her own fingers to delve under my shirt, exploring the bare skin of my sides and back.

"God, Trent. I forgot—how good . . ." She was mumbling softly as she kissed her way down my neck.

"I know." I hadn't forgotten how good we were. It just wasn't something I could let myself think about often without going crazy. But now, it all came back to me, an undeniable wave sweeping both of us along.

I risked moving one hand up to cup her tit, knowing how much she loved it when I touched her nipples. With a quiet moan, she pushed her breast against my fingers, craving more just as I was.

A loud crash came from the direction of my mother's room, and we both jumped, every movement coming to a complete halt. Elizabeth was breathing fast, her chest rising and falling in time with mine. I held her arms again, and she dropped her forehead to my chest.

"I should probably go check and make sure she's not trying to climb out her window." My voice was muffled against Elizabeth's hair. "Or maybe I should just let her do it. God knows I'm sick and tired of being her warden."

"Yeah, I know." Elizabeth turned her head so that her ear pressed against my speeding heart. "I need to check dinner anyway. I made lasagna. I don't want it to burn."

"Okay." I released her. "Let me see what's going on back there, then I'll help you get it all on the table." I dared one more kiss, touching her lips lightly with mine.

Her eyes, clouded and wondering, searched me. I trailed one finger down her soft cheek, smiling.

For the first time in months, my life felt possible again.

CHAPTER SEVEN

Elizabeth

"SO WHAT HAPPENED NEXT?"

I sighed and moved the phone to my other ear. I couldn't help glancing at the closed door to my office. I had a sneaking suspicion that Gladys sometimes skulked down the hall to my office and listened at the door; I'd never caught her at it, but I'd have sworn I saw her unmistakable silhouette out there. She'd made several arch comments about me keeping my door shut, informing me that Clark had *never* done the same.

"I supposed he didn't have anything to hide. No secrets, that man." She'd said it while watching me out of the corner of her eye.

"Or he just knew better than to talk about his secrets here at the office." I'd shrugged and given her my specially-patented Gladys smile, phony as all get-out. She'd harrumphed and stalked away from me.

"Hello? Elizabeth, are you still there?" Cory was getting impatient.

"Yes, I'm here. Sorry, I thought I heard someone at my door." I usually visited Cory at the library a few times a week. In the month I'd been living in Burton, the older woman had become my confidante and my friend. It was such a relief to be able to talk about what was happening at home, with Trent and his mother, and at the office, where Gladys and I continued our daily struggle for control and dominance. But today the rain was coming down in torrents, and since I had a conference call just after lunch with two clients regarding a real estate sale anyway, it didn't make sense to haul my cookies down there.

"Well, don't leave me hanging like that. You two were basically groping at each other, making out like teenagers, and then . . . what happened? Was his mother really trying to escape out her window?"

I sighed. "No, she'd pulled down the clothes bar from her closet, trying to climb up to get something. Trent was afraid maybe she'd somehow gotten booze and hidden it there, so he searched the whole area, but he didn't find anything. She's so secretive, though. And I thought she was going to tear me to bits when I tried to keep her from leaving the house."

"Good for you, for standing your ground." I heard papers shuffling in the background. "But Trent didn't say anything? He didn't kiss you again?"

"Not like before, no." I thought of his face when I'd finally gone to bed much later that night. We'd enjoyed a rare dinner for two, since Donna was still sulking and refused to emerge from her room to eat. I told Trent I'd make her plate, but he wouldn't let me, saying she'd come out if she were hungry enough.

So we'd sat on the floor, with our lasagna on the coffee table, both of us more relaxed and ourselves than we'd been since I'd come to Burton. Trent had apologized that we didn't have any wine in the house to go with our meal; he didn't keep it out of fear his mom would drink anything she could get her hands on.

But we hadn't needed wine to feel a little giddy. I made Trent tell me the whole story about how Mason had come to hire him. I could tell from the light in his eyes that he was excited about the new job.

"He wants you to come down some night, too—both of us. He said Rilla would get someone to watch the kids and come over, too, so we could get to know each other."

I'd winced. "Not sure I'm ready to show my face in the bar yet. Not after making a fool of myself so spectacularly."

Trent had just rolled his eyes. "Honey, if I can go there and work, after all the times I got wasted in that bar, you sure as hell can come over and hold your head high." He'd winked. "C'mon, woman up."

Our conversation had lasted through dinner, into clean-up—Trent never let me wash dishes on my own—and well into the late night, when we'd sat at opposite ends of the couch as the room grew darker.

Finally, I'd stretched and yawned. "I know you don't have to get up as early tomorrow, but I'm exhausted. Apparently being a fucking bitch jailor takes it out of me." I'd made sure that my voice had a teasing note, so Trent would realize

I wasn't serious.

"Yeah, I know. Thanks again for doing that—for making sure she didn't go out. I'd hate to have spent tonight tracking her down instead of having dinner with you." He'd held my eyes, watching me, gauging my response.

I'd stood up, smiling. "I agree. I wouldn't have wanted to miss a minute of tonight." And then, gathering up all my brave, I leaned over the sofa and kissed him.

It was just a good-night kiss, brief, but it was somehow filled with promise. Trent brushed my cheek with the back of his fingers while he whispered to me.

"Good night, Elizabeth. Sleep well."

I'd wanted to snag his hand in mine and pull him toward me, lead him down the hall to the bedroom he'd given up for me, invite him back to his own bed. But I couldn't do it, not with his mother across the hall and everything still so unsettled. So I'd only nodded and walked myself to the lonely bedroom, leaving him on the couch.

"No," I repeated now. "Not again. We just talked until late. It was . . . it was good."

"I'm so glad, Elizabeth. I'm happy for Trent about his new job, too. Please pass on my congratulations." One of the reasons I liked Cory so much was that I could tell she truly did care for Trent. She'd long ago looked beyond the defensive kid with the chip on his shoulder and seen the hurt little boy who pretended his mother made him cookies every day.

"Enough about me." I leaned back in my chair, staring out the window at the raindrops. "No news on the grandbaby front?"

Cory groaned. "No, and I think Flynn's about to drive

Ali around the bend. Every time she sighs or makes a face, he's sure she's in labor. The other day, Bridget told me, 'Grandma, Daddy's a mess!'"

We both laughed. I knew Cory was almost as anxious as her son, but she'd been through this process before. She maintained an air of calm that apparently Flynn couldn't master.

"You'll keep me informed, though, right? Even if I've never met Ali and Flynn, I feel like I know them."

"Of course. And once the baby's here and things get back to normal, I want you and Trent to come over for dinner and meet everyone. I talk about you to the kids, and I'm afraid they think Mom has an imaginary friend."

I giggled. "That sounds like fun. It would be good for Trent to get back in touch with his old friends, too." The prospect of us doing something like that together, like a real married couple, made my heart sing.

"I think you're right about that. Oh, bother—someone just came in. I guess I have to go be a librarian. Talk to you later, dear."

"Thanks, Cory. Bye."

I ended the call and laid my phone on the desk. I had another fifteen minutes before the conference call with my clients, and I hadn't had anything to eat yet. Maybe I could call over to Franco's and see if they'd deliver a salad—

"Ahem." I jerked my head up to the doorway, which was now open. Gladys occupied all the space between the edge of the door and the jamb, regarding me steadily.

"Yes? What do you need?" I picked up a pen and tapped it against the desk blotter. I didn't like being short with her, but it seemed this woman couldn't understand any other way.

"Your conference call with Mr. Jacobs and Mr. Abercrombie is in—"

"—fifteen minutes. I know. Thanks." I pushed away from the desk and stood up. "I told you, Gladys. I don't need reminders for these things. I'm an adult, and I'm capable of keeping my own schedule."

Her mouth tightened. "Of course. Whatever you say. But you haven't met these men, and they're both sticklers for promptness. You wouldn't want to run late."

"You're right, and I won't. Thank you, Gladys." I turned my back, clearly dismissing her the same way I'd seen my dad do with soldiers all my life. I hated having to be like him.

Once I heard the door close again, I picked up the phone and dialed over to Franco's. The man on the other end promised he'd have my salad to me in ten minutes, which I figured would be just enough time to eat a little of it before I made the client call.

As it happened, Franco's delivery boy was actually at the office in five minutes. I complimented him on his speed and gave him a healthy tip as Gladys looked on in silent disapproval. She'd informed me during my first week that Clark had *never* ordered food to be delivered to the office. He ate lunch every day with his dear wife at their home. And when clients were involved, he always took them *out* to eat.

Just to spite her, I left my door partially open as I enjoyed my salad. And out of the same motivation, I might've made some rather loud yummy noises as I crunched the croutons.

In fact, I got so carried away that I nearly forgot my conference call. Wiping my fingers hastily on the paper napkin, I jumped up to close the door and then flipped through the files on my desk to find the right numbers.

This conference call was the first one I'd made in my new job. Back in the Cove, all of my clients were so close that it was easier to just meet in person rather than to do something like arrange a joint phone call. And yeah, I should've looked a little more closely into what setting up a call like this entailed. But I'd figured that it couldn't be too hard. I'd seen the button on my cell phone that said "three-way calling". How much more difficult could it be on a landline?

As it turned out, the answer was that it was very freaking complicated. I started out by dialing Mr. Jacobs' number. As it rang, I searched frantically for the button that would let me add in Mr. Abercrombie. But there was no button. I turned the phone upside down and ran my fingers over every inch of it, but there was nothing.

Meanwhile, Mr. Jacobs was answering the phone. "Well, I was beginning to wonder what was holding us up. Good afternoon, Miss Hudson. Darryl, how are you today?"

I gritted my teeth. "I'm sorry, Mr. Jacobs. I haven't been able to get Mr. Abercrombie on the line yet. Still getting used to the phone system, you know—if you'll give me just a moment—"

"Do not put me on hold." He issued the decree as though he were God on high. "I don't appreciate that one bit. Inane music without words and then half the time you're cut off and no one's the wiser."

135

"I won't, I promise. Just let me see—"

"Where's the lovely Mrs. West? Why didn't she put the call together today?" Mr. Jacobs persisted in talking, which was distracting me from solving our problem.

"She's, uh, she's just down the hall at her desk, but don't worry, I'm perfectly capable of doing this."

At that very moment, another button lit up on my phone. I was afraid that if I pressed it, I might lose Mr. Jacobs, which clearly was a tragedy he couldn't handle. I sat staring at the blinking light, listening to the old man drone on, helpless to do anything. I wanted to cry.

"Miss Hudson." Gladys knocked on my door and leaned in. "I am terribly sorry to disturb your conference call, but Mr. Abercrombie just called in, wondering if he had the wrong time written down. He's been waiting for you to call him."

I stared at her, hating with every fiber of my body the mean triumph in her glittering eyes, knowing that if I'd been a little more patient, a little less cocky, she would've told me how to do the call and I could've avoided this mess.

But it was too late now. I wasn't backing down. I cleared my throat and covered the receiver in my hand. "Thank you, Gladys. Please tell Mr. Abercrombie to hang up and that I'll be patching him in directly."

Once Gladys had closed the door again, I drew in a deep breath and spoke into the phone. "Mr. Jacobs, I am horribly sorry. I have this problem solved now, but unfortunately, it's going to require us both hanging up so I can connect you into the same call."

Mr. Jacobs humphed and sighed, letting me know he

was unhappy, but he finally did hang up. I picked up my cell phone and within a few minutes, I had both men on three-way calling. The quality of the call was not wonderful—Mr. Jacobs kept roaring, "What did you *say*, Darryl?" But we accomplished what we needed, and at the end, both men seemed pleased.

When I hung up, I was a sweaty mess. Who knew that a conference call was such a high-anxiety deal? I made a few notes in the file and dropped my head to the desk. It was my own damn fault. I should have just swallowed my pride and asked Gladys to set it up for me. I would've had to deal with her supercilious smile, but the clients wouldn't have been affected, and I wouldn't be sitting here, wiped out by talking on the telephone.

I sat up and glanced over the other papers on my desk. Nothing was pressing; while nearly all of Clark Morgan's clients had made the transition to me, I'd learned pretty quickly that he'd maintained a light load. Gladys acted as though everything that came through the office was a matter of life or death, but in reality, most of what I saw were property transfers, wills and the occasional traffic violation. If I'd thought practicing law in the Cove was low-key, Burton's legal activity was practically comatose.

I finished a few last minute things, signed a letter and glanced over the calendar. No court dates were upcoming. The days and weeks stretched out in a long line of monotony. Sighing, I stood up and slung my purse over my shoulder. It was only mid-afternoon, but I didn't have any good reason to stay in the office. I wasn't sure where I was going, but I needed to get away.

I intended to walk past Gladys without saying a word, but apparently she had other plans. She cleared her throat.

"Well, *that* was a fiasco." Her hands were folded on the top of the desk. "You may very well have lost two of the most important clients this office has. This is typical of you, isn't it? You don't take anything seriously. You're going to run this practice into the ground, and it doesn't matter to you, of course, because you can just go off on your merry way. But if this office goes under, I lose my job. And I'm not ready to retire yet, not by a long shot. Perhaps it's time for you to think about someone other than yourself."

She spewed her poison at me all the while her face stayed calm and serene, as though another voice was speaking through her façade. I paused, turning to face her.

"Gladys, I took care of the call. Was there a better way? Yes, I'm sure there was. But regardless, I made it happen. Mr. Jacobs and Mr. Abercrombie were both fine. They're not leaving the practice. I'm not running anything into the ground." I stopped to take what I hoped would be a calming breath. "I understand that how I do things isn't how you would. I know I'm not Clark. But believe me, I know what I'm doing. However, when you undermine me at every turn, it makes both of our jobs so much more difficult."

"Undermine? I haven't done any such thing." She rolled her shoulders. "If anything, I've gone out of my way to make sure that this transition runs smoothly—"

"Bullshit." I hissed out the word. "You're sitting up here like a spider in her web, just waiting for me to make a misstep so you can pounce. I don't understand why, though. If you're so worried about losing your job here, I'd think you'd do anything possible to help me succeed. I can only think that despite what you say, proving you're in control is more important than making sure we both do well."

"That's a fine way for a lady to talk," Gladys huffed. "This office has always been one of decorum and class. *I*, for one, plan to uphold that standard, even if you do not. As for everything else you've accused me of doing, I'm not going to justify that with a response. I don't need to lower myself to your level."

I don't know precisely what happened next. Something in me popped, as weeks of her constant sniping and my simmering resentment bubbled to the surface and exploded like a shaken can of soda.

"*My* level?" I bent over the front of her desk, my fingers gripped the edge. "Seriously? I'm the one who agreed to keep you on here for a year, out of the goodness of my heart. Did you know Clark put that in the contract? And I agreed to it? Believe me, lady, if I'd known you beforehand, I'd have run in the other direction. I'm doing the best I can here. Do you think it's easy to come into a new town, where I don't know a soul, and where I'm fully aware people are talking about me, because I'm living with Trent Wagoner? It isn't. I've been moving all my damned life. I'm used to pretending everything's peachy when it really sucks. I can put up with so much shit, it'd make your head spin.

"I'm used to the mean girls, the ones who talk about you out of spite and have a mission to make your life miserable. You know what? That's what you are. Nothing more than a big overgrown mean girl who's been stupid enough to let this fucking law practice become her whole life. You're scared shitless that I'm going to force you out of here, and then what'll you have? Nothing. Because you're a horrid person."

My hands were shaking as I pushed back away from the desk. My heart was pounding, and there was a tinge of red around my vision. I swallowed hard and lobbied my last fatal blow.

"No wonder your husband ran out on you. He probably couldn't stand to be near you one minute longer."

I had the fleeting satisfaction of seeing her face go white and her eyes widened. Humiliation and hurt filled them, and immediately any vindication I felt gave way to horrified remorse.

"Gladys—I'm sorry—I don't know why I said that—" I managed to stammer out a few words before she pushed herself to stand and fled down the hallway, where she wrenched open the door to the restroom and disappeared inside.

Tears filled my eyes. *God, how could I have been so cruel?* One thing I'd prided myself on all my life was never responding, never lashing out against the people who'd made my life difficult. I didn't like Gladys; I hated how she acted, but I had no right to say what I did.

I knew she wouldn't want to see me now. Nothing I could say would take away the pain I'd caused. My sight still blurry, I wrenched open the door and stumbled out into the main foyer.

"Elizabeth?" Will Garth stood in the doorway of his own office space, frowning. "Everything okay? I thought I heard shouting."

I pressed the heels of my hands to my eyes to staunch

the flow of tears. "That would have been me. Sorry. Things got a little out of hand with Gladys, and I'm afraid I lost my temper." I tried to draw in a deep breath, but it came out more like a sob.

"Hey." Will came to my side. For a moment, I was afraid he was going to reach out to touch me, but he didn't, instead rocking on his feet as he stared down, his brows furrowed. "Want to talk about it?"

I shook my head. "No. Thank you, but—no." The last thing I needed was a complication in the form of Will. I'd seen him with a fair amount of regularity over the past weeks; we'd pass in the entry way or out on the sidewalk. It hadn't amounted to more than small talk or exchanged pleasantries, but there was an undercurrent of interest on his part that made me uncomfortable. I liked Will, but my life was screwed up enough without introducing another man into the midst of it.

"You sure?" This time he did reach out and lay a hand on my shoulder. "Let me take you over to Kenny's for a cup of coffee. My treat." He smiled, and part of me wished I could say yes. Will was sweet and easy, and I had a feeling that being with him would be the same way. There wouldn't be any of the angst and uncertainty I felt in my relationship with Trent. I'd have stability and dependability. Maybe the passion and fire would be lacking . . . and if I were another woman, that might be okay. But I wasn't. As it turned out, I thrived on the passion. I needed it. I didn't know where or how Trent and I were going to end up, but I wasn't ready to give up the chance to find out.

"Thanks, Will." I patted his hand and then ducked out

from under his arm. "But I don't think I'm very good company right now. I'm going to get out of here for a little bit, try to get my head on straight. I'll see you later."

Before he could catch up with me again, I pushed open the front door and sprinted down the steps. My BMW was down the street, parked against the curb; this part of Burton didn't have much in the way of public parking other than street side. I climbed into the driver's seat and turned the ignition. The rain had slowed down to a drizzle, but I turned my wipers on intermittent anyway before I pulled away.

I hadn't done much exploring beyond the immediate borders of town. Now I followed the main street past the shops and churches and turned onto the highway, where I opened her up.

Forgetfulness, total mind-numbing amnesia was what I was seeking. I didn't want to remember the words I'd said to Gladys or the ugliness Donna had spouted at me the night before. I didn't want to think about the confused mess of my feelings about Trent or the way Will had looked at me. I wanted to pretend legal briefs, filings of motions and the past month didn't exist.

Out of the corner of my eye, I saw a gold blur coming from the shoulder of the road. Before I could react, a sickening thud hit the side of my car. Braking as hard as I could, I swerved and came to a halt.

"Oh my God, oh my God." I couldn't stop shaking or chanting the words as I grappled for the door handle. When the door opened, I almost fell out of the car in my haste to see what I'd hit.

In the middle of the road, several yards from where I'd

stopped, a golden retriever lay. The dog's sides were heaving, and even from where I stood, I could hear a soft whining.

"Oh, God, what did I do?" I wanted to cry, to lie down next to the poor dog and weep. Once upon a time, when I was nineteen, I'd accidentally rolled a squirrel who'd tried to get across the street ahead of my car. I'd cried for an hour and refused to drive again for a week. But while I was very sorry for Mr. Squirrel, this was a dog, a sweet pup who had only had the bad luck to run into my BMW when it was going a little too fast.

I approached him carefully, remembering that injured animals could sometimes be dangerous. But the dog didn't do anything but watch me with huge brown eyes that seemed to beg me for help.

"I'm so sorry, doggie. I didn't see you. But it's going to be okay, because I'll take you to the vet, and they can fix you right up. Just . . . just let me get you into the car."

I managed to run back to the still-running car and back it close enough that I could lift him into the backseat. From his size and weight, I guessed that he wasn't quite full-grown yet. My heart almost broke when he whimpered as I laid him on the seat.

"Hang in there, buddy. I'm going to find someone to help you." I closed the back door and leaned over the driver's seat to get my phone. Thanking God that I had service out here in the middle of nowhere, I ran a search for local veterinarians. When one popped up only five minutes away, I wanted to kiss my phone.

"Yes! Okay, dog. Just stay still back there, and I'll get you to some place where they can help you."

I added the address of the vet's office to my mapping program and pulled back onto the road, grateful that no other cars had come speeding by while I was trying to save the pup. I drove as fast as I could—but not too fast, since hitting another animal while transporting the first one to get medical attention—yeah, that wasn't part of any plan I had.

The veterinarian clinic was in a newer-looking building just at the edge of town. I pulled up alongside the front, jumped out of the car and flung open the door. The few people sitting in the waiting room looked up, startled. A lady with a bird cage in her lap gave a little shriek of surprise.

The receptionist at the front desk stood up. "Can I help you?" She was an older woman, and her scrubs were decorated with tiny kittens.

"Yes. Sorry for bursting in. I—" *Pull it together, Elizabeth. Don't fall apart now.* "I hit a dog. Out on the highway. He's hurt, and I have him in the back of my car."

If my MO in this kind of situation was utter panic, the receptionist was my exact opposite. She regarded me for a few seconds and then turned. "Smith! We have an emergency here."

The man who came jogging down the hall was hot in a preppy, well-groomed way. He saw me standing in the doorway and pointed. "Out there?"

"Yeah." I led the way, opening the back door of the car. "It was an accident. He came running out of this field, and I couldn't even swerve out of the way in time. I think he hit me more than I did him."

Smith—and I wasn't certain if that was his first name or last—leaned over the dog, crooning comfortingly. "It's okay there, fellow. You're going to be okay." He glanced back over his shoulder at me. "Did the car actually go over him?"

The very thought made me want to gag. "I don't think so. He came barreling into the car, like I said, and as soon as he hit, I turned away from him. I didn't feel the car—you know." I swallowed. "Go over him."

"Yeah, it doesn't feel like he has broken ribs, and his pelvis feels like it's intact. It's possible he sort of bounced off the car. He could have some other broken bones, and maybe a concussion. Let me get a gurney, and we'll roll him in and take a look."

I stood out of the way while the vet, with help from the receptionist/nurse he called Millie, maneuvered the dog gurney close to my car and lifted the animal onto it. They were just moving it around toward the door when an old pickup truck rolled into the parking lot. A woman with long dark hair, wearing jeans and flannel shirt, jumped from the cab and hurried over to us.

"What's going on?" She peered over my shoulder.

"Canine vs. MV. Not as bad as it could be, I think. I'm taking him back to X-ray." His eyes met the woman's. "Why don't you get all the particulars from . . . I'm sorry, I didn't get your name."

"Elizabeth Hudson." I scooted out of the way as Smith and Millie wheeled the dog inside.

"Elizabeth . . . hey, I know you." The woman in the flannel shirt smiled. "My mom was telling me you're the new lawyer in town. She just raves about you, how nice you are, and . . . well, that sounds creepy, doesn't it?" She held out her hand. "I'm Maureen Evans. Cory's my mother."

"Oh my gosh, you're Maureen?" I wanted to hug her. I'd heard from Cory all about her daughter and her recent romance. "So he's *that* Smith, huh?"

She laughed. "I see Mom's been talking to you, too. Hey, why don't you move your car and then come on in, and we'll see what's going on with the dog."

By the time I'd parked the BMW and come back inside, Maureen had boiled water for tea and was waiting for me in her office. She motioned to a chair.

"Have a seat. Tell me what happened between you and that handsome blond in X-ray."

"The blond—oh. The dog." I sighed. "I was . . . I was driving too fast. I'd had a bad afternoon, and I just wanted to get out and be alone and not have to think. I was crying, and then he just came darting out of nowhere. I did the best I could to avoid him." I felt again the thump of the dog hitting my car, and suddenly I fell apart. Burying my face in my hands, I gave up and wept.

"Oh, honey. No, don't cry. Shhhh." Maureen pulled me against her and stroked my hair. She reminded me of her mother, and I let myself relax as all of my pain and guilt from the day poured out.

"I'm a horrible person, and I was terrible to Gladys, and even if she is a raging bitch, she didn't deserve that. And I just—I'm so damned tired of doing something I hate, and living in a place I want to like, but where I'm afraid to get to know anyone." I met Maureen's sympathetic eyes. "If it weren't for your mother, I think I'd have run away that first week."

"Yeah, Mom's a peach, isn't she?" Maureen straightened

up and nudged my tea cup toward me. "Here, have some of this. You should know, though, that my sister Iona and Flynn and me—we're grateful to you. Mom's been kind of coasting through life since my dad passed. At first we didn't notice— she's good at covering, my mother is—but after Flynn and Ali got married, and Iona had her second little guy, we realized Mom wasn't quite . . . there anymore. She showed up and smiled and put on a good show, but her heart wasn't in it. But she's been better since you came to town. She doesn't tell us what you talk about, but she'll say that you came in to the library for tea, and she always seems a little happier." Maureen squeezed my hand. "So thanks for being a good friend to her."

I sniffled. "She's been the only good thing about Burton." A new wave of sadness engulfed me. "I never should've come here."

Maureen was silent for a few minutes. "Hey, you know what? Smith's going to be a little while with all the tests in there. Let me take care of Mrs. Hauvers—she's the lady with the bird in the waiting room—and then I don't think we have any other appointments today. I have an idea."

She jumped up and headed out of the room. I closed my eyes and tried to pull myself together, feeling like an idiot for losing my cool in front of people I didn't even know.

After about fifteen minutes, Maureen reappeared, shrugging into a jacket. "Come on. I want to take you somewhere."

Before I could say yay or nay, she was dragging me out of the clinic and to her truck. "Where are we going?"

She hopped in on her side and turned over the engine.

"Don't you trust me?"

"Ahhh—"

"Don't answer that." Maureen grinned. "When I was a little girl, I was very shy. And very sensitive. My feelings were always getting hurt, and I'd come home from school sad and crying. And my dad—well, he was just about the best man you could ever meet." Her voice went soft. "He would take me to this special place, and we'd sit there together."

"Okay." I found a tissue in my purse and blew my nose. I was silent, watching out the window as we made our way into town. Maureen turned down a side street a few blocks away from my office and pulled to the curb in front of a tiny storefront. Whimsical letters painted on the front window read *Sweetness and Bites.*

We both got out of the truck, and I followed Maureen through the door. Immediately, the wonderful smells assaulted my senses: sweet frying dough, chocolate and caramel mixed with the tantalizing scent of baking bread. I sighed and moaned softly.

"Right?" Maureen elbowed me in the ribs. "See? No one can be sad in this place."

"Not on my watch, anyway." A beautiful woman with long black hair, liberally laced with silver, stepped through swinging doors into the front of the shop. "Maureen, dear one, who have you brought me today?"

"Kiki, this is Elizabeth. She's new to town, and she's had a bad day. What can you do for her?"

Kiki's green eyes perused me, up and down, almost as though she was scanning my body. She frowned, cocked her head and tapped her lips with one long, tapered finger. "Bad day, indeed. I have just the thing." She pointed to the corner of the shop, where a small round table was flanked by tiny chairs. "Go sit. I'll bring it out."

"I don't get to choose?" I whispered to Maureen.

"Not all the time. Sometimes you do. But trust me, Kiki never gets it wrong." She dragged out one of the chairs and sat down as I did the same. I'd just reached for a paper napkin to finish the job of mopping up my pathetic tearful face when Maureen's phone went off.

She fished it out of her pocket, and I watched her eyes take in the text message. "Good news. Smith says the dog probably has a concussion, and one of his legs has a fracture in the distal radius . . . but otherwise, he looks good. No evidence of internal bleeding that he can find, no broken ribs. This was one lucky dog." She put away her phone and grinned at me. "Now you have a reason to celebrate."

"And I have just the thing." Kiki came back in, carrying a tray with a teapot and cups. Following behind her was a younger woman whose red hair was cut short and whose hands toted two plates.

Kiki eased the tray onto our table, pointing to the pastries as the other woman set down the plates in front of Maureen and me.

"For you, Maureen my love, an apple turnover with Dubliner cheddar. You need the protein. For my new friend, an almond horn of joy, because you, dear one, need to find your joy."

I stared first at the cookie and then up at the bakery proprietor. "I do? I mean—how do you know?"

"We don't ask that. We just accept it and enjoy." Maureen cut off a piece of her turnover with the fork. "Oh my God, Kiki, this is sinful."

"Rather apropos for an apple turnover, eh?" Kiki watched us, beaming. "Sydney, darling girl, this is Maureen, who I was telling you about. Reen, dear, my niece Sydney."

Maureen nodded but didn't say anything, since her mouth was full of apple turnover and cheese. I took a tentative bite of the cookie. It melted on my tongue, as sweet almond flavor exploded into my mouth. I couldn't hold back a little groan of ecstasy.

Sydney laughed. "I think that's the best compliment I've had in weeks. Just so happens that I made the almond horns."

Kiki beamed and hugged her niece. "Sydney's graciously agreed to take a break from her own restaurant in Savannah and come mind my shop while I'm away."

The younger woman rolled her eyes, but it was good-natured. "What Aunt Kiki means is that my little hole-in-the-wall place in Savannah went under last month, and she's letting me stay here and run the bakery while she and her boy toy go globe trotting."

I was thoroughly confused. "You're going on a trip?" Of course, I really wanted to ask about the boy toy, but since I'd just met this woman, it seemed wiser to stick to the travel plans.

"I am." She mock-glared at Sydney. "She's teasing, though. Troy isn't my boy toy. He's the love of my life. He just happens to be twenty years younger than me. Oh, and he's sort of a big deal in country music."

The pieces were beginning to fall into place. "Your

Troy—is he Troy Beck? *The* Troy Beck?"

Kiki smiled serenely. "He is. Isn't he a hottie?" She leaned toward me. "And if you think he looks good with his clothes on, you should see him without them." She fanned herself with one hand.

"Aunt Kiki!" I could tell Sydney was equal parts amused and mortified. "Honestly. The things you say."

Maureen was laughing so hard that she was nearly falling out of her chair. "The things she says are one of the main reasons I love her. I always tell Kiki that when I grow up, I want to be just like her."

"And I tell you, growing up is something I never plan to do." Kiki shrugged. "Sorry if we're making you uncomfortable, Elizabeth. But I spent the better part of my life trying to please other people, saying what I thought they wanted to hear and doing what I thought they wanted. I turned fifty and said to hell with that. Now I dress like I want. I say what I want to say, as long as it's not hurtful or harmful to others. And I do what I want, with whom I want."

"Bravo." Maureen clapped. "See, Elizabeth? Isn't she awesome?"

"She is." I felt so comfortable in this place, with all the smells and these amazing women surrounding me. For the first time in years, I was in a cocoon of familiarity, as though I'd stepped into the world where I was meant to be. All of my angst from this day was melting away with each bite of the almond cookie. I took a sip of my tea and thought I never wanted to leave this place.

Kiki narrowed her eyes as she watched me. I had the sense once again that she was reading me, examining my thoughts. "Elizabeth, do you have some free time this weekend?"

I thought about it and nodded. "Actually, I have nothing but free time." Weekends were not usually fun for me, since I had no desire to sit at the apartment and spend quality time with Donna. Trent took our clothes to the Laundromat on Saturdays and did yard and house work for Mrs. Price on Sundays; I suspected he too tried to avoid being stuck in the apartment with his mom. But this weekend, Trent was going to be at the Road Block as Mason trained him. My options were going to my office and pretending to work or wandering around town, since the library closed at noon on Saturdays and wasn't open at all on Sundays.

"I thought so. Perfect." She rubbed her hands together. "Come in Saturday about ten, and Sydney and I will teach you to make the horns of joy. That way, you can have them whenever you need them."

I wrinkled my forehead. "Can't I just come get them from you?"

Kiki shook her head. "I hope you will when you can, but in this life, we need to be able to make our own joy sometimes. You have to be prepared to take it with you. What will you do when you leave Burton? Never eat these delicious cookies again? I think not."

Sydney leaned her hip against the counter. "You might as well just plan to be here. She never gives up, and she's always right. Drives me batshit crazy, but it's true."

I shrugged. "Hey, I'm not going to complain about spending a day here, learning to make cookies. It beats any other plans I might have by a long shot."

"Good." Kiki grinned. "It's a date then." She tilted her head at me again, her lips pursing. "Tell me, how's that handsome husband of yours?"

My mouth opened, but I didn't know what to say. Since I'd come to Burton, I'd only shared my marital status with three people: Trent's mother, Cory Evans and Clark Morgan. Donna never left the house, and as far as I knew, she didn't have many if any friends in town. Clark might've told someone, but it seemed unlikely—and he'd been in New Mexico for a month now. I knew Cory hadn't told anyone. She was the very soul of discretion, and that hunch was borne out by the expression of shock on her daughter's face just now.

"Are you *married* to Trent?" Maureen's voice was incredulous. "Trent Wagoner? Oh my God. I mean, I'd heard you were living in the same apartment, but when I asked my mom about it, she told me there was some kind of mix-up with the rental company and you were letting his mom and him live there until they could find something else."

I gave an inward sigh. *God bless Cory*. She'd managed to keep my secret without telling a lie.

Sydney quirked an eyebrow at me. "I have no idea what's going on, but apparently this is shocking news. Who's Trent? And why is it so surprising you're married to him?"

Kiki patted her niece's back. "Patience. Let Elizabeth talk."

I glanced up at her. "How did you know?"

She smiled beatifically and lifted one shoulder. "I have a connection to Trent. I've known him since he was a little boy, when I used to sneak him treats whenever he stopped in. I keep track of those who're special to me, and he is." She paused and cast her eyes up as though listening to something I couldn't hear. "I saw him when he came back to town, and I knew his heart was broken. I lured him in here under the pretense of needing help with a bag of flour, and then I coerced him into eating chocolate chip cookies. They're his favorite." She added that last almost as an aside to me.

"And he told you about me?" I couldn't imagine my taciturn husband spilling his guts to the bakery lady.

"Not in so many words. He told me what he'd been up to, that he'd lived for a time in Florida, and that he'd left abruptly. I happened to notice that he was wearing a wedding ring, and when I asked, he told me it was complicated."

It made sense now. "And then I came to town and moved in with him . . ."

Kiki nodded. "Exactly. All the pieces clicked, except for the one where neither of you is telling anyone that you're married to each other. That one I still don't get."

I swan dived back into our old stand-by. "It's complicated. We got married fast, and then—well, stuff happened. And now we're not sure where we stand."

Kiki blinked once, slowly. "Do you love him?"

No one had asked me that up until now. Any prevaricating I might've done felt wrong here, in this place with these women. I dropped my gaze to the table. "I thought I did. I think I still do. But I'm not sure I can trust him. He left me in Florida without telling me why. He didn't give me any warning." Tears sprung to my eyes again.

"That happens sometimes." Kiki laid an arm around my shoulder. "But sometimes we have to lose something—or someone—temporarily to realize how much we need him."

"Maybe." My head was spinning. Between the aftermath of hitting that poor dog and the calming effects of the tea and cookies, I felt like I could lay down and sleep for a week.

"I'm beginning to feel like I stepped into the middle of a counseling session here." Maureen's teasing broke the silence. "And as fascinating as I find it, Elizabeth and I need to get back to the clinic. Smith's going to think I abandoned him, leaving him with an emergency on his hands."

Kiki took hold of my hand as I stood up to leave. "I'll see you here on Saturday. Wear comfortable shoes." She leaned forward and kissed my cheek. "And give your husband this kiss from me."

"I will," I promised, and suddenly, I couldn't wait to get home to do just that.

CHAPTER EIGHT

Trent

WHEN I WAS GROWING UP, I never thought about having a career. In my world, men had jobs—jobs they tolerated for ten or twelve hours a day, five days a week, so they could earn the right to sit at the bar on Friday nights and bitch about their bosses or their co-workers. The only exception was my Uncle Nolan, whose passion about his Christmas tree farm was a different animal altogether. But I saw Nolan rarely in my childhood; he was only around if my mother needed some kind of help, or if he and the family were passing through town on their way to one of their infrequent Florida vacations.

When I'd begun working as a teenager, I was willing to take any job that would pay me the most for doing the least. In Burton, that meant manual labor, and it didn't end after I graduated high school. Once I'd turned eighteen, I began spending my summers out at Benningers' farm, working the fields. Grady Benninger had one of the largest operations in the area, and every year he hired on a few guys as hands. At first, it had felt grown-up and kind of exciting; he had a bunk house, just like I'd seen in old movies, where the hired guys lived. Room and board were part of our salary, and for a kid who wasn't always sure where his next meal was coming from—or when—three squares a day, a comfortable bed and three months of stability were pure heaven.

I'd managed to hold onto the gig for a long time. During the off-months, I'd move back to town and find something temporary to do. Working at the hardware store had been my favorite winter job, and I thought I was good at it. That, and then working for Nolan, had been the high point of my working life so far.

But after my first few weeks at the Road Block, I realized I had a new favorite. I thought I'd enjoy working there, for Mason, but I hadn't known I'd flat out love it.

Part of it was the atmosphere. Mason was a good boss, who treated all of us like gold. There was a spirit of cooperation among Darcy, Rocky and me. I'd worried they might be resentful of me, a know-nothing who was coming in to help run the place. But there'd been none of that. Rocky told me privately that knowing Mason was hiring help took a big load off his shoulders.

"I love the guy, you know? So if he asks me to do something, I do it. I told him, though, I like my job now. I don't want to be here any more than my regular hours. But I'd feel bad if I knew he'd been working extra and needed some help. Now I don't have to feel guilty."

Later that same day, Darcy had said something similar.

"Hey, you know, I never signed up to help run this joint. All I want to do is serve up drinks and bar food. I don't want to mess with schedules and all that other shit. You being here means I can do what I like best."

The wait staff were pretty cool, too. They were patient when I asked a million questions about how and why they did things. They didn't freak out when I got in the way, which I did, even though I tried not to. And they told me what was especially good to eat, since Mason had made it clear I was welcome to all the food I liked.

After I'd been training for a week, Mason had called me into his office. I didn't have time to get nervous about why, since he started speaking as soon as I closed the door.

"So I think things are going well. You catch on quick, you're fitting in great with everyone else, and you take it seriously. If you're good, I'm ready to make this permanent."

I was more than willing, but I only nodded. "I'm good. I like what you've got here, and I think I can handle what you need me to do."

"Excellent." Mason leaned back in his chair and laced his hands together behind his head. "And Elizabeth's cool with you working here? The hours and everything?"

"Yeah." I thought about the past week. Elizabeth had been preoccupied the day I'd gotten home from the first day at the Road Block. I'd been excited to come back to the apartment and tell her all about it, but she'd been in her room, in bed. When I'd knocked on the door, she'd stuck her head out.

"I'm sorry." Her blonde hair was tousled and her eyes were swollen. "I had a shitty day. Well, some of it was. Most of it, although . . . well. I'm sorry I didn't make dinner. Your mother is sulking in her room again, because I wouldn't go out and get her a bottle of scotch. If you don't mind, I'm going to sleep now."

My mood had immediately deflated. After our time together the night before, especially the kiss, I'd been hoping things between us would be better, but she was shutting me out—both literally and figuratively.

"Hey, what happened today?" I'd risked reaching out to brush a strand of hair out of her face. "Do you want to talk about it?" I was clueless when it came to women. I knew that. But from our time together in the Cove, I'd learned that Elizabeth always felt better after she'd dumped on me about a bad day—and I didn't mind it when it was my wife doing the dumping.

She hadn't shied away from my touch—*that was good*—but she'd shaken her head. "Thanks, but right now, I just want to hibernate and forget this day happened. Work was horrible, your mother—ack." Elizabeth had rolled her eyes. "And I hit a dog." Her eyes welled up. "He's going to be okay, but Maureen and Smith can't find the owner, and I was so freaked out." She'd drawn in a ragged breath. "Like I said, bad day. Tomorrow'll be better, right?"

"Gotta be." Since she hadn't dinged me for touching her hair, I got cocky and cupped her face with my hand. "Sorry about my mom. It's not you. She's mad, and she's sick. You're just a handy target."

She'd closed her eyes and leaned into my palm. "I know. Still not my idea of a good way to be welcomed home. Anyway." She stood back a little, away from me, and then her lips curved just a little. "I'm going to bed, but first, I need to deliver this." She'd risen onto her toes and kissed my cheek. "That's from Kiki."

I wasn't sure if the warmth spreading over my face was from Elizabeth's kiss or her words. "You met Kiki?" There were a few people in town who stood out in my memories of growing up. They were always the ones who reached out to me, who paid me a kindness or stood up for me against others. I hadn't spent a lot of time with Kiki; I knew she owned the bakery, and sometimes, if I was particularly hungry or frightened, I'd go in and just breathe the air. Kiki never made a big deal about me being there, but I always left with something to eat and one of her oddly accurate encouraging words.

"I did. Long story, and I'm too tired to tell it now." She began to back into her room but then paused again. "She said you were wearing your wedding ring."

My thumb immediately went to rub the third finger on my left hand, the one that still felt bare even though I'd only worn the gold band for a few months. I'd kept it on even after I'd left, only tucking it into my pocket for safety's sake when I was working at Grainger's. I was sure Elizabeth hadn't noticed it had been on my finger the night I'd picked her up at the Road Block. But when I'd seen her ringless finger, I'd left mine off, too.

Elizabeth hadn't really asked a question, and I hadn't wanted to dive into that kind of talk when she was clearly dealing with other crap. So I only nodded and stepped back. "I'm going to get something to eat. Let me know if you need anything."

She'd apologized a few days later for not making a bigger deal over the first day at my new job, but I'd shrugged it off. And since then, we hadn't seen much of each other, since I'd been working hard, and she'd been busy, too. I had a vaguely uneasy feeling that something was going on, since she'd asked me if Mrs. Price would be watching out for my mother on Saturday while I was at the bar. She'd only say that she was going to be out most of the day, which did nothing to help ease the knot in my stomach or silence the voice in my head. The one that suggested maybe my wife had already found someone better than me.

Now, as Mason waited for me to elaborate, I just shrugged. "She doesn't really care as long as she doesn't get stuck watching my mother."

"Hmmm." Mason's brows knit together. "You should bring her in here. Elizabeth, not your mom."

I gave a flicker of a smile. "I figured that's who you meant."

"Like we talked about. I can see if Rilla could get a sitter for the kiddos. Sometimes Millie—" He broke off, and I understood why. Millie was Jenna's mother. Didn't seem likely that she'd want to babysit so that Rilla could come double date with the man responsible for her daughter's attempted suicide. "Well, we could work it out. Maybe Meghan and Sam could watch them."

I shook my head. "Can't do it right now. I need to be home at night to keep an eye on my mom. She's been a handful lately."

Mason sighed. "Forgot about her. That can't be easy."

"Right now, it's more of a pain in the ass than anything

161

else. The first few weeks, when she was detoxing physically?" I shuddered. "That was nasty. And a little scary. Now she's just mean. And demanding. It's like having a two-year old."

Mason whistled. "I said it before, man—what you're doing here is above and beyond. How much longer until she qualifies for the rehab deal?"

"About four weeks." I was mentally marking off the days. "And then things should get a little easier for me." Maybe. It would be a huge relief to not be constantly worried about my mother, where she was and what she was saying. But my initial plan to move out of Burton and find a place closer to the facility wasn't very appealing anymore. I liked this job, and I didn't want to walk away from the commitment I'd made to Mason. And even though everything was iffy and uncertain with Elizabeth, I found I didn't want to walk away again. Not without maybe giving the idea of us another try.

I was thinking about that possibility as I drove home that afternoon. If I could just get Elizabeth to hang in here with me for the next four weeks, then maybe I could work on proving to her—and to myself—that I was worthy of her. It was an unfamiliar thought; I'd never set out to win a girl's heart. Before Elizabeth, I hadn't cared, and back in the Cove, she'd been mine from the minute our lips had touched. It hadn't been a matter of convincing her we were meant to be. But then I'd been an idiot and thrown all that away, which meant I had to work double time to get her back for good.

I knew I could do it. Or I hoped I could. I was feeling more optimistic these days than I'd been in a very long time.

But all that feeling evaporated when I turned the corner to the apartment and saw at the curb an unfamiliar dark blue car with the crest of the county justice system on its side.

Shit. What had she done now? What had someone heard? To my knowledge, my mother hadn't left the apartment unsupervised since the night I'd bailed her out of jail. I'd taken her with me to the Laundromat and the grocery store now and again, but even there, she'd been in my sight the entire time.

I trusted Mrs. Price—I'd gone to great lengths to impress on the elderly lady how important it was to watch my front door. But still . . . people had needs, and it was possible that my mother had managed to sneak out while our neighbor was taking a bathroom break.

Pulling my truck behind the car, I climbed out slowly, dreading what was coming next. I couldn't see through the tinted windows, so I was surprised when the driver's side door opened and Judge Roony stepped out.

"Afternoon, son." He held out a hand, and automatically I reached to shake it. "Glad I timed this right. I wanted to catch you before you went inside the house."

I nodded. "Everything okay, sir? I've been doing exactly what you said. As far as I know, my mother's kept out of trouble. I can't watch her twenty-four/seven and still support us, but I've got a lady watching her—"

"Whoa there, Trent." The judge held up one hand. "I'm not here to rap your knuckles." He pointed to the cement stoop, the same one where I'd sat with Elizabeth the afternoon after she'd come to Burton. "Can we talk a minute?"

"Of course." I followed him to the step and sat down after he settled himself on the concrete. Glancing up at the house, I wondered if my mother or Elizabeth knew we were there.

"First of all, son, I want to say I'm impressed. When Jock Reiner and I made you that proposition for keeping your mother out of jail, I never thought you'd be able to make it work. Not because of you," he hastened to add. "But because I know people like your mom. They're cunning. They work the system. They manipulate, and when they want something, nothing and no one stands in their way. I knew you had, uh, limited resources, having to make this happen in a town where you don't have much support, and I figured we'd be seeing your mother back in my court in a few weeks."

He turned to face me more fully. "But you proved me wrong. I've lived in Burton my whole life, and I have a lot of people who keep their eyes on things for me. Everything I've been hearing about you is exemplary. You've done a bang-up job."

"Thank you, sir." I still felt a little unsettled. People like Judge Roony didn't just stop by to give out a pat on the back and an attaboy. The other shoe was probably about to drop.

"Now I know you're a busy man, so I'll get to my reason for being here. When Jock and I made you that offer, we may have padded the time required just a little. We weren't trying to mislead you, but I knew before I could give you that referral, I had to know if you were serious about making the commitment. But you didn't even blink. And since you've stuck to the letter of the deal, I'm here to give you this." He reached into his suit jacket and pulled out a long white envelope, handing it to me.

I took the envelope and turned it over in my hands.

"What's this?"

He smiled. "It's confirmation of your mother's reservation and paid-in-full status at the rehab facility in Devlin. They expect you—well, her—there tomorrow."

My head felt fuzzy, and nothing quite made sense. "I don't understand, sir. I thought . . . I didn't expect this for another month or more."

"I understand. Look at this as parole for good behavior." He winked at me. "Yours, not hers." With a groan, Judge Roony stood up and gripped my shoulder. "You be okay to get her there? Think your truck can make the trip?"

"Um, yes, sir. She doesn't look like much, but I keep her tuned up."

"Good man. Well, best of luck." He fished into his pocket and produced a business card. "This is my personal phone number. If you need anything, you give me a call, you hear? If you have any questions or . . ." He lifted his gaze to the apartment. "If she won't go quietly, you know. We can make this happen even if she gives you a hard time. Don't be afraid to ask for help."

"Yes, sir."

He put his hand on the car door handle and paused. "Like I said, I hear a lot of things. One of the things I hear is that you've got a woman living here with you. The town's new lady lawyer."

Discomfort prickled my backbone. "Yes, sir. Well, sir—"

"I looked her up. So she's your wife, huh? And she's been living here with you and Donna?"

"She has, sir. It hasn't been easy on her."

"And y'all just got married on New Year's Eve. Hell of a

honeymoon, to move into a small apartment with your new mother-in-law." *Especially when she's a belligerent dry drunk.* The judge didn't say the words, but I knew he was thinking them. "She must be quite a gal. I'll look forward to seeing her in my court one of these days."

"I'll pass that on, sir."

He grinned. "You do that. Travel safe, Trent. Keep in touch."

"I will, sir. And Judge Roony—"

He turned just as he was about to get into his car.

"Thank you, sir. For everything. And please tell Mr. Reiner thanks, too."

He gave me another wink and a nod before he pulled away. I sat where I was for a few minutes, just absorbing everything. I felt like I'd just gotten my get-out-of-jail-free card. It was a lot to take in, considering I'd been primed and ready for another four weeks of warden duty.

An unfamiliar sense of excitement and anticipation bubbled up inside me. Once my mother was safely at the rehab place, I could start working on convincing Elizabeth to stay married to me. I could take her on a date to the Road Block, like Mason had suggested.

That reminded me that I'd have to call up my boss and ask him for the day off tomorrow, so I could drive my mother to Devlin. I didn't think he'd give me any problem with it, especially since I'd have a lot more time to give him once I didn't have to be on Ma duty at nights. I could spell him during early evenings if he wanted dinner with his family.

But first things first. I had to go inside and tell the women the good news. Well . . . I was pretty sure at least *one* of them would think it was good; as to the other, right now I didn't really give a damn what she thought.

The drive to Devlin was long and monotonous, cutting across the state of Georgia and maneuvering around Atlanta to the small town. We'd left Burton just before dawn, since I was determined to make it there and back in one day; the trip was a solid four hours, each way.

As I'd expected, my mother had thrown an unholy fit when I had announced we were leaving for rehab the next day. It went on for about fifteen minutes, but then she abruptly stopped yelling, turned around and went into her bedroom. I waited for the slam of the door, but it never came.

Elizabeth had looked at me in surprise. "Well . . . that was interesting. How do you think you're going to get her into the truck come tomorrow morning?"

I'd shrugged. "Not worried about it. She's going if I have to hog-tie her, gag her and toss her into the cab. It's happening. She can either get on board or get handled."

Elizabeth had grinned. "You know, I think I kind of like take-charge Trent."

The look in her eyes had warmed me. No, dammit, it had made me downright hot. I'd wanted to scoop her into my arms and make her shriek as I hauled her into the bedroom and reminded her of why we'd fallen in love in the first place.

But first things first. Priority one was getting my mom

where she needed to be. She hadn't come out of her bedroom the rest of the night, but right before I'd gone to sleep at ten o'clock, I'd knocked on her door and called to her.

"Ma, we're leaving at six tomorrow morning. If you want to take anything with you, better have it packed and ready to move by then, because I'm not messing around."

I hadn't held out much hope that she'd even be awake, let alone packed, by six the next morning, but when I knocked on her door and opened it, she was dressed and sitting on the edge of the bed, a small plastic grocery bag at her feet stuffed to bursting. She'd stood up and followed me out, but she didn't speak at all. In fact, she didn't do much more than grunt the entire way there.

When we were about fifteen minutes away from the facility, I turned down the radio and cleared my throat. "Ma, I know you probably hate me for this. Hell, maybe you've hated me my whole life. I don't know. Felt like it sometimes. But believe it or not, I'm doing this for you. I want you to have a chance at life, and I think this may be your last shot. I'm doing everything I can to make it happen for you, but I can't do more than get you here. I hope . . . once you get inside, I hope you do the work to get healthy. Not for me, not for anyone but you."

She didn't answer me, but I thought I saw her eyes flicker a little.

The rehab center was just outside the town of Devlin. I'd read the instructions the night before; I was to pull into the check-in area, let my mother out, and someone would be there to greet us and take her inside. And then I had to leave. They didn't want family members hanging around, and honestly, I was okay with that.

The building was a typical one-story institutional-looking place, about what I'd expected. The grounds were pretty, though, with trees and well-trimmed hedges. I slowed the truck as we pulled under the awning. Two people, a man and a woman, both in scrubs, emerged from the glass doors as I put on the parking brake and shifted into neutral. Before I could get out, the man had opened the passenger door and offered my mother his hand.

"Ms. Wagoner? Welcome to Devlin Horizons. Let me help you down from there." He reached up to guide her down as the woman took the grocery bag Ma'd had on her lap the whole time.

I came around the side of the truck, watching them. The man ushered my mother toward the doors, and his partner turned toward me.

"We're all good here now. Thank you for following our instructions. You'll receive weekly updates via the email address you provided, and we'll inform you through those updates when you're allowed to call the patient. Do you have any questions before you leave?"

I shook my head. "No, thanks." I watched my mother approaching the glass doors, which opened automatically. An unexpected lump rose in my throat.

"Trent." She paused before she stepped inside, speaking for the first time that day. She didn't turn to look at me, but her voice carried anyway. "I never hated you."

She kept walking over the threshold and disappeared into the building. The woman in scrubs patted my arm. "We'll be in touch. Have a safe trip home."

169

The drive back to Burton was just as silent as the one over had been, but with each mile I drove, I felt a little lighter. A little more free.

I stopped for gas and a bottle of water an hour away from home, taking the opportunity to text Elizabeth to let her know when I'd be back at the apartment. She responded with a simple, "See you then" and a smiley face, which I figured was about as good as I could expect.

But that was okay, because the whole time I drove, I was making plans. And those plans included making my wife remember why she'd been attracted to me in the first place, why she'd loved me. I wanted to be a better man for her, for both of us. And with that in mind, I made a couple of telephone calls, too, as I covered the last miles into town.

Her car was parked in front of the apartment when I got home. I rolled up behind the BMW and hit the parking brake before jumping out of the truck and taking the steps two at a time. Suddenly, I couldn't wait to get inside.

When I opened the door, a familiar and delicious smell greeted me. I might've moaned a little, just because I couldn't help it. Something wonderful was baking in my kitchen.

"Hey!" Elizabeth leaned out of the kitchen, hands behind her back, her face alight with a welcoming smile. "You're home."

"Yeah, I am." For the first time in months, that felt true. "What're you doing in there? Something smells like heaven."

"Well, if heaven for you is a chocolate chip cookie, you're

in luck." She brought her hands to the front, and damned if she wasn't holding a plate of chocolate chip cookies.

A storm of emotions battled inside me. All at once, I was a kid again, walking home from school while I listened to the other kids bragging about the cookies their moms baked for them to eat after school. I'd pretend I knew what it was like, and in my head, I wove an elaborate fantasy where my mother was waiting at the kitchen table with cookies and milk, wanting to hear about my day. Since my reality was my mom hung over in bed, grousing at me to be quieter so her head didn't explode, the make-believe world was a much better place to live.

These cookies, though—not only did they look and smell amazing, they sparked another, better memory for me. In my mind, I saw Kiki leaning over the counter to hand me a white paper bag as she whispered conspiratorially, "These are very special cookies made only for you. I'm usually in favor of sharing cookies, but in this case, don't. Each of them is for you."

"They're not going to bite you." Elizabeth sounded equal parts amused and nervous as she lifted the plate a little higher. "Try one. Turns out I'm pretty good at this baking deal."

I obeyed, choosing a cookie in the very center of the plate. The first bite melted in my mouth, an enticing mixture of butter, vanilla, chocolate chips and something else I couldn't describe. I closed my eyes and just enjoyed.

"Do you like them? Are they good?" She sounded anxious.

"Baby, these are the most incredible thing I've ever put into my mouth." I smirked and raised one eyebrow. "Well, maybe second best. But a real close second."

Her cheeks went pink, and she shook her head, smiling. "You're incorrigible."

"And that's why you love me." The words came out of my mouth before I could stop and think. Elizabeth met my eyes and held them, the tip of her tongue darting out to trace her lips, but she didn't speak.

"Elizabeth." I moved closer, nudging her chin up with two of my fingers. Her throat bobbed as she swallowed, and her chest rose and fell a little faster than normal. I wondered if I'd find her heart pounding if I covered her breast with my hand.

"Hmmm?" She hummed a little, questioning.

"Would you go out on a date with me?"

Surprise flashed across her face. "A date? Where would we go?"

I shrugged. "That's for me to know, and you to guess. Do you trust me?"

She didn't answer right away, but finally, she nodded. "Yes. I think I do."

"Cool." I framed her face with both of my hands. "Then let's go."

"Now?" She glanced around us, as though something might keep us from leaving. "Right now?"

"Right this very minute. C'mon. You look amazing, and don't worry, I'm not taking you anywhere fancy. You know I don't do fancy."

Elizabeth laughed. "Fine by me. Just let me change my shirt, okay? I got flour and stuff on it from baking."

I ran my hands down her sides, just skimming her

tempting curves. "I don't know. This shirt smells pretty damn tempting." I burrowed my nose in the crook of her neck, just above the scoop of her shirt, and took a big sniff. "Mmmmm, yeah. Elizabeth and cookie dough. If you could bottle this scent, men would go wild for it."

She was breathless as she playfully shoved me away. "Let me go, you goof. I'll change and be right out." She darted away from me, giving me a tantalizing view of her sweet little ass as she shimmied down the hall to her bedroom. I thought about her peeling away the cotton shirt from her silky skin and had to adjust the crotch of my jeans. She was going to kill me, this woman.

Good as her word, Elizabeth was back out in a minute, slinging the strap of her handbag over her shoulder. "Okay, I'm ready. I look like a hot mess, though, so you better not take me anywhere people will see me."

I snagged her hand and laced our fingers together. "The only one who's going to see you tonight is me, baby." *And if I got really lucky, I might get to see a lot of her. As in naked her.*

As if she could hear my thoughts, she smiled big and lifted her eyebrows. "All righty then. Sounds like a plan."

I helped her into the truck, reminding her not to lean on the loose passenger side door. Once we were on the road, I made one stop, running into Franco's to pick up sandwiches, and then pointed us out of town, cruising into the country.

"Watch your speed. It was right around here that I hit that dog." She stuck out her lip, sighing.

"I'll keep my eyes open. Any word on finding his owner? And is he okay?"

She shook her head. "Nothing on an owner. Smith says

he doesn't have a chip they can scan. But he's doing really well. Apparently he's up and walking around. They said he'll make a full recovery."

"Excellent." I wondered if Elizabeth would want to bring the pup home, provided his owners never appeared. I doubted pets were allowed at the apartment, but if things went my way, we'd be finding a better place to live pretty soon, anyway. Having a dog might be nice.

"I told Maureen I'd help find him a home, if no one claims him. I'd take him myself, but I'm horribly allergic."

There was my answer. "Ah, I didn't know that."

She sighed. "I guess that's one of the many things we never got around to talking about before. But yes, I'm allergic to dogs and cats. I love them, but I sneeze and swell up. I had to go get my car vacuumed out last week. I was having an attack every time I drove, after having the dog in it even for that short time."

The sun was beginning to sink lower in the sky as we drove. We had a few hours until dark, and I wanted to take full advantage of them. I turned the truck onto a small hidden dirt road, slowing as we bumped along. It hadn't rained much lately, which was good; if it had, this road could be a muddy mess.

"Where are we going?" Elizabeth craned her neck to look around us as the road wound into the woods. "Please tell me you're not taking me into the forest to kill me and dump my body."

I laughed. "Honey, there's a lot of things I want to do to your body, but dumping it in the woods isn't one of them." I caught her hand in mine and lifted it to kiss the knuckles.

She shivered, and gladness rose up in me.

Around the bend, the small lake came into view. I parked the truck as close to the water as I could before I switched off the ignition.

"It's beautiful out here." Elizabeth leaned forward to stare through the windshield. "Is this someone's property?"

"Yeah. This is actually right at the border of two farms, the Reynolds' and the Nelsons'. I went to school with Ali Reynolds and Alex Nelson, so we used to hang out here sometimes." I pointed to our left. "The river's that way. That's where everyone used to go to park." I waggled my eyebrows at her.

"And you didn't take me there?" She grinned at me, teasing.

I pretended to be offended. "I brought you here on a date, Miss Elizabeth. I have nothing but honorable intentions. No ulterior motives." I put on what I hoped was an earnest expression.

"Damn." Elizabeth feigned disappointment. "I was hoping for ulterior motives."

I leaned closer to her, sliding one arm behind her back. "Baby, I can give you what you want. I can *always* satisfy your . . ." I let my voice trail off. "Your needs."

Her cheeks went pink and when she spoke again, her voice was husky. "Right now, I think my biggest need is . . ." She batted her eyelashes. "That delicious smelling chicken parm sandwich sitting between us."

Laughing, I eased back and reached for the sandwiches. "Your wish is my command. One chicken parm for you, one hot roast beef for me."

We unwrapped the food and demolished it, talking and laughing as we tried to avoid dripping sauces on our clothes.

"Hey, I think you got some gravy on your shirt." She trailed a finger down the middle of my chest. "That might leave a stain. Maybe you should just take it off."

"Huh." I pulled the material away from my skin. "As the person who does the laundry, I can say I'm motivated to avoid stains any way I can." I began unbuttoning it.

"Ah, ah, ah." Elizabeth brushed my hand away. "I can do it better."

"You always could, baby." I sucked in a breath as her fingers teased the skin on my stomach. "Hey, I've got a blanket behind the seat. I know it's kind of chilly, but want to sit outside for a little bit?"

She eased the shirt over my arms. "I think I can do that. But since your shirt is off, I might have to keep you warm."

I fished around behind us until I closed my fingers around the blanket. "Think you're up to it?"

She smiled and raised one eyebrow. "Pretty sure I am."

It was a clear night, and there on the lake, it felt as though the stars were as close as the tree tops. I spread out the blanket a few feet from the water's edge, and Elizabeth sat down, kicking off her shoes and hugging her knees to her chest. I tried to keep from shivering as the air chilled my bare skin.

"Is it okay that we're here?" She glanced over at me, watching me tug off my boots before I joined her on the blanket.

"Yup. I made a call just to make sure."

"When did you do that?" She scooted closer to me, her

body warming my side.

"On my way home from Devlin. I called Mason to let him know how everything went, and I asked him to check with Sam, see if we could come out here tonight for a picnic."

"Hmmm." She snuggled closer, and I wrapped my arm around her. "Planning ahead, were you? Was I so much of a sure thing?"

"No, baby." I touched my lips to her temple. "You're never a sure thing. I was just optimistic."

We were quiet for a minute, enjoying the quiet. "So how did it go? Today, I mean. Taking your mother up there." She hesitated, as though trying to find the right words. "I didn't ask before in case you didn't want to talk about it."

"Not much to say, really." I stared out at the dark surface of the lake, rippled by the soft breeze. "She was ready to go this morning, and she didn't talk the whole way there. They took her inside as soon as I pulled up, and that was about it." I wasn't ready to share my mother's parting words yet. "It was fine. Felt a little weird when I left, like I was just abandoning her there, you know? Even though I know it's for the best."

Elizabeth laid her head against my shoulder. "I'm sorry you had to do that."

I shifted, pulling her to sit between my legs. "I am, too. Not sorry I did it, but sorry I had to. But I don't want to talk about my mother anymore tonight. I think she's messed with our lives enough, don't you?"

She laughed softly. "Oh, I don't know. The apartment's going to be pretty quiet with her gone. I don't know what

I'll do when I come home from the office and she's not there to remind me that I'm the fucking bitch ruining her life because I won't let her go out and get plastered."

"There is that." I held her a little closer, chafing her arms. "But I want you to know, Elizabeth, how much I appreciate you letting her stay there. Us, I mean. I know it wasn't a picnic, and you were really great about it. And I also want you to know, I'm done now. Whatever my mother decides to do next, it's up to her. I've given all I can."

"I think that's reasonable." She arched her neck to kiss my jaw. "You deserve a future. And now with your new job . . . you really like it there, don't you? At the Road Block, I mean."

"Yeah." I twisted a lock of her hair around my finger. "I do. I know it sounds crazy, but it feels good to work with people who treat me like I have a brain, you know? And I think it's really helping out Mason, too." I kissed the column of her throat, where it was exposed. "I was thinking . . . once I get a few months under my belt, maybe we could think about finding a better place to live. We could look at houses outside town, like we said before." My heart began to beat a little faster. "If you wanted to, I mean."

Elizabeth leaned her head back against my arm so that she could look into my eyes. I couldn't read her face, and I wondered if I'd pushed too hard.

"I want that, too." She spoke so low that it was nearly a whisper. "I'm just not sure . . . I need us to take it slow, okay? We jumped into everything so fast last time, and I thought we both wanted the same things. And then you left me." The pain in her voice was raw, and her eyelids drooped to half-mast, as though she didn't want me to see too much. "I can't do that again, Trent. I can't open myself up to you and trust in us unless I know you're in this for the long haul. You're my one. I need to be your always."

I traced her cheekbone. "You are. You never stopped being my always. I just . . . got lost for a little while."

"How do you know you won't get lost again?" She caught the corner of her lip between her teeth.

"Because I found out you're my beacon. You're the light who guides me home, baby."

She sighed then, relaxing against me. "I don't feel like a very good beacon. I'm so mixed up half the time." Her hands came up to grip each other behind my neck, holding on tight. "I think I made a mistake buying the practice. I realized over the last few months how much I really don't like being a lawyer."

"Huh." I digested that for a few minutes. "So if you don't want to be a lawyer, what *do* you want to do?"

She lifted one shoulder. "I have no fucking idea. Which, ironically, is why I ended up getting into law anyway. Process of elimination."

"Well, what do you enjoy doing? What makes you happy?"

Her mouth twisted into a smirk. "The library makes me happy. The bakery does, too. Making cookies and pastries with Kiki and Sydney."

A puzzle piece fell into place. "The cookies you made me today—did Kiki give you that recipe?"

"Yep. Actually, she taught me how to make them. Why?"

I shook my head. "They brought back good memories."

"I'm glad about that. I was hoping they would." She wriggled a little, her ass teasing against a part of my body that liked it a little too much. My dick hardened, pushing against the zipper of my jeans. Elizabeth froze for a minute, and then she arched her back, gazing at me upside down. Her gorgeous tits were thrust out in that position, and it took all the control I had not to roll her onto her back and take her, right there.

"I've missed this." She spoke quietly. "When you left, my house was so quiet. So lonely. I missed talking to you, eating with you, just hanging out . . . but I'd be lying if I said I didn't miss you touching me, too. I'd lie in my bed every night and just ache."

I pulled her a little tighter and angled my mouth to seal against hers. Our kiss was tentative and testing, but she opened to me and let me sweep my tongue over hers. I broke the connection just long to whisper in her ear.

"I ached, too. There wasn't a minute after I left that I didn't wish I hadn't." I settled her back against my chest, locking my hands around her waist mostly to make sure they didn't go somewhere they shouldn't. "I know we're taking it slow, and I think you're right. But even just being able to touch you like this feels like I'm in heaven." We were both quiet.

The wind picked up a little, and a chill shook me.

"It's getting colder." Elizabeth pushed to sit up. "Maybe we should head back home. You've got to be exhausted, anyway, after driving eight hours today."

"You're not wrong. But hey, at least tonight I can sleep in a real bed. I won't be sorry to be off that couch."

She tilted her head at me in questioning, and I rushed to clarify. "I mean, I can sleep in the other bed now, since my mom's not here." I stretched, standing up. "Don't worry. I'm not trying to push you into anything, babe. I heard what you said about moving slow. Right now, I'll be happy if you let me kiss you good-night."

"Oh, I think that can be arranged. I might even be persuaded into some heavy petting." She helped me fold the blanket and patted my ass as we went back to the truck.

"In that case, I might break some speed limits on the way home." I shrugged into my shirt and boosted Elizabeth into the cab before I climbed into the driver's seat. She slid over the bench to lay her head on my shoulder as we drove home through the dark. We held hands, and I sang along to a slow love song playing on the radio. Elizabeth sighed, her breath tickling the bottom of my jaw. I felt content. Peaceful. Maybe we hadn't solved all of our problems yet, but I thought we'd made a good start.

And the prospect of another good-night kiss and maybe a little more, combined with the feel of Elizabeth's body pressed against my side, meant I was primed for action by the time we got back to the apartment.

"Hey, who's car is that out front?" I leaned forward, squinting. "Are those Virginia plates?"

"Oh, shit." Elizabeth peered through the windshield and then scrambled to the other side of the truck. "Shit, shit, shit. They wouldn't—of course they would." She closed her eyes, pressing her lips tight together, then took a deep breath and looked over at me. "Listen, just follow my lead, okay? Go with it. And try not to freak out."

181

"Why would I . . ." I stopped speaking when the doors of the car in front of us opened. From the driver's side, a man in a uniform stepped out, just as a woman whose hair was the same color as Elizabeth's emerged from the passenger side. I got out of the truck in time to hear my wife's voice carry through the clear night air.

"Well, this is a surprise." She glanced back at me, her blue eyes pleading. "Trent, this is my mom and dad. Mother and Dad, this is Trent. My husband."

CHAPTER NINE

Elizabeth

ONCE, WHEN I WAS A little girl, I'd asked my father what his job was. I knew he was in the Army, and I knew he went away a lot. But I hadn't figured out exactly why or what he did when he was at work.

He'd thought about it for a minute, probably trying to explain the duties of a regimental commander to a six year-old. Finally, he'd said, "I take care of my men. I make sure they're doing their jobs, and that they're ready if we're called into action."

I'd considered that briefly. "But what do you have to do? Missy's dad fixes cars. What do you *do*? What's the most important part?"

Dad had grinned. "I have to make sure I'm never surprised. No matter what my men tell me, I never let them see me react. So that's what I do. I work hard so that nothing surprises me."

As I grew up, he proved to be a master at that job. I'd never said or done anything that had shocked my parents, or at least my father. And tonight didn't prove to be any different.

I'd no sooner introduced Trent to my parents that my dad was reaching out for a handshake, as though he'd known all along that I was married. "Trent. Good to meet you. Elizabeth, give your mother a hug. She's ridden a long way just to see you."

My mom was hanging back, watching all of us, and I moved obediently to step into her embrace. I was a little taken aback when she held me extra tight and a bit longer than usual. She pulled back and searched my face, cupping my chin in one hand. "Look at you. You look wonderful! Doesn't she look wonderful, Mitch?"

Dad was watching both of us. He nodded and opened his arms. "Of course she does. Elizabeth always looks beautiful." He enfolded me in a hug, and out of habit I breathed deep, taking in his scent. It was a mixture of the cologne he'd worn for as long as I could remember, the starch of his uniform and something else I could only ever describe as eau de Army.

When I'd been very little, my mother had given me one of my dad's T-shirts to sleep with whenever he was away. I'd never dealt well with separation; apparently, I'd missed the training that most other Army brats seemed to get in utero, the lessons that taught them to take in stride frequent deployments and months away from one parent or another. As I got older, I'd gotten in the practice of breathing in his scent every time he hugged me, just to remind me when he inevitably went away again.

"Uh, it's very nice to meet both of you." Trent spoke in his respectful voice, and I was grateful. "Why don't we go inside? Elizabeth and I were just sitting out at the lake, and I think she's pretty chilled through."

Even if I suspected he might be putting on a little bit of a show for my parents, I appreciated how solicitous he was. And I was even more thankful for the hand he slipped into mine as we led my parents into the apartment.

"I know we should've called first." My mother glanced at me. "Daddy had a meeting at Ft. Benning, and we decided to drive down from Virginia so that we could stop in Hilton Head for a few days on the way back. But then we were so close to you, and it just seemed a shame not to stop to say hello." She paused before adding, "Since we haven't seen you in nearly two years."

Ouch. I pasted on a bright smile. "Well, it's been a busy time, hasn't it? You've both been traveling, spending holidays with the boys."

"And you've been getting married, apparently." My father drilled me with the same look that used to bring me to tears. "Without telling your parents, let alone inviting them to participate in the wedding of their only daughter."

And the hits just keep on coming. "It was a very quiet wedding. Just the two of us."

"Uh huh." My mother's eyes swept over the tiny, dingy living room. "Then you moved to Georgia. We did appreciate you sending us your forwarding address when you left Florida."

There wasn't a good answer to any of these statements,

so I fell back into my old familiar stand-by: ignoring whatever I couldn't handle.

"Sit down." I spread my hand over the dilapidated sofa. "Do you want some coffee? Or something else? Trent and I had sandwiches down at the lake, but I can whip up something fast if you're hungry."

"Coffee would be fine, thanks." My father sat down, and unfortunately, he chose the end of the couch Trent and I knew to avoid, since the springs there were iffy and the frame weak. Consequently, he ended up sitting a lot deeper than he'd expected. I bit back a snort of laughter at the look on his face as he tried to right himself.

My mother, learning from his example, perched on the very edge of her cushion. "What a sweet little place, Bethie." She cast a smile at my dad. "Reminds me of our first place, Mitch, outside Ft. Meade. Remember that? Every time I opened the oven door, the pilot light went out."

Dad nodded. "That place sure was a dump." But he smiled a little, too, which made his words sound more like fond reminiscence than complaint. "When MJ was born, we had to keep him in a dresser drawer at first, because we couldn't fit the bassinette in our bedroom."

I shook my head at the thought of my hulking big brother tucked into a tiny dresser drawer. "I'll be right back with the coffee." I took the few steps into the kitchen and pulled out the glass pot from our cheap little coffee maker.

"Bethie, huh?" Trent's low murmur at my ear made me jump. "I like it."

Rolling my eyes, I flipped on the tap and filled the pot. "Family nickname. No one calls me that but my parents and my brothers."

He pushed my hair out of the way and pressed his lips, hot and coaxing, to the back of my neck. "I always thought you were more than just an Elizabeth. And hey, as your husband, I think I'm allowed to use family nicknames." He skimmed his hands up my sides, his fingers teasing the undersides of my breasts.

I blew out a breath of frustration. "I can't believe we finally get rid of your mother just in time to have *my* parents here. It feels like we can't catch a break."

"Hey." Trent turned me to face him. "Elizabeth, it's fine. They're your parents, and they seem like great people. I think it's kind of sweet they drove out here to surprise you." He hesitated a few seconds before going on. "I get why you didn't tell them we got married. I mean, I'm sure they wanted you to marry some doctor or another lawyer or maybe someone in the military, right? I'm not exactly wonderful son-in-law material. But why haven't you seen them in so long?"

Scooping ground coffee beans into the filter, I shrugged. "I didn't plan for it to happen, but it did. Like I said, they were traveling, and I couldn't afford to leave the practice in Florida, not when I was struggling to pay everything off after Darcy." I slid the filter drawer into place and hit the ON button. "And I don't really care about what kind of son-in-law they expected. I chose you."

Trent studied my face. "I want you to be able to be proud of me. To be proud of that choice. I don't want you to regret it. Ever."

I raised myself up and kissed his lips. "I don't regret

marrying you. And that has nothing to do with your past, your family or your job." I ran my fingers through his hair. "It's because you're the only one who sees me the way I am and loves me anyway." I paused. "Or loved me. Sorry, I'm not trying to rush us back into anything."

"Elizabeth." He stopped me from moving away. "Don't be afraid of saying the words. I do love you. I have, since that first day when you asked me to dig through your purse to find your car keys. I fell in love with you that day, and every day since, I've only learned how to love you more. I was stupid and scared for a little while, but I never stopped loving you, even then."

I couldn't manage any words, but I nodded. Trent blew out a long breath. "Okay. I'm going to be a really generous person and share my cookies with your parents. I'll put them on a plate, and you pour the coffee. Let's get through this."

And get through it we did. We sat in the living room—my parents on the sofa and Trent and I on cushions on the floor—and made small talk for an hour. My parents updated me on my brothers, their careers and their families. MJ and his wife had had their first baby, a boy, last fall, and my mother showed me pictures of my nephew on her phone.

"Trey's such a good baby, and Courtney's a wonderful mother. She and MJ love living in Germany." She stared at the photo, her face turning pensive. "His next tour is in Korea, unaccompanied. He's going to miss so much of the baby's first year."

"Now, Dulcie. Don't get started on that." Dad gripped her hand. "They'll be fine. Don't forget, Courtney and the baby are coming to stay with us for part of the time, so you'll get all the grandma time you want."

"I think it sucks." The words shot out of my mouth before I knew what I'd said. "I think it's horrible that MJ has to leave his baby and go off alone. Mom's right. By the time he gets back home, his son won't even know him anymore."

My father shrugged. "That's Army life. MJ knew better than most what he was getting into. It is what it is. The sacrifices of the family—"

"That's bullshit." A mix of rage and pain rose up in me. "I'm sorry, Dad. I know you don't want to hear this, but it's true. All that crap about the military families being brave and making sacrifices? No one likes it. It's not a noble, honorable thing. It's painful, and it hurts the kids and wives and the husbands."

"Elizabeth—"

"Do you know how hard it was for me every time you left us again? Did you even know? After all the hoopla of the goodbyes were over, did you know I'd cry myself to sleep every night for a month? And when I was little, and I didn't understand yet that you'd be back, and I just stopped eating, did you have to deal with that? The boys were told they had to be brave and not show anyone that they missed you, but they did. Henry used to get in trouble for fighting while you were gone. And Mother—she'd shut down for days on end, so then I didn't really have a mother or a father." I sucked in a ragged breath. "I'm sorry. I know you were doing what you had to do, and I understand it's the way it is. But we don't have to pretend it's some noble calling."

I dropped my forehead onto my knees, willing the threatening tears to pass me by. I felt Trent's arm encircle me, pulling me against his body, and I waited for my father to yell.

But he didn't. Instead, I heard a choked sob from the other end of the couch, and when I glanced up, my mother was covering her face as her shoulders shook. My father glanced from her to me, his face troubled.

"Elizabeth. Bethie." His voice broke, and then I was crying. "I never . . ." He stopped speaking for several beats, inhaling a deep breath. "I knew it was hard on all of you. I hated leaving my family, believe me. But it was what I had to do. It was my job. I made a commitment to our country, and it was one I had to keep. Still, I had no idea you were still so . . . troubled by it. By the time you were a teenager, my leaving didn't seem to bother you anymore. I figured you were used to it."

"I never got used to it. I just got better at hiding how I felt." I leaned into Trent, drawing comfort from his strength. All the rage was spent now, and only the grief remained. "I'm sorry, Daddy. I didn't mean to yell at you. I know you were only doing what you had to."

"I was. But maybe I should've been more aware of how much it affected you. I'm sorry, too, Bethie." He stood up and then knelt next to me, brushing my hair away from my face. "I'm sorry you were hurt, and that you felt like I was abandoning you. I can't undo that now, but I can be better about listening when you need to talk about it. Is that a good start?"

I pressed my lips together and nodded. "Mmmhmmm."

His mouth crooked into a half-smile. "And maybe you could come home a little more often, so your mother and I don't have to chase you down." He flickered his eyes to Trent. "I'd like to get to know my son-in-law."

Trent tightened his arm around me and answered for both of us. "I think that can be arranged, sir."

It was well after midnight by the time we all went to bed. Since there were no hotels anywhere near Burton, my parents slept in our extra bedroom, in the room Donna had occupied up until the night before.

Which meant that Trent slept in my bed.

We didn't really have a choice, since my parents assumed we shared a bedroom, as most married couples did. And Trent and I did an admirable job of playing it off as though it was no big deal.

"I'm sorry." I leaned against the closed door. "I didn't think tonight was the time to share with my parents that maybe our marriage hasn't been everything they think it is."

"Hey." Trent framed my face with both his hands. "It's fine. Anyway, I hope they never have to know we've been anything but blissfully happy together." He sealed his lips to mine, gentle and full of promise. "And I'm never going to complain about sharing a bed with you. Not that I expect us to do anything other than sleep," he added, murmuring against my mouth.

"I'm not sure I could handle anything other than sleep

right now. Emotional catharsis exhausts me."

"I was proud of you for that. You opened up and let your parents know how you felt. I know it wasn't easy." He trailed his mouth over my cheek and down to my neck. "And I realized something else, too. When I left you in the Cove, it wasn't just us having an argument and me taking off like an idiot. You must've felt like it was your father all over again."

I raised my eyes to his. "The men I love always leave."

"Baby." With a low groan, Trent gathered me close. "I promise you, no matter what happens between us, I'll never leave you again. We can fight it out, we can yell and scream. You can tell me I'm a shithead. But I won't leave. I'm with you for the long haul. You and me, sweetheart. My dysfunction and yours. You're stuck with me, for always."

I wrapped my arms around his neck. "Always sounds like the best idea you've ever had."

We had breakfast with my parents the next morning before they left. I made pancakes, and our conversation was easy and light after the night before.

"Tell me how you two met. And I want to hear all about your wedding." My mom glanced from Trent to me.

I smiled. "Trent was working with his uncle, selling Christmas trees in our parking lot down in Crystal Cove. We got to be friends, and then . . . more." I held his hand, gazing into his eyes. "We got married on New Year's Eve. It was fast, yes, but when you know, you just know."

My mother sighed. "How romantic. Still, Bethie, you've

broken my heart by denying me a wedding to plan. Remember when we used to dream about your perfect wedding gown?"

"I'm sorry." I glanced at Trent. "Maybe after MJ comes home, we could have a big party to celebrate both that and our marriage. Wouldn't that be fun?"

"What a wonderful idea. Trent, does your family live around here?"

He shook his head. "My uncle and aunt live up in Michigan. My mother . . ." He slid his eyes to me. "She's an alcoholic, and she's in a rehab facility just north of Atlanta."

To their credit, my parents only nodded. My mother reached out to squeeze Trent's hand. "I'm sorry about that. It must be so difficult for you."

My father cleared his throat. "So you're in the restaurant business now, are you?" He looked at Trent with interest. "I've always thought running a bar or a diner would be fun."

"Since when?" My mother snorted. "This is news to me."

Dad shrugged. "Just something that's crossed my mind for our retirement years." He winked at my mom. "Got to keep you guessing, honey."

"If you want to come over and check out the Road Block, sir, you're welcome to ride over with me." Trent folded his napkin and tucked it under the edge of the plate.

"I'd love to do that some time, but today, Dulcie and I need to hit the road. We've got a little bit of a drive ahead of us to Hilton Head. But I'd definitely like a rain check." His eyes met mine. "For the next time we come visit, assuming we're invited back."

"Definitely." I smiled.

"And maybe we could see your office, too, Bethie," my mother put in. "You haven't said much about your new job. Do you like it?"

Old Elizabeth would've put on a happy face and described a few clients, made the practice sound better than it was. Instead, though, I shrugged. "Honestly, I don't think I do. It's going well, for the most part, but I'm beginning to think that I might not be cut out to be a lawyer." I held my breath, waiting for the fallout from the parents who'd paid for three years of law school.

"You don't want to spend your life doing something you don't enjoy." My father took a sip of his coffee and regarded me thoughtfully over the edge of his cup. "What is it you think you'd like to do instead?"

The germ of an idea had been evolving since Trent had asked me the same question the night before. "I'm not sure yet, but I'm thinking . . . I might want to do something with baking. I've been spending a lot of time with the woman who owns the bakery here in town. She's been teaching me, and she says I have a knack for it." I lifted one shoulder. "I know I've just started, and I don't know what I can do with that, exactly. Burton doesn't need two bakeries, for sure. So unless I want to drive to Savannah every day, or maybe see about opening a place in another small town nearby, I'm kind of stuck."

"I wonder if you couldn't do something on the internet." My mother tilted her head, considering. "You could have an on-line store front, like my friend Carla who sells jewelry."

I nodded. "That's a great idea, Mother. Maybe I could talk to Carla about it, if I decided to go that way?"

She smiled, pleased. "Of course. I'd be happy to help in any way I can."

My father checked his watch. "Dulcie, we need to get on the road. And I'm sure Trent has to leave for work." He stood up and offered his hand to Trent. "It's been good to meet you, son. I look forward to getting to know you better."

My mother didn't stand on such ceremony. She pulled Trent into a tight hug and then wrapped me in her free arm, holding us together. "You two be good to each other, you hear? And come up to see us in Virginia." She patted my cheek. "If you come visit in a few months, you can see Courtney and meet your nephew."

"I'd like that." I kissed her and then turned to my father. "Dad, I'm glad you came."

He wrapped me in his arms, and this time when I sniffed deep, it was a smile. "I love you, Bethie. Never forget that. I have since the first minute I held you, and I always will." He released me and stepped back, flicking my nose with his finger. "You'll always be my little girl."

"I love you, too, Daddy." I kissed his cheek. "Have a good time in Hilton Head."

Trent stood behind me, his arms around my waist, as we watched my parents drive away. He kissed my ear lobe. "I need to go, baby. What're you going to do today?"

I smiled. "I'm going into the office for a little bit. I think I'm going to list the practice for sale. I'm tired of doing something I don't like." I glanced up at him. "Are you okay with that?"

He dropped a quick kiss on my lips. "If you're happy, so am I."

"And then I might run by Kiki's to see if she has time to give me some pointers on my scones. I want mine to be light and airy, like hers."

"Practice makes perfect, right? I'm always willing to help you practice." He slid his hands lower to squeeze my ass, fitting me to his body. "I never did get that heavy petting you promised me."

I hauled his head closer to mine for a deeper kiss. "Anticipation is a good thing. See you tonight."

CHAPTER TEN

Trent

"SOMEONE'S IN A GOOD MOOD." Mason smirked at me when I came into the bar whistling. "I take it the date at the lake went well? Did y'all scare some fish?"

I laughed, shaking my head. "Not quite. That water would be damn cold this time of year. But yeah, it was a good date. We talked a lot. I think we've actually got a chance of making this work."

"Dude." Mason held out his fist for me to bump. "I'm happy for you. And I'm going to follow that up by asking for a favor. We've got a pretty big name coming in to play tonight. She's getting to be well-known in the folk music scene, and we expect a pretty big crowd. Can you hang out a little later tonight to lend a hand?"

"Of course." I joined him behind the bar. "You've been great about giving me the time I needed. I'm all yours."

Mason nodded. "Thanks, I appreciate it. Let's tackle that inventory while it's still quiet."

We worked for several hours, doing all the various mundane tasks that kept the bar running smoothly. I loved that my job had both variety and predictability; it kept me interested without stressing me out.

Just after the lunch crowd began to slow down, the door swung open and a group of four people walked in. Leading them was a petite blonde who paused just inside and surveyed the room. Hands on her hips and a saucy smile on her face, she called out, her voice carrying into the bar.

"Hey, where's the owner of this dump?"

"Crissy Darwin!" Mason came out from behind the bar, drying his hands on a rag and grinning big. "Look at you. All grown up! Come here and give me a hug."

With a little giggle, Crissy leaped into his arms as Mason folded her into a bear hug. "I'm so glad to see you! God, it's been forever, hasn't it?" She stepped back and looked around the club. "This is amazing, Mason. Really. Wow. You've done good."

One side of his mouth lifted in a smile. "We like it. We've got everything set up for you all to run sound check. Anything you need, just ask me or Trent." He hooked a thumb in my direction. "Oh, and hey, think you can come by the house for breakfast tomorrow? Rilla's heard so much about you, she's dying to meet you. And then you can see the kids, too."

Crissy nodded. "Piper's got to be getting so big. She was just a tiny baby last time I saw her, back in Nashville." She patted Mason's arm. "I'm so happy you found someone to love again, Mase. You deserve all the best. I can't wait to meet the woman who roped you this time."

Mason laughed. "She's amazing, though it was more me who did the roping than her. Now come on, let me show you around."

I stayed behind the bar, keeping my eye on everything while the band began to set up and run sound check. Mason came back over a while later, frowning.

"Hey, Trent, give me a club soda, no ice, please. Crissy's guitarist isn't feeling well."

I pulled the hose and filled a clean glass. "Here you go. Hope he's okay."

"Yeah, thanks. He's afraid he got a bad burrito from a gas station." Mason rolled his eyes. "You'd think a man used to being on the road would know better than that."

"True. You've known Crissy a long time, huh?"

Mason nodded. "She was just a baby, really, the first time I met her in Nashville. I think she must've been about fifteen. She'd been playing the fair and festival circuit, and one of our scouts caught her act, alerted us about her. We brought her out, and I wanted to sign her, but after we talked, her parents decided she wasn't quite ready yet. I think it was a good call. She just signed a contract with a big recording studio."

I whistled. "Nice."

"Yeah." Trent grabbed a paper napkin from the bar to wrap around the glass. "She had a rough time last fall. The guitar player who'd been with her from the beginning was killed. And so was her new publicist. Turned out she had a crazy fan. Anyway, the guy who's playing for her now is just a temporary sub until she can find someone else who gels." He lifted the glass. "I better get this over to him."

I served up another set of beers to the two guys killing time at the end of the bar, pausing just long enough to shoot the breeze with them. I'd just turned back, chuckling at something they'd said, when another man slid onto a barstool a few feet down. I made my way over to him.

"Hey, there. What can I get for you?" Up close, I realized the guy looked familiar. I couldn't quite remember where I'd seen him before, though.

"You got a hell of a nerve, hanging around this town after what you pulled." He spoke through a clenched jaw, his eyes flashing fire. "I heard a rumor you were working here, and I had to come see for myself. Couldn't believe Mason's hiring your kind these days. Didn't think he'd really give a job to the man who raped his wife's cousin."

I remembered now where I'd seen this man before. It had been the day at the hardware store, when I'd gone to talk with Larry about getting my old job back. He'd been there, too, whoever he was, and he'd spit venom at me then. I had the vague sense that he was working for Larry.

I swallowed. I couldn't lose my cool, not here. I had to keep in mind that I represented Mason and the bar, and regardless of what lies he was spewing, this man was a customer.

"Look, buddy, I don't even know who you are. But I think you got some wrong info. I didn't—" I lowered my voice. "I didn't rape Jenna Sutton. Or anyone else. What happened between us is just that, between us. I was sorry, real sorry, to hear what happened last year. If she was hurt by me, I'm sorry about that, too. I used to be—well, I wasn't very good when it came to women. But I'm not that man anymore."

"You ruined her. You took her innocence, and you threw it back in her face. You're going to burn in hell for that, boy. And no one in this town will ever forget what you did. You can pretend you've changed, but we all know what you did."

I sucked in a deep breath and gripped the edge of the bar. "I'm sorry. I can't go back and undo what happened, but I'm sorry I couldn't be who she wanted. I—"

"What's going on here?" I hadn't heard Mason come back over, and now he stood next to me, his massive arms crossed over his large chest as he glared at the man. "Nick, what the hell do you think you're doing?"

"I could ask the same." Nick stood up. "Nice family loyalty there, Mason. Hiring this asshole? How could you do it?"

"You need to leave." Mason spoke quietly, but his voice was pure steel. "If you can't be a sane and decent person, get the hell out. I'm not having some idiot come in and hassle my staff. Trent works for me, and he's damned good at his job." He leaned over, hunching his shoulders. "And no one in Jenna's family, not my wife, not Jenna's mother or father, has said anything to me about Trent working here. So you either shut your fucking mouth and sit down, or you get the hell out and don't come back."

Nick muttered something I didn't catch—which was probably a good thing—and pushed away from the bar. He kicked a chair that was in his path on his way out and nearly yanked the door from its hinges.

Mason let out a long breath once he was gone. "Trent, I'm sorry about that. Nick—he's a hotheaded idiot. Don't pay him any mind."

I shook my head. "Who is he? I don't think I remember seeing him around town until I came back. He works for Larry?"

"Yeah, at the hardware store. He moved here right after you left, I think, or maybe right before. I don't know much about him, except he's got an aunt in town. Larry hired him, and he's been hanging around Jenna. I guess they've dated on and off, but I never got the feeling it was anything more than casual."

I ran a hand over my face. "The way he talked, I would've thought they were pretty serious." I met Mason's eyes. "He accused me of raping Jenna. Mason, you know I would never—I didn't. It was just a bad decision."

"I know it. Jenna always made that clear. She never blamed you for anything, Trent. She told Rilla that you never led her on."

"I was stupid. I knew she was young, and on some level, I even knew she had a crush on me. I just didn't realize how far it would go."

"Who would've?" Mason rolled his shoulders. "God, this was the last thing I needed today. Rilla just texted that the baby's sick, and she's harried. Crissy's guitar player is in the back, puking out his guts, and I don't think that guy's going on tonight. I'd jump in and play for her, but I'd really like to go home to help Rilla." He glanced at me out of the corner of his eye. "You don't happen to know anyone who plays guitar, do you?"

I didn't even think about what I was saying when I heard myself replying, "I can play."

Mason straightened up and stared at me. "You can?"

"Yeah, some. I haven't in a while, because I couldn't afford a guitar. I hocked the one I had to help me get up to Michigan last year."

He hooked his thumbs in the front pockets of his jeans. "How long did you play?"

I rolled my eyes up to the ceiling. "Started when I was a sophomore in high school, and I kept it up. Used to play out at Benningers' when we were all sitting around at night. I can read music, but I mostly play by ear." I shrugged. "Like I said, though, I haven't played in a year. I probably can't help you out."

"Hold on there. Let's not jump to conclusions. Come on over here with me."

I followed Mason over to the club side, where Crissy was set up on the stage adjacent to the dance floor. "Hey, Crissy. I might have a sub for you. Can he borrow Ronnie's guitar?"

Crissy smiled and waved her hand. "Of course. Come on up and give it a try."

I felt like an idiot, climbing onto the stage. What'd I been thinking? I was just a punk who sometimes messed around with a guitar. I hadn't even much thought about it in the year since I'd sold mine. No, that wasn't really true. I'd wished for it now and then, wished for the outlet it gave me. When Elizabeth and I were first together, I'd wanted to play for her. But I'd never seriously considered playing for anyone else.

Picking up Ronnie's guitar, I sat down on the empty chair and gave it a testing strum before I plucked out a few chords and then a familiar riff or two I knew by heart. Crissy was watching me, her eyes alight.

"Do you read music?" She leaned down over her guitar case and shuffled some papers, emerging with a sheet of music. "Let's try this one."

I scanned the bars and then flipped it over. "I think I can handle this. Can you play it through once, though? I do better by ear. If I can hear it and read the music, I think I have a better shot of actually making music that sounds decent."

"Sure." Crissy turned her body to face me, closed her eyes and began playing a haunting, lovely ballad. I listened intently for a few minutes and then joined in, playing along and singing harmony where the words repeated. When we reached the end of the song, Crissy didn't pause; she went back to the beginning, and I went right along with her. By the time we reached the middle, I'd forgotten to be self-conscious and was so caught up in the music that I wasn't even thinking about where we were.

Our voices rose together at the end, and in the moment of silence that followed, applause and whistles rang out.

"Trent! You dog. You've been holding out on me." Mason put his hands on his hips and mock-glared at me. "You're awesome, dude."

I shook my head. "Nah, I'm just messing around." I stood up and tried to pull the guitar strap off my neck, but Crissy laid a hand on my arm.

"If you're just messing around, then I can't wait to hear what you sound like when you're serious. Damn, baby. I want you up here playing with me tonight." She looked over my shoulder. "You're cool with that, Mase, right? I can hijack your man here to help me make some pretty music?"

Mason nodded. "Hell if I'm going to stand in the way of something that's meant to be. Trent, Rocky can cover everything on the floor tonight. I'm going to run home for a while and see if I can give Rilla a break, but I may try to sneak back to hear you two tonight. I have a feeling it's going to be something no one wants to miss."

I'd texted Elizabeth earlier that I was going to be working late, and she'd responded, telling me she'd see me when I got home. I was almost tempted to tell her about the change in plans, that I was going to be on the stage, not behind the bar, but I chickened out; if I turned out to be an utter disaster, I really didn't want her to witness that train wreck.

"You ready for this?" Crissy emerged from one of the back rooms that doubled as a dressing room during live gig nights. I was leaning against the wall, tapping the toe of my boot on the floor.

"I don't know. I'm afraid I'm either going to throw up from nerves or completely melt down up there and forget everything we practiced this afternoon. Either way, I apologize ahead of time."

Crissy laughed. "Stage fright is one thing I've never had to deal with. But after this year, I can safely say that nothing that could happen on the stage would surprise me."

I remembered what Mason had said about her guitarist and publicist both being killed. "I don't know how you went through that shit and still get up on stage now. I think I'd still be rocking in the corner, sucking my thumb."

She gave me a half-smile. "The show must go on. Music is who I am, and there's nothing else I want to do. I figure the best tribute I can pay Maddy and Dell is to keep on going." She jerked her chin in the direction of the doorway to the club. "You have anyone out there tonight to hear you play?"

I shook my head. "No, I didn't want to tell my wife in case I crash and burn. If it goes okay, I'll tell her after."

Crissy regarded me curiously. "Won't she be hurt that you didn't ask her to be here? I thought the whole purpose of being in a committed relationship was having some-one there to console you in crash and burn scenarios." She winked at me. "Not that you're going to do that. You're going to be great. Just relax and let the music flow."

I quirked a dubious eyebrow. "For your sake, let's hope it works that way."

Darcy stuck her head around the doorway. "I'm about to introduce you. Y'all ready?"

I couldn't answer for panic, but Crissy gave her a thumbs up. "Go for it. We're good on this side."

A few seconds later, we heard a shrill whistle followed by a hush falling over the club floor. Darcy's voice floated back to us.

"Tonight we're pleased and proud to welcome folk mu-sic sensation Crissy Darwin to the Road Block! Let's give her a big Burton welcome!"

I was pathetically relieved that Darcy hadn't said anything about me, but I didn't have time to think about it before Crissy grabbed my hand and pulled me to the stage.
The lights on us were bright and blinding, which was perfect
since it meant I couldn't see anyone in the audience. I found
my chair, my borrowed guitar and settled myself in, breathing deep and begging myself not to pass out.

Crissy stood at the microphone, launching into an up
tempo number as I tried to just keep up. I gave her some
back up vocals on the chorus, and by the time we'd finished
that first song, I felt better.

She segued into a slower song, a sort of teasing love
song, before she took a short break to speak to the crowd,
thanking them for coming out tonight.

"This is my first time in Burton, and I have to say . . .
y'all are blowing off my socks!" The crowd roared, and Crissy laughed. "I want to thank Mason Wallace, who was one of
the first people I knew in Nashville way back when. Mason's
always been supportive of my career, and I'm real tickled to
be here playing his club."

"Took you long enough!" I recognized the bellow from
the back of the room and grinned. Apparently Mason had
made it back in time to catch part of the show.

"Love you, too, baby!" Crissy shot back, and laughter
followed. "I also need to say a real special thanks to my guitarist tonight. Ronnie Gardins, who's been playing with me
the last few months, got sick tonight, and your own hometown boy Trent Wagoner jumped in to help me. I think he's
doing a wonderful job, don't you?"

I held my breath. There was every chance that her words

would bring as many boos as cheers, but to my relief, I heard only polite applause and a few shouts of encouragement.

"This next song is one I always dedicate to my late friends Maddy and Dell. It's about love and loss and moving on to find new hope. A new start. It's called "After You.""

Crissy moved back to sit next to me. She caught my eye and counted us in as we began the ballad I'd sung with her this afternoon.

I'd closed my eyes to forget about the audience, to focus on the music, but when I opened them in the middle of the chorus, I spotted Elizabeth standing at the edge of the stage. The lights were lowered, and I could see her clearly, watching me with soft eyes, her mouth curved into a delighted smile. I gave up on forgetting the crowd and instead concentrated on the face of the woman I loved more than life. The woman who *was* my life.

We finished the song to thunderous applause. Crissy led us through five more numbers before she again thanked the crowd, asked them to keep up with her through social media and said goodnight. To my surprise, she yanked me to my feet and made me take a bow as well before the lights went down and we left the stage.

"Oh, my God! That was the best show I've done in months." Crissy clapped her hands as soon as we were back in the hallway. She turned and pulled me into a quick hug. "You were amazing. Seriously. We had so much energy on that stage."

I laughed. "I was so freaking terrified, I don't really remember much of it. I'm glad it was okay."

"Okay? It was better than okay." She spun on her heel

as Mason opened the door and approached us. "Mason, tell him. Wasn't he unbelievable?"

My boss grinned. "He was pretty damn good." He punched me in the arm. "Of course, you weren't as good as me."

"Who're you kidding—he was ten times better than you. Mase, no offense, buddy, but his vocals ran circles around yours."

"Please, Crissy. No more gushing over me, or you'll make me blush." Mason rolled his eyes, then relented and slapped me on the back. "Dude, she's right. You looked like you were born up on that stage." He glanced down at the phone in his hand and sighed. "Okay, rock stars, you did good. Both of you. Crissy, it was pure pleasure hearing you again. I got to get back to the sick house before my wife runs off and leaves me. Oh, and speaking of wives . . ." He turned his head and looked back toward the door, where I spotted Elizabeth slipping through as Darcy showed her the way.

Everyone else disappeared. All I wanted to do was get to my wife, hold her close and share some of what had just happened. I had no idea how she'd come to be here, but I was glad she had been; the night wouldn't have been complete if she hadn't come to the bar to watch me.

"Baby." I caught her in my arms and swung her around. "How did you know?"

"Mason texted me." She raked her fingers through my hair, wrinkling her nose when she found it still damp with sweat. "My only question is, why didn't you?"

I exhaled hard. "I wasn't sure how it was going to turn out. I was scared shitless, babe. If I'd screwed it up, I didn't want you having a front-row seat." I held her face between my hands and kissed her, coaxing her lips apart and tracing the inside of her mouth with my tongue. Turned out performing made me horny as hell. If we'd been alone in this hallway, no telling what I might've done.

"Ahem." Crissy came over to us, smiling big as she chugged a bottle of water. "Hey, there. You must be Trent's wife." She winked at me. "At least I hope you are. I'm Crissy."

Elizabeth laughed. "I am the wife, for sure." She squeezed my hand. "I'm Elizabeth Hudson. Nice to meet you, Crissy. Your show was amazing."

"Thanks. Your husband here was a big part of that." The singer paused for a moment. "I'm going to be in town a few more days. I want to see Mason's family and take a few days of downtime. Think we could meet for lunch tomorrow? Say, about one, right here?"

I glanced at Elizabeth. "Sure. I can do that. I'll be here anyway, working."

"Cool." Crissy held out her fist for me to bump. "I have to go find Trina and Roland, and then I'm heading out to my bus to get some rest. See you both later. Trent, thanks again for stepping in. You rocked the joint."

"Thanks. I appreciate the chance. Kind of a once-in-a-lifetime deal, you know? Something I can tell my grandchildren."

Crissy shrugged. "Maybe, maybe not. We'll talk. Bye, now." She went back into her dressing room, and I shifted to face Elizabeth.

"I still have to hang out until closing, to make sure everything runs smoothly. Can you stay with me?"

She nodded. "I can do that. Just remember, if I ask you to pour me shots of Jameson's, say no." She looked a little queasy, and I remembered her first night here.

"You got it, sweetheart. C'mon, I'll get you set up out here."

We were wending our way to the bar when someone caught my arm. "Trent. Shit, man, you were awesome tonight."

Flynn Evans stood up from his table to talk with me. I hesitated a few seconds before I took the hand he held out. "Thanks, Flynn. I appreciate it. Just filling in for the regular guy."

"I'd totally forgotten you played in high school." The woman who poked her head around him had light brown hair and was heavily pregnant. Ali beamed at me. "And I'd forgotten how good you are."

"Thank you." I was relieved that seeing Ali Reynolds— *Ali Evans*, I reminded myself—didn't affect me one bit. She was just an old friend, someone I'd once known.

"Hey, Trent." From the other side of the table, Sam Reynolds waved, and his wife looked distinctly uncomfortable. I wondered why. "Nice job tonight."

"Thanks," I repeated. I didn't know what else to say until I remembered Elizabeth standing next to me, still holding my hand. "Oh, uh, this is Elizabeth." I glanced at her and made a decision. "My wife, Elizabeth."

There was silence around the group for a minute, and then Ali laughed. "Okay, this is ridiculous. We all know Elizabeth is your wife. Maureen spilled the beans." She smiled big. "Congratulations, Trent. And it's wonderful to meet

211

you, Elizabeth."

"Why don't you guys sit down and join us?" Sam nudged out a chair. "We're just having drinks and bar food."

"Thanks, but I need to get back to work. Mason had to go home to check on Rilla and the kids."

Ali leaned forward as far as her enormous stomach would let her. "Elizabeth, why don't you sit down with us, at least? We can get to know you while Trent's finishing up."

She glanced up at me, as if for permission, but before I could say yes or no, she spoke. "I'd love that. Thanks so much."

I wasn't sure how I felt about Elizabeth hanging out with people who'd known the old Trent. People who remembered all too well what I'd been like before last year. But on the other hand, I'd have to get used to this, if we were going to make a life in Burton. I'd have to learn to trust that each day of being a new person, a better man, would bury a little bit more of the old one.

I kissed the top of Elizabeth's head as she sat down in the chair Flynn had dragged over. "Have fun. I'll send y'all over a round of drinks." A small cheer went up as I walked away, smiling.

It was weird, but I had to admit, I was beginning to feel like I finally belonged in my own hometown.

CHAPTER ELEVEN

Elizabeth

WATCHING MY PARENTS DRIVE AWAY that morning while I rested safely in the circle of Trent's arms, I finally felt a measure of peace, a sense that I was where I was meant to be. Seeing my mother and father had been a huge surprise, of course, but being open with them at last, sharing who I really was instead of who I thought they wanted me to be? That had been freeing in a way I'd never imagined. I hadn't understood up until last night how much of my life I'd lived trying to make other people happy.

That was over, now. As soon as Trent took off for the Road Block—after giving me a searing kiss that promised we'd make up for lost time, and soon—I got dressed and headed into the office. Since it was Saturday, I didn't have any appointments, but I planned to catch up on some correspondence and begin the process of listing the practice for sale.

The old building was quiet when I let myself in. One of the biggest perks of coming in on the weekends was a total lack of Gladys, who was a stickler for keeping to her regimented work hours. Actually, she was a stickler for just about everything . . . which, I decided, was why she was such a thorn in my side.

I'd apologized over and over for losing my temper. I'd tried to explain how I felt, without excusing what I'd done, I'd used every form of conflict resolution I'd ever been taught and I'd offered every olive branch at my disposal. Nothing worked. Gladys didn't speak to me unless it was absolutely necessary and related to the practice of law. She never looked at me, even when she did speak, and she ignored me if I tried to initiate conversation.

Consequently, being at the office during the week had become something I dreaded even more than I had before my blow up. I'd only gone in if it was absolutely necessary, and I'd been spending more and more time at Kiki's and the library. It was a bad situation, I knew. Something had to give, and I was pretty sure it was going to be me.

I settled in at my desk and flipped through my messages and letters. I'd just begun to type a response when my phone buzzed; it was Maureen, sending me an updated picture of the dog I'd hit. Or more accurately, the dog who'd hit me. He had made an amazing recovery and won the hearts of everyone at the clinic. There was still no word from his owner, although Smith and Maureen had posted signs around town and pictures on social media.

I was just tapping out a response to her text when I

heard a sound at my office door. Will Garth stood there, leaning inside. "Knock, knock. Sorry, didn't mean to startle you. I knocked at the main door, but I guess you didn't hear."

"No, and my dragon lady isn't here to *not* tell me someone's on his way in. Sit down?" I pointed to my visitor chair, across the desk.

"Just for a minute." He sprawled in the chair the way only men seem to do. "I saw your car out front and thought I'd check in. You haven't been around much lately."

"No." I fiddled with a pen on my desk. "The atmosphere around these parts has been less than friendly. I practically get a stress ulcer just from walking in the door. So I've been working at home or at the library. And then drowning my sorrows in pastries over at Kiki's."

"That sucks. Why don't you just fire her?"

I sighed and leaned my chin on my hand. "Can't. I agreed to keep her on for at least a year when I bought the practice." I hesitated. "But I think it's about to become a moot point. Don't tell anyone yet, but I'm planning to sell the practice."

Will frowned. "Why? Because of that bitch? Don't let her get to you. Want me to have a talk with her?"

"No, thanks." I shook my head. "And it's not her. Well, it's not *just* her. I'm finally in a place where I'm ready to admit how much I hate being a lawyer."

He nodded. "Okay. So what're you going to do next?"

"That's the million-dollar question, isn't it? I'm not sure. I have some ideas, but nothing's solid yet."

"And here I was going to harass you about that interview you've never given me. Guess I'll have to change the headline from 'Burton's Newest Legal Eagle' to . . ." He paused for a minute, thinking. "'Changes Afoot for Burton's Former Lady Lawyer.'"

"Ugh! No." I laughed, tossing my pen at him. "You'll get no interview from me with that headline, buddy." My phone vibrated again, and I glanced at Maureen's response. "Hey, you're not by any chance in the market for a dog, are you?" I turned the screen toward him. "Isn't this guy gorgeous?"

Will leaned up and squinted. "He really is. Is he yours?"

"Nah. I just ran into him. Literally. On the highway outside town. Well, actually *he* ran into *me*, but no one seems to understand how important a distinction that is." I dropped my phone back onto the desk. "He's fine, though. We just can't find his owner, and he's really too big for Maureen and Smith to keep at the clinic much longer. Oh—maybe you could run something in the paper about him. You know, a feature story, some pictures . . . might either suss out his owner or find him a new one."

"Sure." Will shrugged. "Animal stories are always popular. I could run over there now and take some photos. Want to come with?"

I bit the corner of my lip. I hadn't been upfront with Will about my marital status, and while we'd had a friendly flirtation—more friend on my side, more flirt on his—I didn't want to mislead him. "I think I'd better stay here and get the rest of my work done."

"Oh, come on." He stood up and eased a hip onto my desk, his green eyes a little too warm for my comfort. "We'll interview the dog, and then I could take you to lunch afterward. Have you been out to the Road Block yet? They make a mean burger."

This was my perfect opening. "I've been there. Actually, my husband is the assistant manager."

What flared in Will's eyes wasn't surprise, but it was definitely disappointment. "Ah. Your husband, huh?"

I nodded. "Yeah. I know I haven't mentioned much about him—"

"No, you never mentioned *anything* about him. I'd heard that you were living with some guy, but since you never said anything, I figured it was just a roommate situation." He glanced at my hand. "You don't wear a wedding ring."

"No. Things haven't been settled between us, but we're better now. I'm sorry. I didn't mean to mislead you. I haven't said anything to anyone, really. I wasn't sure what was going to happen."

"And now you are? Sure, I mean?" He raised one eyebrow. "Are you sure you're sure?"

"I know I'm committed. I know I'm not interested in anyone else." I met Will's eyes. "We've both had things to work out, but in the end, Trent's the only one I see. He's my always."

"Okay then." Will sighed. "I can't say I'm thrilled to hear that, but I guess I'm happy for you." His mouth twisted into an almost-smile. "Maybe it's my turn to go drown my sorrows in pastries."

"Tell you what." I hit save on the letter I'd been writing and closed my laptop. "I'll walk over to Kiki's with you, and I'll treat you to one of her specialties. It's the least I can do, right?"

"What's her specialty?" Will followed me out of the office.

I grinned at him over my shoulder. "That's the coolest part. We won't know until we get there and she sees you. Once that happens, she'll know what you need."

"Sounds a little weird, but what the hell. Lead the way."

I'd just finished my chocolate croissant when my phone went off again. I rolled my eyes and lifted it up to show Kiki. "Maureen keeps sending me pictures of this dog. I'm starting to feel like he's stalking me." I glanced at the screen and frowned. The number of this text wasn't Maureen's. I opened it up and scanned the message.

This is Mason. Thought you might want to know Trent is playing guitar tonight with our act. You should come over and catch the show. PS I didn't tell him I told you.

"Everything okay?" Will licked some raspberry jelly from his thumb. Kiki had pronounced him in need of a double-jelly Danish, and from the looks of it, she'd been on target as usual.

"Yeah. Apparently my husband is playing at the Road Block tonight." I knit my eyebrows together. "I wonder . . ."

"You're going to go, right?" Kiki stood on the other side of the counter, hands on her hips and eyes questioning.

"I guess so. But he didn't ask me to be there. Mason did."

Kiki shook her head. "You need to be there. Trent will never tell you he wants your support, but he does." She shot an arch glance at Will. "Men sometimes don't know what they want or what's good for them. It's up to the women to let them know."

Will snorted and said something else, but I was too busy staring at the phone to pay attention. Before I could change my mind, I typed a response.

I'll be there.

He was good.

No, better than that. He was amazing.

My husband was a freaking rock star.

Okay, so he wasn't playing rock; it was folk music. Still, he was phenomenal. Watching him up there on the stage with the pretty blonde singer, I fell in love with him all over again, on an entirely different level. Since I'd met him, Trent had been fighting just to keep his head above water, certain he was destined to get the raw end of every deal and the short end of every stick. Life hadn't been kind to him.

But tonight, with his eyes closed and his fingers moving over the guitar strings as his voice joined with Crissy Darwin's, he was different—lighter and more alive than I'd ever seen him.

I knew the moment he spotted me. His eyes lit up, and it felt like energy flowed between us, a spark that shot straight to my core. Even with the throngs of people pushing me as I stood alongside the stage, it was almost as if we were alone. I wanted to crawl across the stage and slide my body up against his until he fell on me, pressing every inch of his strength into me.

"He's good." Mason's voice was suddenly at my ear. "He's damned good. I had no fucking idea." He sounded delighted, like a kid on Christmas morning. "Did you know? Have you heard him play?"

I shook my head. "I knew he used to play. We went to see a band at the Riptide back in the Cove, and he mentioned it. But he told me he'd sold his guitar for gas money to Michigan when he left to work for Nolan. I remember thinking I'd get him one for his birthday, but then . . ." I lifted my shoulder. "You know. Stuff happened. I just forgot."

Mason nodded. "He's too good not to be doing something with it. I'm going to talk to him tonight. I've still got connections in Nashville, and I could get him linked up with a promoter, maybe get him into play for a recording studio. There're no guarantees, but it's worth a shot."

"If you can talk him into it." I sighed as the tempo of the music changed, morphing into a sweet love song that threatened to melt me into a puddle. "Now go away. I want to soak in every minute of this."

Mason chuckled and fell silent, though I knew he stayed close to my side. When they finished and the lights went down, he leaned down to me again.

"They'll be in the back, right through the door next to the kitchen. It says Employees Only, but come on back when you're ready. I'm going to say goodbye before I take off."

I turned to follow him, but for some reason, I hesitated. The Trent I'd seen on stage had been almost a stranger, and I was a little shy about going to see him. I'd never been a groupie, but tonight I felt like one. Plus, he hadn't told me he'd be performing tonight. I wondered if he was going to be pissed that I'd shown up unexpectedly. Maybe he didn't even want me here.

I'd nearly talked myself into sneaking out and driving home when someone grabbed my arm. "Hey there. Bet you don't remember me."

The woman smirking at me was probably a good fifteen years older than me and looked a little familiar, but I couldn't quite place her.

"I'm Darcy. We met your first night in town."

Now I did remember. A little. "Oh, yes. You have the same name as my best friend from law school." I winced as memories from that night flashed through my mind. "I'm sorry if I was rude that night. I was a little, um, nervous about moving here."

Darcy laughed. "Oh, honey, I've seen much worse. Don't worry about it. Come on, I'm going to take you to see Trent. You looked like you might be a little lost." She pulled at my arm, and I had no choice but to let myself be moved.

She kept talking as we walked. "We just love Trent. He works hard, he's always willing to lend a hand, and he's not full of himself, you know? He's made a big difference here." She stopped by a door, turned the knob and gave me a slight shove. "Here you go. See you later."

I stumbled into the hallway, glancing around. A few feet away, Mason was chatting with Trent and Crissy. When he spotted me, he nodded in my direction, and Trent turned. Before I could say anything, he was on me, catching me in his arms and spinning me around.

"Baby, how did you know?" His face was glowing. That was the only way I could describe it. Gladness swelled in my heart.

"Mason texted me." I reached up to touch his hair, which was still slick with sweat. "My only question is, why didn't you?"

He blew out a long breath. "I wasn't sure how it was going to turn out. I was scared shitless, babe. If I'd screwed it up, I didn't want you having a front-row seat." He cupped my face between his hands and lowered his lips to mine, nudging my mouth open and teasing me with his tongue. When he pressed his body against mine, I felt a surge of the same connection I'd experienced when he was performing, and judging by the hard ridge under his fly, I guessed he was on the same page.

All I wanted to do was drag him home—or some other dark, private place—and cover every inch of his skin with my mouth. But before I could make this suggestion, Crissy came over to introduce herself to me. I tried to smile and play nice, but it wasn't easy with Trent's fingers teasing at my hip, rubbing the skin just above my jeans.

Crissy wanted to talk with Trent before she left town, and the two of them set up to meet for lunch the next day. I wondered if she had the same thoughts as Mason about Trent's talent and future in music, but honestly, I just wanted her to leave so that I could have my husband all to myself.

"I still have to hang out until closing, to make sure everything runs smoothly. Can you stay with me?" Trent held me close again, brushing my hair away from my face.

Staying here was the last thing I wanted to do, but I agreed. I wasn't very excited about sitting at the same bar where I'd gotten wasted and embarrassed myself a few months back, but I followed him out into the club anyway.

Someone at a table called his name, and once they began chatting, I realized that the man who'd yelled for Trent was Cory's son Flynn. His very pregnant wife sat next to him, and the guy at the far end of the table was her brother Sam and his wife Meghan.

When Trent explained that he was still working, they invited me to join them while I waited for my husband. I glanced at Trent, wondering if he wanted me to say yes or no, but the prospect of staying here, instead of at the bar, made me agree quickly.

They were a friendly group, quick to include me in their conversation. Ali leaned across the table and squeezed my hand.

"Between Cory and Maureen, I feel like I know you. Maybe once I finally pop out this kid, we could get together some time."

"I'd like that." I smiled and turned to Meghan. "It's good to meet you. I know your mom and Logan pretty well. Logan rented me the space for my law office back in the Cove."

Meghan nodded, but she seemed uncomfortable. I wondered if she'd heard something about me she didn't like.

"Jude and Logan are great, aren't they?" Sam slung an arm around his wife's shoulders. "So you met Trent down there, and then you moved up here?"

"Yes." I decided there wasn't any need to go into detail about how we'd happened to end up in Georgia. "I had to close up my law practice in Crystal Cove before I came up to Burton, and Trent had some issues to take care of with his mother." I figured they probably already knew all about

Donna and her history.

"I'm so glad Trent found someone like you." Ali beamed. "We were all in the same class, Flynn and Trent and me, and we used to hang out together. He was always so sweet, but he dated the skankiest girls."

"Ali." Flynn laughed, shaking his head.

"It's the truth," Ali protested. "And if you're wondering why my sister-in-law is looking so guilty over there, it's because she was one of Trent's less-skanky conquests. Back before she met my brother, of course."

"Ali!" Meghan's face was aghast. "Seriously, who says things like that?"

"Only my sister." Sam patted his wife's back. "Relax, sugar. It's in the distant past. Your taste in men has only improved with time." He winked at me. "No offense to you or Trent."

Meghan covered her face with her hands and peeked at me between her fingers. "I'm sorry. I was drunk and stupid and blowing off steam."

"But if you hadn't gotten drunk and stupid, I wouldn't have met you." Sam kissed her head. "And you could've done a lot worse than Trent, if you had to blow off steam with someone."

"Meghan, don't worry about it. Trent was honest with me about his past when we met. No hard feelings on my part." I smiled. "And in the interest of full disclosure, the first night I got to town, I got drunk and stupid, too, right here in this bar. So believe me, I'm not throwing stones."

Meghan seemed to relax after that. We chatted about people we both knew in the Cove, and she told me a little about her job teaching art in the Burton elementary school. I was having a grand time when Flynn announced it was time for him to take Ali home.

"He's scared I'll turn into a pumpkin for real if he keeps me out too late." Ali stood up and stretched her back. "Hopefully the next time you see me, I'll have a flat stomach and a new bundle of joy."

After they'd all left, I wandered over to the bar. It seemed as though the evening was winding down, and most people were heading out. I sat down on a barstool as Trent oversaw the closing time tasks.

"Hey, babe. Almost done here." He came over and leaned over the bar, twisting a strand of my hair around his finger. "Thanks for being patient."

I raised myself up to be closer to him, touching my lips to his with the lightest of kisses. "I think I'm tired of being patient."

His forehead wrinkled in consternation until he got my meaning, and then a smile spread over his face.

"All good things come to those who wait." He tugged on my hair, urging my head back so that my throat was exposed to him, and ran his lips down the column.

"I don't want to wait anymore for all the good things. I want them now." I dug my fingers into his shoulders.

"I think we can make that happen." Trent's eyes smoldered with the same fire that was currently building inside me. "Give me two minutes."

225

Trent was as good as his word. Two minutes later, he grabbed my hand and pulled me off the stool, through the darkened club and to the back door, where he paused just long enough to set the alarm.

"Crud." I came to a halt as he began to move toward his truck. "I have my car here, too, remember? We'll have to drive home separately."

"Nuh-uh." He shook his head. "I'm not letting you get that far away from me tonight. We'll leave my truck here, and you can drive me back tomorrow, okay?"

"Sounds perfect."

We stepped carefully through the pitch-black night until we came to my BMW, parked in the far corner of the lot. I held up my key to Trent.

"You want to drive?"

"Nope." In the dim light from the safety lamp above, his eyes glinted predatorily. "You drive. I want my hands free."

I opened my car door and slid behind the wheel. "What's that supposed to mean?"

"You'll see." Trent shot me a cocky grin. "Now drive me home, woman."

I cut straight across the empty lot to the highway. It was deserted this time of night, but I still drove carefully, mindful that animals were out and about, just waiting to dart in front of my car.

"Are you still flying high?" I glanced at him sideways. "You were so incredible tonight. I knew you could play the guitar, but up there—oh, my God."

"It was a pretty surreal experience." He shifted in his seat so that he faced me. "I was so nervous, I thought I was going to pass out. Then I settled down into it, and it was cool." He reached across and with one finger traced the inseam of my jeans, just above my knee. I shivered.

"And then, just when I thought I was probably going to make it through without crashing and burning, I saw you." His finger inched a little higher, a little closer to the spot that was pulsing, waiting for his touch. "When I saw your face, any possibility of doing anything other than rocking that show went out the window."

"Mmmmm." I was listening to him, but a good part of my attention was focused on his finger on the inside of my thigh.

"You know why? Because you make me want to be a better man. You make me want to be someone you could be proud of." He hovered for a second right where I wanted him but instead of touching me, he moved to the other side and ran the tip of his finger down. I wanted to cry in frustration.

"All I could think of when I saw you watching me was that I could do this. I could . . . blow you away." He crept his hand up, up . . . closer . . . My breath caught. "I could rock your world."

As he spoke the last word, two of his fingers pressed between my legs, and I thought I was going to fly through the roof. I arched up, desperate to have more of his touch, wishing like hell we were already at home.

"So are you going to rock my world?" I managed to eek out a whisper.

"Baby, count on it." He rubbed a little harder.

"God, Trent." I was panting. "I'm going to run us off the

road."

"Can't have that." He withdrew his hand to my knee. "Just get us home fast."

I growled in frustration, and Trent laughed softly.

"You're mean. And you're a tease." I gave the gas pedal a little more pressure.

"Nope. I wasn't teasing. I was just giving you a little appetizer. Preview of coming attractions." His grin was wolfish, and I shivered.

He kept his hand on my leg for the five minutes it took to get us home, but he didn't say anything else until I pulled up to the curb in front of the apartment. The minute I took the keys out of the ignition, he ratcheted his seat back as far as it would go and reached for me, dragging me onto his lap.

"God, I'm dying for you." He mumbled the words as his hands raked through my hair, gripping my neck and pushing my face down until our mouths collided in a rush of tongues and lips. I heard small, desperate sounds and realized they were coming from me.

Trent's tongue plunged against mine, and his hands slid to my hips, then under my shirt and up to cup my breasts. I arched, my breath coming in short bursts.

"What do you want, baby? Tell me what you want." He teased his thumbs just under my nipples, over the silk of the bra.

"You. I want you. All of you." I grasped his wrists and moved his hands to where I wanted them, writhing as he curled his fingers to tug down the cups. With one hand, he shoved up my shirt and lowered his mouth to fasten on one aching nipple.

"Baby." He whispered the word with my breast still in his mouth, making me moan. "You taste so fucking good. I've missed this so damned much."

"Harder." I ground against him. "Oh, God. Trent, should we—inside?"

"We will." His teeth nipped lightly at me. "But first, I'm going to make you come right here. Right out here, in your car, with your legs spread on my lap." He shifted his mouth to the other nipple and drew it deep into his mouth. "Just to take the edge off. Make it better."

"God, yes."

"Ride me, baby. Grind down against me. Make yourself feel good."

With a cry, I did as he said, every fiber in my body focused on where our bodies met. I found the movement that brought me ever closer to the edge before I plunged, straining against him as I cried out his name.

I fell against his chest, my ears ringing and my extremities tingling. Trent rubbed my back, soothing me.

"That's some edge you just smoothed." My voice was muffled against his shoulder. "Pretty sure I'm not going to be able to walk into the apartment."

"I'll carry you." He wrapped both arms around me and held me tight. "Don't worry, baby. I'll take you anywhere you want to go."

I pushed up a little, just enough to see his face. "To bed. Take me to bed."

A beautiful smile spread over his face. "I was hoping you'd say that." He opened the car door and stood, lifting me with him. I clung to his shoulders as he took the cement steps to our apartment two at a time, pausing at the door just long enough to fumble for his keys and unlock it.

Then it was closed and he was striding back to the bedroom—to the room he'd given up to me without a second thought, to the room where for months I'd been wishing he'd come climb into bed with me.

I thought he was going to lay me on the bed and fall next to me, but instead he stood there for a moment, staring down into my face.

"Elizabeth." It was a caress, as subtle as the lightest touch. "Elizabeth, I love you. Baby, I can't . . . being without you was the hardest thing I've ever done in my life. I've been through shit you can't imagine, and I don't want you to know it. Times I thought I might die. Times I wished I would. But Elizabeth, I never felt so dead inside as when I drove away from you in the Cove. I knew it was the worst mistake I'd ever make, but I couldn't stay when I was afraid I might ruin you."

I reached to brush my fingers over his cheek. "You could never ruin me. When stuff happens, we deal with it together."

"Together is all I ever want to be." He kissed my forehead. "Together, and inside you." He bent, lowering me to the bed, and then pausing only to pull off his boots and his shirt, climbed in to lie next to me.

"Hi," I whispered, stroking his hair.

"Hi." Trent smiled. "Anyone ever tell you that wearing clothes is overrated?"

"Actually, yes. My husband told me that. On our wedding night."

"He sounds like a very wise man." His lips teased the sensitive spot just beneath my earlobe.

"He is." I leaned away to strip off my shirt. "And if he were really smart, he'd take this opportunity to get those jeans off."

Trent wagged his eyebrows at me. "Sounds like my wife is propositioning me."

"You know it."

He rolled away just long enough to get rid of the jeans, and I did the same. We landed back alongside each other at the same time.

"You still aren't naked." Trent covered my boobs with both his hands. "I thought we had a deal."

"I know how proud you are of being able to unhook any bra with one hand. I didn't want to deny you that pleasure." I kissed him open-mouthed and demanding. "Show me your stuff, baby."

With a soft laugh, he reached behind me and flicked open the hook. "Show me *yours*, baby."

I wriggled my arms out of the straps. "I'm all yours."

His eyes darkened and slowly, much too slowly, he covered one nipple with his mouth, sucking it deep and circling it with his tongue. I hummed in pleasure and pressed the back of his neck to pull him closer.

"I love when my mouth is on one of your beautiful tits, and your hips start arching like crazy. Like you can't wait for me to touch you there."

"I can't." I slipped my hand between us and found him, hard and hot under smooth skin. "I want you to touch me and then I want you inside me. It feels like I can't wait."

"I can't, either." Trent groaned. "Especially if you keep that up. Your hands on me—God, baby. Nothing better."

"Nothing?" I rubbed the head of his cock over my slickness. "Nothing like this?"

"*Fuck.*" He shook a little, holding himself over me. "You're driving me crazy."

I rolled, forcing him onto his back. "Oh, honey, I'm just getting started." Easing down his body, I traced each line of muscle with my tongue. He inhaled sharply when I reached his lower abs, and when I took his cock into my mouth, I was pretty sure he started speaking in a foreign language.

His fingers threaded through my hair. "Oh, God, your mouth . . . baby . . . ohhh . . . *fuck.*"

I hollowed my cheeks on the way back up, sucking and then swirling my tongue around the head when I reached it. His hips canted upward, and I could feel the pulse thrumming beneath my lips.

With one last teasing kiss, I slowly crawled back up, straddling him. Taking his erection in my hand, I lifted myself up and eased myself down onto him.

"Don't move." His tone was steel, and he held me in place, hands on my waist. "If you move, I'll lose it."

I sat perfectly still, only my chest rising and falling. Trent lay beneath me, his jaw clenched and eyes closed. Slowly, he relaxed and brought one hand to the place where we were joined. He stroked over my folds, finally finding the one spot that drove me so insane, I couldn't help moving. Almost on instinct, I began lifting myself up and then sliding back down his cock until my sex ground into his.

"Elizabeth—baby, oh, God. So good. Never stop. Oh,

fuck, baby, faster. Tell me you're going to come. Tell me you're going to come with my dick inside you—"

Pleasure rose so sharply and with so much intensity that for a minute, the world went dark and silent. Everything froze, everything stopped; it was as though time stood still, and we were the only two people who existed. Trent cried out my name, his fingers digging into my ass and holding me to him.

I collapsed onto him, my ear pressed to his chest. Trent's heart was pounding, and I smiled. His hands rubbed small circles on my back.

"That was incredible." His breath tickled my ear. "But way too fast. You drive me wild. I can't help myself when you touch me. It's like I have to be in you." He rolled me to lie on my back and leaned over me. "But the good news is, we have all night."

"You think you're good for it?" I teased, tracing his lips with the tip of my finger.

"Baby, I'm better than good." He kissed me, aggressive and full of promise. "I'm a sure thing. And I'm going to rock your world. Again."

Oh, yeah.

CHAPTER TWELVE

Trent

"TRENT, CRISSY'S HERE. I JUST set her up at a booth in the back." Niki, the hostess, came over to the bar where I was working on a liquor order.

"Okay, thanks. I'll go over in just a minute."

"Hey, dude. I'll finish that." Mason held out his hand for the note pad I'd been using. "You don't want to keep the lady waiting."

I shrugged. "I don't think it's a big deal, Mason. Pretty sure she just wants to say thank you for pitching in last night."

"Trent." He laid a hand on my shoulder and stared me down. "If Crissy Darwin wanted to say thank you, she wouldn't be taking you out to lunch here, at the restaurant where you work. Keep an open mind, bud. You've got potential. Don't let this chance get away."

"Mason, that's really nice, but I've got a job here. And Elizabeth's happy in Burton." I thought about the night before, about Elizabeth's face when I was holding her. "She's my top priority."

"That's great. It's the way it should be. I'm just saying, don't say no right away. Think about it. Talk it over with Elizabeth. Consider the possibilities." He swatted me on the head with the notepad. "Now get over there."

Crissy was sipping a glass of tea and glancing at the menu. She smiled when I slid into the booth opposite her. "Well, if it isn't my favorite guitarist. How're you doing this afternoon?"

I laughed. "I'm good, thanks. How're you? And how's Ronnie?"

"Oh, he's going to be fine. Food poisoning's no joke, but he'll recover." She paused, playing with a corner of her napkin. "Thing is, though, Ronnie's just a temporary guitarist. That's his gig. He played a few recordings I did, and he agreed to come on the road with me to some dates that were close by. But he's from Florida, and he really doesn't want to go any farther away than we are now. I need someone who's willing to go to Nashville with me and take that next step. Someone who can travel to all our gigs."

I nodded. "I understand that."

"And Trent, I think that someone might be you."

I would've been lying if I'd said I hadn't had a clue Crissy was going to ask me to think about going on the road with her. I knew she was happy with our set last night, and I trusted that Mason wouldn't have said anything if he hadn't been pretty sure, too. But part of me had been in denial until she actually said the words.

"That's . . . really flattering. I'm honored you would even ask. But I'm not a guitarist. I'm not a real musician. I'm just a guy who messes around with music. Or who used to, anyway. I'm not a professional. I'm sure you could get any number of guitarists who'd kill for a job like this. So why me?"

"A couple of reasons. First of all, I'm going into Nashville as a novice. I've been playing all these small venues for years, since I was a teenager, and I feel pretty confident about my own talent. But this is going to be a whole new world for me. I want to have someone with me who I can trust, and if Mason says you're that guy, I believe him. Second, I'm fussy about how my music is played. Any guitarist who's been on the circuit for a while, I'm going to have to fight to teach him how to do things my way."

I grinned. "So you're looking for someone you can mold to be who you want?"

"You got it." Crissy laughed. "Hey, I'm nothing if not honest. I'll always tell you the truth. And with that in mind, you should know that guitarists aren't exactly knocking down my proverbial door. After what happened to Dell and Maddy last fall, there's a rumor that I have a black cloud following me around. You know, that it's bad luck to be connected with me. Never mind that the nut doing the killing's been in a mental hospital since November."

"I'm not superstitious." I hesitated. "But I don't want to disappoint you, Crissy. I don't want to give up my job here, talk my wife into moving and then find out I'm not who you're looking for."

"I understand that. I'm willing to commit to six months,

with the option for us to renegotiate at that time for a longer contract. And Mason said that if it doesn't work out, he'll give you back your job here. So the way I look at it is, nothing ventured, nothing gained. For both of us."

Excitement rippled through my stomach. *Could I really do this?* Or was I being an idiot to believe something this wonderful could really happen to me, to Trent Wagoner?

"Listen, do me this favor. Think about it. Talk to Elizabeth. And then call me." She slid a business card across the table.

"When do you need an answer?" I picked up the card and turned it over in my hand.

"Tomorrow would be great. By the end of the week would be fine." She flipped over her menu. "Now tell me what's good here, and let's order lunch and pretend you already said yes. We can talk hypotheticals about the next few months."

I'd had a bunch of long days, not to mention a very—ah—*busy*—night. Not that I was complaining, but I was yawning big by the time the truck rolled to a stop in front of our apartment that evening. I was looking forward to a quiet dinner with Elizabeth, who'd promised me her chicken pot pie, and an early bedtime.

And then I saw the dark blue car again. My heart fell through my chest. *Shit.*

This time, though, the judge wasn't still sitting in his driver's seat. The car was empty. Frowning, I climbed up to our front door and pushed it open.

Judge Roony sat on our ratty old couch, a cup of coffee in his hands as he chatted with Elizabeth. She turned when she heard me come in, and I could see the worry in her face.

"Hey, Trent." She stood up, taking my hand and kissing my cheek. "You look like you're asleep on your feet."

"Yeah." I nodded, but I was numb. "Judge Roony."

He rose, too. "I'm sorry to be here when you got home, but I'm afraid I have some bad news."

I nodded. "She left, didn't she? She ran out on rehab."

The judge sighed. "I got the call this afternoon. They thought she was adjusting well, and then she took off this morning. It's not their policy to pursue patients, but they won't accept her again, either. This was her last shot, and she threw it away."

"I understand." I clenched my jaw. "Will you . . . will there be an arrest warrant issued?"

He shook his head. "Not at this time. Now, if she comes back into town and causes a problem, then we'll have to re-think that. But I don't see the point in wasting any of our state's resources to hunt down a woman who's probably going to end up in a local jail somewhere anyway."

"Thank you for that." I was pathetically grateful for that small favor. "And thanks for coming over to tell me in person."

"Of course." He set down his cup and glanced at Elizabeth. "Thanks for the coffee, and good luck with your plans." He started for the door and then paused next to me. "Son, just remember, you did everything you could for your mother. No one could say any different. But at some point, she has to stand up and make her own choices. You can only do so much, but the final decision is hers."

I cleared my throat. "Yes, sir. Thanks again."

He shook my hand once again and let himself out. I stood rooted to the floor, staring after him. Elizabeth came up behind me and slipped her arms around my waist.

"I'm so sorry. I wish . . . I hoped that she was going to be different this time. That she'd think about you, if not about herself. But she's sick, babe. You know she is."

"Yeah, I know." I covered Elizabeth's hands with mine. "I did everything I could. I got her sober and I sent her to the best rehab place around. I got her a freaking scholarship to the place. The only thing she had to do was stay there. And she couldn't even fucking do that." I shook my head. "I'm done, baby. I can't put us through this anymore. She's my mother, and I wish things were different, but they're not. So that's that."

"I'm still sorry." She laid her head on my back and we stayed like that for a few minutes. It was strangely comforting to feel her against me, to know that she was there.

"Do you want to eat? The pot pie's in the oven. Should be ready by now."

"Yeah." I sighed, kissed her hand and released it as she slipped away toward the kitchen. "Let's sit down, eat and have a glass of wine. I want to tell you about my lunch with Crissy."

Elizabeth glanced at me over her shoulder. "Oh? Anything exciting?"

I leaned against the doorway. "Depends. How do you feel about being married to a musician?"

Elizabeth was quiet as I told her all about Crissy's offer. She got out the chicken pot pie while I set the table, and she didn't say much of anything until I'd finished my first helping of dinner.

When she spoke, her voice was low and intense. "Trent, you have to do this."

I raked my hand through my hair. "But babe, we'd have to move. We'd have to leave Burton and go to Nashville, to start. And then I'd be on the road." I reached across and touched her cheek. "You wanted a home. Remember you told me that? Your dream is having a hometown, a place where you can be settled and feel like you're a part of it. You could have that in Burton. I've got a job, we've got a community . . . you've made friends. I can't tear you away from that."

Elizabeth slid down from her chair and came around the small table to kneel in front of me. She gripped my hands in hers, and when she looked up into my face, her eyes were shining.

"Trent . . . yes, I told you I wanted a hometown. I wanted a home. And I found that home. You are my home. It's not a place or a house or a job. It's you. We can live anywhere, as long as we're together. I want you to have this dream, and I want to live it with you. I'll move to Nashville or anywhere else, as long as we're both going."

"What about your future? You were talking about doing something with that. I don't want you to give up your dream for mine."

"I wouldn't." She smiled. "I'm not ready to jump into my own business yet. I know that. But I can keep studying and learning, and when I'm to that point, maybe a new door will open for that. Meanwhile, I have some savings, and I can just be your groupie for a while."

I traced the line of her jaw, and she turned her head to press her lips into my palm. "I'd like that. Will you wear tight shirts and short skirts?"

"Not in public. But if you're very good, I might dress up in private."

"Oh, baby. I already told you. I'm better than good." I winked, smirking. "I'm a fucking rock star."

CHAPTER THIRTEEN

Elizabeth

THE NEXT TWO WEEKS WERE a whirlwind of insanity. Once Trent gave Crissy his answer, everything kicked into high gear. It felt like every day, something new was happening.

"I can't believe you're leaving." Cory sighed as she took the library books I'd just returned. "I'm going to miss you terribly."

A lump rose in my throat. "I'll miss you, too. So much. But you won't have time to even know I'm gone, not with that new granddaughter of yours. Go on, show me the latest picture. I know you have one."

Cory beamed. "Of course I do. She's just the darlingest little thing." Cory held up her phone, and I smiled at the sweet little face. Colleen Maeve Evans had come into the world about ten days before, after a peaceful labor and delivery. Cory reported that the small family was blissfully happy.

"Just as you and Trent will be. Oh, yes, I'm going to miss you, but I'm thrilled for you two. What an adventure you'll have. And promise you'll come back and visit us."

"Oh, we will. After all, Burton is still our hometown." I smiled.

"So tell me about your plans. Any bites on the practice? And were you able to get out of your lease at the apartment?"

"Maybe and yes. I talked to a lawyer from a firm in Savannah. They're looking to franchise their practice, and so they may be interested in acquiring our space and client roster. We'll see."

"And what does Gladys say?" Cory raised one eyebrow.

I wrinkled my nose. "Gladys still doesn't say anything to me. But she left a letter on my desk yesterday, informing me that she has no desire to be part of any sale. She intimated that Clark Morgan making her employment part of any agreement was the same as indentured servitude. So . . . seems that's a problem solved."

"Excellent. And the apartment?"

"Rented the same day the landlady put up the ad. As a matter of fact, I'm just on my way to the hardware store to pick up a replacement for the closet rod Trent's mother broke. We want to make sure we get my security deposit back."

Cory came around the desk to give me a hug. "I'll see you before you go?"

"Oh, yes. Kiki's leaving for her trip with Troy right around the same time we head to Nashville, so we thought we'd have one big party, probably out at the Road Block. I'll let you know when we've set up the details."

"Sounds good. Let me know if you need help with anything, sweetie."

I swung out of the library, humming to myself. It was amazing, really, how easily everything was falling into place. And although I'd had a little twinge of regret over leaving Burton, I was so excited now by our plans for the future—plans Trent and I were making together—that it felt right. Moving to Nashville would be the new start we both needed.

The hardware store was just down the street from the library, and since all of my errands that afternoon were in those few blocks, I'd left my car at home and walked. It was a beautiful afternoon, with a soft breeze that promised warmer days coming soon. The sun was shining, flowers were blooming, and the birds were singing. Living in Florida, I'd forgotten how much I loved spring.

The bell over the door rang as I stepped into the hardware store. I'd never been here since moving to Burton, but I'd passed it several times. It was small but neat, with wide aisles and filled shelves. I hunted for the closet rod I needed—I'd measured the space before I'd left the apartment—but I couldn't find the exact one I needed.

"Can I help you?" The man who came up alongside me was about my age, I figured. Maybe a little older. He smiled at me and pointed to the bins of rods.

"I hope so. I need a replacement rod, and I don't see the size I need."

He nodded. "That's all right. We can cut a larger one down for you. What's the length?"

I handed him the paper with the numbers on it. "Thanks so much. We're getting ready to move, and we wanted to replace this before we leave our apartment."

"Sure, no problem. I'll cut it and be right back." He disappeared around the corner to the rear area, where I assumed they had their saws.

An older man wandered up to the front counter, near where I stood. He was carrying a pricing gun.

"Good morning. I'm Larry Wexler. I don't think we've met." He smiled. "Are you new in town?"

"Kind of. I've lived here a few months, and actually, my husband and I are getting ready to move now. I'm Elizabeth Hudson. Oh, sorry, Elizabeth Wagoner." I grinned, holding up my left hand, where my wedding ring glinted, once again in its rightful place. "Sometimes I forget to use my married name."

The man who'd first helped me was just coming back to the front as I spoke. He stopped suddenly, his friendly face darkening.

"Wagoner? Is that what you said your married name is? Is your husband Trent Wagoner?"

A twinge of uneasy rippled through me. "Yes. Do you know him?"

The man's mouth twisted. "Unfortunately, I do."

"Nick." Larry spoke in a quiet, warning tone.

"Did you know that your husband is a rapist, Mrs. Wagoner?"

All of my blood drained from my head, and my heart began to pound. "Excuse me? What the hell are you talking about?"

"Nick—stop this. You're saying things—"

"Oh, so he didn't tell you? He didn't tell you how he

met an innocent girl—Jenna Sutton—at the Road Block last year, and he took her home and stole her virginity? Got her drunk and God knows what else he gave her, and then forced her to have sex with him?"

I shook my head. "No—Trent would never do that. Why're you saying this?"

"And then afterward, Jenna was so devastated by what happened, she tried to kill herself. Did he tell you that? Did he tell you how he destroyed a girl's life?"

In the back of my mind, I heard Trent's voice from last Thanksgiving, the first day we really talked. I'd asked him why he was avoiding sex.

I slept with a girl who took things between us to be more serious than they were. It wasn't the first time it happened, but this time . . . it went further. She was really hurt when I told her I didn't feel the same way she did.

No matter what this Nick was saying, I didn't believe for one minute that Trent had raped anyone. He would never have done that. But clearly he hadn't told me the whole story. He hadn't included Jenna's attempted suicide. Not back then, not when we got married, and not when we were both living in Burton, in the same town where all this had happened. I remembered now a dozen or more snide comments, glances I didn't understand or arch remarks that hadn't made sense. Now I knew what everyone had been thinking, while I went on in blissful ignorance.

I pushed away from the counter and began walking toward the door, my hands shaking. I heard Larry calling after me, but I didn't stop until I was outside the hardware store, where he caught my arm.

"Don't listen to Nick. He doesn't know what he's say-ing. He's got a hard spot where Trent's concerned and—" He sighed. "It's not like he said. Listen to me, please. Jenna's my niece. I think I know a little more about it than Nick does. He wasn't here the year before last, when Jenna and Trent were both working for me. He didn't see Jenna throw-ing herself at Trent day after day, flirting, making it clear how she felt—and Trent was real nice, without encouraging her. Jenna went after Trent. And she didn't stop until the night she turned twenty-one and convinced him that she was ready for a—" The man's face turned red. "Trent was who Trent was. Any girl who chose to go home with him knew what she was in for. He didn't do girlfriends. But Jenna thought she was different, and when he wouldn't play along, she took a bunch of pills. Tried to end it all."

"But she's okay?" I needed to know this girl was still alive.

"She is." Larry nodded. "And she'll tell you—or she would, if you saw her—that she doesn't blame Trent." He paused. "Look, Trent's a good guy. He worked for me for several years, and I liked him. I've heard he's turned his life around now, and I'm sure you're part of that. Don't let Nick's lies ruin what you have."

I shook my head. "I need to—he lied to me. He never told me about Jenna. How could he not?"

"Give him a chance to explain." Larry laid a hand on my shoulder. "Please. Give him that much."

I nodded and turned to walk home. I was numb, and all I could hear was Nick's voice, the hate in it as he told me the story. I climbed the steps to our apartment and walked inside.

"Hey, there you are." Trent came out of our bedroom, toweling off his hair. "I just did Mrs. Price's lawn, so I grabbed a shower. Did you . . ." He caught sight of my face, and his voice trailed off. "What's wrong?"

I licked my lips and tried to swallow, but my mouth was too dry. "Tell me about Jenna Sutton." The words came out as a rasp.

Trent's face lost all its color. He closed his eyes. "Shit. I'm sorry, babe. I know I didn't give you all the details—"

"All the details? You never told me anything at all. Back at Thanksgiving you said there was a girl who took sex a little seriously. That was it. That was all. You call a girl trying to end her own life over you 'taking sex a little too seriously'?" My voice rose to a near-shriek. "Why didn't you tell me, Trent? Why did I have to hear it from some jerk at the hardware store who's calling you a rapist?"

"He's an asshole, Elizabeth." Trent crossed his arms over his chest. "Yes, it's true. I slept with Jenna, she wanted more, I didn't, I blew her off, like I did every other girl after I slept with her. But Jenna took it hard, and she . . . she tried to kill herself. Yes." He ran one hand over his face. "God, I was . . . I felt so guilty. I wanted to do something. But I'd already done the damage. I'd treated her like a throw-away girl, and so she tried to throw away her life."

"And that's why you were on a sex fast when we met." I rubbed my temples. A wicked headache was brewing between them. "Maybe you didn't lie outright, Trent, but by not telling me, ever, that's a lie of omission. You let me marry you without knowing the whole story. God, how could you do that?"

His face was stony. "I didn't think it would matter. I thought about telling you several times, but it never seemed right. And then I figured someone would tell you here in Burton, but no one did."

"Until today." Suddenly everything that had felt so shiny and new in my life was ugly and tarnished. "God, Trent, if you could hear what this guy was saying . . ."

"And who did you believe, Elizabeth? Did you jump to your husband's defense, or did you buy what that jerk Nick said and come running home to scream at me for who I was a year ago? What good is trying to change if you're always going to assume the worst of me? Why are we even starting over if that's the way it's going to be?"

I stared at his face, filled with hurt and anger. "I need to—I need to get away. I want to be by myself." Tears filled my eyes and made it hard for me to see. I turned and groped blindly for the door.

"Elizabeth—wait. Come on, let's talk about this."

"There's nothing else to talk about." I stopped, my hand on the doorknob. "You'll leave. You'll go to Nashville, and you'll just—you'll leave. It was what you were going to do eventually anyway, right? You leave. That's the way it works. So go ahead. You might as well go now and get it over with." I choked back a sob. "Just leave me. Let me go."

I wrenched open the door and ran down the steps to the sidewalk, then up the block, going as fast as I could without running into anyone. I kept moving in a half-walk, half-run until I reached my destination. My safe place. My sanctuary.

And I hid.

Trent

For a moment, I couldn't move. I was frozen in shock, in guilt and in regret. Everything that had haunted me since the day Jenna attempted suicide—all of it came roaring back in its ugly truth.

Your fault. Guilty. Good for nothing. Not worth anything.

And then something snapped. I was staring down at the sofa where I'd slept for months so that my mother had a shot at health and life, and so that Elizabeth had her own space. I remembered that what Jenna had chosen to try wasn't my fault. I'd been irresponsible, yes. But I hadn't made the choice that day. Jenna had. I wasn't the Trent I'd been two years ago. I was a new man, a better man.

A man who wasn't going to just let his wife walk away. A man who sure as hell wasn't going to lose the most important person in his life.

I took off then, running down the steps and scanning the block for Elizabeth. I didn't know if she'd gone right or left, and after a frantic few moments of trying to figure out which way to go, I finally ran to the left, down the street, shouting her name.

People stared, and some even pointed. I didn't give a damn. I wanted my wife.

I went past the house where her law office was, thinking she might've gone there to hide, but something told me she wouldn't risk going in with Gladys still there. I kept running while my brain repeated a steady refrain. *Find her. Find her.*

I was just passing the library and about to head for Kiki's when I heard my name. Cory Evans stood in front of the building, her face etched with worry and her arms hugging her middle.

"Trent." She met me at the edge of the sidewalk. "She's here. She's inside."

I made as if to go around Cory, but she caught my arm. "Wait a minute. She's upset, Trent. She thinks you lied to her." She looked up at me, no judgment or condemnation in her eyes. "Listen. You need to go in there and make sure she knows the truth, about everything. Don't hold back." Cory gripped my arm. "I believe in you. I've always known you're a good boy, Trent. I know you can be a good man. Don't make me regret believing that."

I shook my head. "No, ma'am. I just want to see my wife."

She nodded. "Go ahead. She's in my office. I'll make sure no one disturbs you."

I went into the cool silence of the library, my heart beating so loud, I was sure Elizabeth could hear it. It felt odd to walk around the counter and into the inner sanctum of the librarians, but I opened the swinging door anyway.

My wife was curled up in a wing chair, her blonde hair forming a curtain that blocked her face from my view. Two long steps brought me to her side, and I sank to my knees.

"Elizabeth. Baby." Brushing her hair out of my way, I cupped her face in my hand. "Baby, I'm so sorry. I never meant— I was wrong. I should've told you everything about Jenna from the beginning. I guess . . . I thought I could leave it behind. You were always so perfect to me, so beautiful and good, and I didn't want to tell you about what I'd been. What I'd done."

She met my eyes, and my heart broke. Those gorgeous blue eyes were swollen, filled with unshed tears, and her face was wet. "You didn't trust me."

"No, baby. I was an idiot. I'm sorry. I—I blamed myself for what happened with Jenna, and I ran to Michigan to get away from my guilt. I was still punishing myself when I met you, and I knew I didn't deserve you. I couldn't have someone as wonderful as you, not when I'd fucked up so many other lives." I swept my thumb under her eye to clear away a tear. "But I told you, Elizabeth. I'm not leaving you. Never. I won't. I'm here, baby."

She shook her head. "You will. You always do. You did before."

"I was stupid before. I told you that. I'm not so dumb anymore. I know who my heart wants. You're my home. You're my peace and you're my life. Nothing works without you, and nothing makes sense if you're not by my side. I love you, baby. I love you, and I'm never going to stop."

I repeated the words, over and over, a litany of promise and vows of fidelity. "If you don't believe me today, I'll keep telling you. I'll keep saying the same thing, every day, for the rest of our lives, until you finally believe me. I love you, Elizabeth Hudson Wagoner. I love you."

At last, when my voice was hoarse, she reached out, laying one cool hand against my cheek. She swallowed, her eyes begging me for more reassurance.

"You'll never leave me?"

My throat tightened. "Never."

She sighed. "I'll never leave you. You'll never lie to me? Even to protect me?"

I pressed a kiss to her palm. "Never. You don't need my protection. You're the strongest person I've ever known."

She managed a tremulous smile. "You love me? For always?"

I pulled her down from the chair, into my lap. "For always. For all the always there are. And then some."

She linked her hands behind my neck. "I'm sorry I let Nick upset me. I'm sorry I freaked out. I'm still scared. Trusting is hard."

"I know it is. It doesn't happen in a day. We'll build our trust. Together."

Elizabeth leaned her forehead against mine. "Trent Wagoner, you're my home and my heart. I've loved you since the moment I saw you. You're mine. For always."

I covered her lips with mine, pouring into the kiss every promise and vow we'd made and all the hope for days to come.

Always.

EPILOGUE

"I CAN'T BELIEVE YOU'RE LEAVING TOWN after we just got to be friends." Maureen sighed and took a swig of beer.

I laughed. "Sorry. But you and Smith can come visit us in Nashville. And if Crissy plays anywhere near Burton, we could always meet."

"True. And you'll come back for my wedding, right?" An antique diamond ring sparkled on her left hand. "I mean, it's not going to be a big deal. I'm totally not a lace and flowers girl, no matter what my mother wants. But still. We want all our friends there."

I glanced across the restaurant to where Trent was standing behind the bar, talking with Darcy and Rocky. The Road Block was closed today for the big going-away party Trent and I were sharing with Kiki and Troy Beck, but the place was still filled to capacity. Mason was leaning against the other end of the bar, his infant son Noah tucked into the crock of one arm. Rilla was riding herd on their daughter

Piper while chatting with Cory.

"Of course we'll be back for that. I wouldn't miss it. And your mom made me pinky swear I'd be there." It was going to be hard to leave this little town that had been briefly my home, but more even more, I'd miss the people who'd come to be my friends.

"You're going to have such a blast, being on the road. You're going to be a total groupie." Maureen turned around to look up to the stage, where Crissy Darwin was having an impromptu jam session with Troy. "Look at that. They're just like regular people. I saw Troy's picture in *People* magazine last week, and tonight he's here in Burton, at the Road Block. I feel like I'm hanging out with famous people now."

"He's really cool. He and Crissy were talking last night, and he's asked her to think about playing some dates with him, if they can work it out. Trent's walking on air, just thinking about it."

"I bet." She smiled. "Everything's okay with you two? Things are better?"

"Much better." I touched my wedding ring, turning it around my finger. "We still have things to work on. Both of us come with a whole cartload of baggage. But we're taking our time, and we're talking a lot." I lifted one shoulder. "What can I say? He's the love of my life. He's not perfect, but God knows I'm not either."

"None of us are. I guess it's a matter of finding the person whose imperfections match our own."

"Speaking of matching . . ." I nodded to a table a few feet away. "Is that one there? Will and Sydney?"

"Oh, God, not if Sydney has her way. He keeps asking

her out, and she keeps telling him no. He thinks he's going to wear her down, but she's pretty damn stubborn."

"Language, Maureen." Cory slid an arm around each of us. "This is such a nice party, isn't it? It was sweet of Mason to put it together."

"I told him he's like our fairy godfather." I smirked. "He didn't like that so much." The image of the huge man wearing wings and a tutu made all of us laugh.

"Hey, ladies, what's the joke?" Trent joined us, crooking an arm around my neck and pulled me close for a kiss.

"Ah, it's an inside deal." Maureen poked him in the ribs. "Oh, hel-heck. Is that my fiancé climbing onto the stage? Excuse me, please, y'all. I need to stop this before someone hands him a mic." She darted through the small groups of people, making a beeline for Smith.

"Those two." Cory shook her head. "Good thing they found each other. Would be a shame to ruin two families." She winked at me and patted Trent's arm. "I promised Ali I'd come and sit with the little ones so she and Flynn could stop by tonight. But before I leave, I wanted to tell you both how proud I am of you. I know you've had a rough road. You didn't give up on yourselves or on each other, and no one's happier to see you together than me." She gave me a quick, tight hug and then stood on her toes to kiss Trent's cheek.

"Be happy, sweethearts. Be good to each other." She blinked rapidly, making me suspect she was battling tears. "And always remember that you have a hometown waiting for you, no matter where you go."

Cory squeezed my hand one more time and then turned to leave. Trent wrapped his arms around me from behind and kissed the side of my neck.

"Are you ready to begin the rest of our life together, baby?"

I covered his hands with mine and tilted back my head against his chest.

"As long as it's always with you."

Trent and Elizabeth's story begins with the Christmas short
Underneath My Christmas Tree

The Burton Books began with
The One Trilogy

The Last One
The First One
The Only One
The One Trilogy Box Set

And continued in
The Always Love Trilogy

Always For You
Always My Own
Always Our Love

Will and Sydney's story is coming!

My One and Always
A short in the anthology
Love Paws
April 18, 2016

ALWAYS MY OWN PLAYLIST

Peace – O.A.R

Home – Blue October

Goodbye Girl – David Gates

Hold Each Other – A Great Big World

I Breathe In, I Breathe Out – Chris Cagle

Slowdown – A Sunset Diary featuring Plugin Stereo

Back to You –Coconut Records

Acknowledgements

Trent first came on the scene in *The Last One*, where he was introduced at Mr. Sexy Cowboy. He was never meant to be anything more than just the town's conveniently easy man-whore. So imagine my surprise when during the planning of the second Burton trilogy, Trent wouldn't go away. He wanted his story told, and when I realized just what his story was, I knew he was in.

What happened between Jenna Sutton and Trent, and her subsequent response, has been an undercurrent in this series. We've heard about it from Trent, from Maureen Evans and from a few other Burton folks. But it's time for Jenna to tell her own story. *Always Our Love* will be out in the summer of 2016.

My first thank you is to my wonderful readers, who wanted to go back to Burton. I love this small town in Georgia, so rest assured, there will be more Burton books, even after the Always Love books are finished. Thank you for enjoying it as much as I do!

Gratitude and appreciation to my usual team, who never fails to amaze me: Kelly Baker, proofer; Stephanie Nelson, cover artist; and Stacey Blake of Champagne Formats. Hearts and hugs, ladies!

Thank you to my author support team, including Olivia Hardin and Mandie Stevens, and to Jen Rattie, Maria Clark and Andrea Coventry for keeping me in line.

To my awesome Temptresses, big hugs! Special love to my betas: Sue Ann Brooks, Carla Edmonson, Christy

Durbin, Anne-Marie Marcoux, Kara Schilling and Julianna Santiago.

And as always-always, thank you to my family for your support and patience. Love you all to the moon and back!

ABOUT THE AUTHOR

Photo by Heather Batchelder

Tawdra Kandle writes romance, in just about all its forms. She loves unlikely pairings, strong women, sexy guys, hot love scenes and just enough conflict to make it interesting. Her books run from YA paranormal romance through NA paranormal and contemporary romance to adult contemporary and paramystery romance. She lives in central Florida with a husband, kids, sweet pup and too many cats. And yeah, she rocks purple hair.

Follow Tawdra on Facebook, Twitter, Instagram, Pinterest and sign up for her newsletter so you never miss a trick.

If you love Tawdra's books, become a Naughty Temptress! Join the group for sneak peeks, advanced reader copies of future books, and other fun.